THE
SERIALIST

DAVID GORDON

Simon & Schuster Paperbacks
New York London Toronto Sydney

Simon & Schuster Paperbacks
1230 Avenue of the Americas
New York, NY 10020

First Simon & Schuster trade paperback edition March 2010

SIMON & SCHUSTER and colophon are registered trademarks of Simon & Schuster, Inc.

For information about special discounts for bulk purchases, please contact Simon & Schuster Special Sales at 1-866-506-1949 or business@simonandschuster.com.

The Simon & Schuster Speakers Bureau can bring authors to your live event. For more information or to book an event contact the Simon & Schuster Speakers Bureau at 1-866-248-3049 or visit our website at www.simonspeakers.com.

Designed by Jill Putorti

Manufactured in the United States of America

10   9   8   7   6   5   4   3   2

Library of Congress Cataloging-in-Publication Data
Gordon, David
The serialist / David Gordon.
1st Simon & Schuster trade pbk. ed.
      p. cm.
Subjects: 1. Authors—Fiction. 2. Serial murderers—Fiction. 3. Murder—Investigation—Fiction. 4. New York (N.Y.)—Fiction. 5. Black humor (Literature). I. Title.
PS3607.O5935S47   2010
813'.6—dc22   2009024126

ISBN 978-1-4391-5848-7
ISBN 978-1-4391-5977-4 (ebook)

For My Parents

THE
SERIALIST

PART ONE
April 4—15, 2009

1

The first sentence of a novel is the most important, except for maybe the last, which can stay with you after you've shut the book, the way the echo of a closing door follows you down the hall. But of course by then it's too late, you've already read the whole thing. For a long time, when I picked up a new book in a shop, I would feel compelled to flip right to the end and read the last sentence. I was unable to control my curiosity. I don't know why I did this, except that I knew I could, and if I could, I had to. It's that old childish impulse, peeling away the wrapping paper, watching horror movies through our hands. We can't resist peeking, even at what we know we shouldn't see, even at what we don't want to see, at what makes us afraid.

The other reason I really want to start this book off right, with a strong first line, is that it's the first I've written under my own name, and in my own voice, whatever that means. I want to make sure I set the right tone, connect with the reader, and win you over to my side. Establish that intimacy of the first-person voice, so you'll follow me anywhere, even if you begin to suspect, after it's too late, that I am one of those unreliable narrators you learned about in English class. But don't worry, I'm not. This isn't one of those tricky books. I'm not the killer. Like I said (did I mention it?), this is a true story and I intend to tell it straight.

Up till now I was just a ghost. I hid behind false names or the names and faces of others. And really, even this story wasn't mine to start with. It began as a hired job, what we in the book business call an "as told to." But the teller is gone, permanently ghosted, and he left the story with me, whether I like it or not. Of course, now that it is mine, who will bother to read it? Who cares what the ghost has to say?

Still I'm a professional, of sorts, and since this is a Mystery/Suspense (shelve accordingly), I want to open in the classic style, with a hook, a real grabber that holds the reader hostage and won't let go, that will keep your sweaty little fingers feverishly turning the pages all night long. Something like this:

It all began the morning when, dressed like my dead mother and accompanied by my fifteen-year-old schoolgirl business partner, I opened the letter from death row and discovered that a serial killer was my biggest fan.

2

I've been a working writer, more or less, for twenty years, and in that time I've told many stories, true and false. Those of you who used to read *Raunchy* magazine back in its glory days might remember me as the Slut Whisperer. Ring a bell? I had an advice column on how to handle girl problems, how to "break" a rebellious, high-spirited wench and reduce her to an obedient sex slave, or coax a shy, reluctant girl into acts of insane depravity, often with methods involving leashes, belts and treats. My girlfriend Jane used to howl as she read my copy in our bed on a Sunday morning, while I made coffee and softly boiled eggs, which she liked with buttered toast fingers. Sometimes she even ghosted it for me when I was stumped by a letter (Dear Slut Whisperer, How do I ask the girl at the office to pee on me and then get my wife to film it?) or when I was busy ghosting something else, one of my innumerable freelance projects, a book of stock tips from a senile millionaire, say, or a puppy owner's manual "by" a trainer to the stars. We tried the star techniques on Jane's dog, but they didn't work like they did for Barbra Streisand's shitzu. (Editor—Sp? Shit's who?) The damned mutt still hopped right up onto the bed with us as soon as I yelled *No!* But I did manage to work a lot of the tools (shock collars, positive reinforcement, the old stick and carrot) into the perverted sex advice column.

It never occurred to me until it was too late, when Jane was long gone, married and living in a Brooklyn brownstone with a real writer (by real I mean a successful one who published real novels under his own name and with whom she cofounded *The Torn Plaid Coat*, a journal that asked the literary question Why *can't* experimental writing be as cute and unthreatening, quirky but ultimately reassuring as indie cinema or alternative rock?), and I came across her picture on the back cover of *A Preponderance of Autumn*, the novel she wrote (which was really two novels, one beginning on the first page of the book and another beginning on the back page, so that by switching back and forth, chapter by chapter, or page by page, you followed the separate—yet parallel!—stories of two lovers who keep just missing each other and crisscrossing paths by taking the same subway, dreaming interwoven dreams, going to the same pizza place for the same favorite mushroom calzone, one even losing in the wind a scarf that the other finds, and finally meeting, on a fall night on a street corner in Brooklyn, right in the center of the book), and there, in the Employees' Picks section, was her husband's equally successful and formally innovative book *Underland* (which was about a young boy who, fleeing family problems and a bad fever, discovers a world of wonder under his bed, and get this, that portion of the novel was not only in footnotes at the bottom of the page but upside down as well, which is even more original and groundbreaking)—it was only then, standing in Borders alone and staring at the back of her book, holding her face in my hands as it were, and gazing at her clear smile, her very fine and sometimes brittle brown hair, her slightly oversized bottom lip and slightly crooked nose and I swear golden eyes, that it crossed my mind: maybe all that giggling and blushing over whips and collars, all that collaborating, was really a cry for help which I, stone-deaf, ignored. Maybe it would have all been different, and she would still be Her Master's Sweet Little Slut and not Some Rich Asshole's Wife, if I had only had the guts to bring my loving but firm hand down on her yielding but equally firm bottom and, like Barbra, command in a warm, even, but firm tone of voice, *Stay.*

3

Don't get me wrong. It's not like I haven't written novels too. Twenty-three at last count, I think. What happened was that the Internet killed *Raunchy*, like it killed all magazine publishing, just as TV and the movies killed books before that, and even earlier, something or other that I can't remember killed poetry. Or maybe that was a suicide. In any case, finally even the perverts quit reading and my porn career dried up. But one of the former *Raunchy* editors got a job with a sci-fi imprint and I found work, writing books under various other names. (I mean other than my porn names, of which there were many, but mainly Tom Stanks or, if I needed a feminine nom de plume, Jillian Gesso.) The Zorg sci-fi series came first. It was a kind of transition for me, since Zorg was a soft-core planet that featured a lot of sexual enslavement, light bondage and eroticized torture in between battle scenes. It was a place I thought of as existing in the future ancient tense, a world of castles and starships, of battles fought with laser and sword, where overbreasted miniwaisted women and bearded, brawny, weirdly busty men rode dragons, flew rockets and drank mead from horns. I wrote those as T. R. L. Pangstrom. *Whoremasters of Zorg* was the most popular, but I think I had the most fun with *Zorgon Sexbot Rebellion*, in which the girls turn the tables for once. I even dedicated that one, *For J.*

Then I started up my inner-city African-American novels, the genre they call urban experience. This series features a former Special Ops lieutenant, a veteran of Afghanistan and Iraq, who picked up a dope habit after he was wounded. Back home in Harlem, he kicks cold turkey, becomes an honest cop, but still gets thrown off the force when his past comes out. So he ends up as an unofficial private eye, an independent contractor dealing out street justice for two hundred a day plus expenses. I made the main character a black Jew of mixed Ethiopian and Native American descent: Mordechai Jones, the ghetto sheriff. By J. Duke Johnson. What readers learned in an interview I did, with myself, for a magazine called *The Game*, was that the J actually stands for John. But everybody always calls me Duke.

Lately, however, I've been getting into the vampire business, which seems, potentially, to be the most lucrative of all. For some reason vampire mania is sweeping the shelves. Go to Barnes & Noble, you'll see yards of them. Why? Beats me. It's got something to do with a whole kind of nouveau goth/horror/industrial club culture. With all the piercings and black clothes and stockings and such, my slut skills fit right in and I found I was able to squeeze out a living, while literature languished, writing pulps for the nerdy and the perverse: when books become a fetish, only fetishists will still read books.

The catch, according to the twenty-six-year-old editor at Phantasm, the imprint, was that all these vampire books are pretty much told in the first person voice of a young woman. Writingwise, this was no problem for me, since many of the stories I wrote as Jillian Gesso for *Sweet Young Thing* magazine began, "It was my eighteenth birthday and as captain of the cheerleading squad . . ." But when it came to a name and an author photo, I ran into a snag.

For my other names the hassle was minimal: T. R. L. Pangstrom was I, in a fake beard, thick dark-framed glasses and a pillow under my shirt. I pictured him, or rather his readers, as chunky, geeky guys and tried to look like a slightly cooler, aspirational version of them. J. Duke Johnson was this friend of mine, Morris, who owns the florist's shop down the street. He's extremely gay but also extremely big, with thick, dark skin, long, heavy braids, and a massive, kingly face that looks to me like Duke Johnson's would—tough and wise and unlikely to take any shit. I just couldn't let him grin in the photos because he has dimples and the cutest gap in his teeth. We dressed him in a suit and hat, borrowed some rings, and I bought dinner and wine for him and Gary, his slim Vietnamese boyfriend. Drunk and bored and sleepy, he finally achieved the perfect world-weary, royal, don't-fuck-with-me glare, which I snapped with a disposable camera. In both cases one small, indistinct black-and-white photo was fine. I simply sent them out for all PR requests, of which there were very few, believe me.

But apparently the vampire reader required more: better photos, more contact with the author. And she had to be a woman, because, who knows why, the readers, mainly female, only trusted and really believed first person female vampire stories if they were written by a fellow woman. Preferably one who was attractive but not too young or too thin. Which is how my dead mother got in on the act.

4

She wasn't dead to start with. She was still quite lively in fact, still in the same Queens two-bedroom where I grew up and where, sadly or perhaps happily, I live again now. Sadly because it is a constant reminder of my life's extremely limited progress, ten feet from the smaller bedroom to the larger. Happily because of the soup dumplings. The Jewish-Italian-Irish neighborhood where I grew up, and which was on its way back then to becoming mainly Hispanic, had taken a wild left turn somewhere and ended up almost completely Asian. Hence the soup dumplings.

And what are they exactly? Don't I mean dumplings in soup? No, my friend. Let's say you order six crab and pork. A few minutes later, they appear, steamed, plump as little Buddhas, sitting on lettuce in their tender skins. But don't bite. Lift one carefully in your spoon and gently nibble its tip. Out dribbles hot soup. That's right. I shit you not. Soup inside the dumpling. It's a kind of miracle, a chaste, doughy nipple dispensing warm broth, the sort of thing that makes life worth living and gives you the strength to hang on, if only for one more novel.

Back when I started with the vampires though, I wasn't living in Queens. I was over in Manhattan, renting a sublet uptown. I rode out on the 7 line to visit my mother, bringing along her favorite salted H&H bagels and her favorite salty belly lox, neither of which were easy to get anymore, because of the yuppies and all those rich people who moved here from other places, like Europe and America, and who preferred nova lox and less extreme peasant food in general. The magical age of egg creams and knishes and loud, crunchy, blindingly sour pickles is over. No more the ancient heroes of Salamis. This is a time for mortal men and their earthly food.

I sliced the bagels while she put out the lox and sturgeon (I splurged to get on her good side). She used the same plates, brown with a daisy, that she'd had forever. Then I waited for her to ask, as she always did, "So what's cooking?"

And this time, instead of "Nothing much," which was my usual reply, I said, "I've started a new book series."

"Pirates?" she asked.

"What?"

"Is it about pirates?"

"No, not about pirates. Why would it be?"

"I saw something on TV about how everybody loves them and thought maybe you'd be writing about them too. I made a note. Where are my glasses?" She checked in her hair, a high red shrubbery that could easily hide a family of partridges.

"Who loves them?" I asked. "Since when?" She went to search her bedroom and I realized that this was why after all these years I had learned, when she said, "What's cooking?" to just say, "Nothing much."

She came out wearing her glasses and then picked up the pad that sat by the phone in a little wooden holder with a pencil. "Here it is," she said. She tore off the top sheet and handed it to me. It read *Pirates*.

"Actually it's not about pirates," I said. "It's about vampires, although that's not even the point."

"Vampires?" She looked unconvinced. "Are you sure? Let's face it. You need to get something going here." Like many mothers, she was both my sworn defender and my mortal foe, all without actually reading anything I wrote. As far as I could tell, every scrap of text I'd produced was lovingly archived in this apartment, although the porn was in a closet out of sight, rather than out on display with the novels in the glass case she called the "étagère." Nevertheless, despite proudly showing my collected works off to everyone, and refusing to lend them out ("Let them buy!"), she hadn't read a word since the few short stories I gave her ages ago, when I had hoped, briefly, to write serious fiction. As always, her critique was pithy and unequivocal: "Not my cup of tea," she pronounced after a quick perusal. "No wonder no one wants to publish it. You just write about lost souls with sad lives. My book club would never read that." And of course she was right, she was right.

As we sat down to build our bagels, with tomato and onion and lemon and, in a nod to modern health awareness, Philadelphia whipped cream cheese, I assured her that vampires were extremely popular, enjoying a renaissance in fact, and that I had already been contracted to write the first book.

"Huh," she said, as if amazed she hadn't heard about this yet in the building's laundry room. "Who knew?"

"The thing is I need a woman's name."

"How about Esmerelda? I always liked that name."

"No. For the author. These books are usually written by women, so I need a woman's name and I was thinking, if it's OK, about using yours. Your maiden name I mean. The old way." My mother's name was Sibyl and her married name was Bloch of course, like mine. But her real first name, which she never used, was Sibylline and her family's name in full was Lorindo with Gold as her mother's maiden name. Sibyl Bloch might write a nice bar mitzvah card, or at best a decent pirate story. But Sibylline Lorindo-Gold? That said vampire.

"Sure," she said. "Why not?"

"Well," I added, eyeing her red curls and wondering what it would take to straighten them into the luxurious long tresses of Madam Lorindo-Gold. "The thing of it is, I'm not just talking about your name."

And so, after prolonged negotiations, my mother's name and slightly altered visage have ended up appearing on three vampire books so far, as well as in various magazines and newspapers. We avoided live personal appearances by characterizing her as a recluse who never went out in public, but she did try a single telephone interview after the first book in the series, *Crimson Vein of Darkness*, came out and shocked everyone, most of all my mother, by becoming a minor (very minor) hit. Suddenly, chatter about my vampire lovers, Aram and Ivy, appeared all over MySpace and numerous vampire websites, along with my Mom's image. Phantasm agreed to boost my next advance check up into the mid four figures, but only if "I," that is to say, My Dark Mistress, Mom, played ball by at least doing a phone chat with a blogger from a site called the Vampyre's Web. There was something sad about that spelling to me, like an undead PC feminism, and sure enough when I checked it out, I saw that, alongside the pentagrams and goat heads and the bloodsucker's forum matching "drinkers and donors," the site also contained a stern warning against any discrimination or offensive, "exclusionary" language regarding sexuality, race, religion, gender or transgender. Apparently vampires, despite living forever, flying, and tearing out the throats of peasants, are still extremely sensitive and fragile about being called "dork" or "homo" like they were back in the locker room, before they grew fangs.

Anyway, we scheduled the interview and prepared carefully, with me listening on the bedroom extension, scribbling answers on a pad, and passing them to my young pal Claire, who relayed them to my mother, who sat in the kitchen in her housedress.

My worst fears were realized immediately, however, when within five minutes she announced that vampires were "nothing" compared to Germans, that they lived mostly in Pennsylvania (she later blamed this on my handwriting), had "a thing" for crosses, and died from silver bullets.

"That's werewolves," I hissed, standing in the bedroom door and frantically miming a stake driving into my chest.

"Oh yeah," she added into the phone. "Garlic gives them heartburn."

After this she declined all requests. And there were some, because Madam Sibylline Lorindo-Gold was popular, my most popular writer by far. Though of course popular in my world meant a $4,500 advance on a 350-page novel, requiring that I keep up my strict diet of ten manuscript pages a day. God, I hate to think of the forests I've felled, just to pay the rent and keep my lights on. When it comes to literature, I'm a furnace. I'm a wildfire. I'm the inferno of American Fiction.

5

All in all, my mother was very pleased with her virtual celebrity, and it was a fun thing for us to share, answering her fan mail, getting her hair and makeup done, choosing the clothes and taking pictures. And I'm glad we at least had that, because three months after that first book was published, she was diagnosed with lymphatic cancer. A year later—after *Crimson Darkness Falls* and *Darkly Crimson, My Sweet*, after I had moved back into my old room to look after her, to count her pills and bring her to her chemo appointments, after her hair no longer needed to be straightened for the photos because it had fallen out and we got a red, straight wig—she finally died, quietly, one night while I slept next door. I found her around noon the following day, since even then, in her last extremity, she was always the early riser and I was the dead log of a sleeper who had to be awakened with nudges and coffee every morning.

And that is how, on the day my death row fan letter arrived, I found myself in a midtown photo studio, wearing my mother's red wig and one of her black "Lorindo dresses," as we once called them, as well as thick makeup, lipstick, eye shadow, foundation and rouge, all applied by Claire, who was accompanying me to the shoot for the new portrait I needed for *Crimson Night and Fog*, which was due to come out soon. Needless to say I resemble my mother quite a bit, although my hair isn't red. But then again neither was hers. Not really, I mean. In truth I don't know what her natural color was, and neither did she.

Claire leaned over me, breathing bubblegum into my nose and frowning in concentration as she struggled with my eyebrows, which presented a special problem. So did my greasy forehead, my pronounced, bristly jaw and my Adam's apple, but Claire managed to overcome these failings with her clever deployment of wardrobe, hair and a bag full of products about which I knew only that they itched. But my eyebrows were particularly recalcitrant, since despite her many cogent arguments, I refused to have them plucked.

"They're just so bushy," she muttered to herself, snipping away with a tiny scissors. "It's like I'm lost in a forest."

"Don't exaggerate. Of course they're bushy for a woman."

"For a human. And your mom's were so nice and elegant."

For the record, my mother was one of those women who essentially have no eyebrows, merely a dusting of microscopic hair. She then drew in her own with the same little colored pencils she used for her shopping list.

"I probably have my dad's eyebrows," I offered.

"Then this must be his ear hair too," she said, wrinkling her nose in distaste. "You should be writing about the wolfman."

At last she sorted me out by somehow disappearing my beastly brows with makeup, then painting new, ladylike curves on my forehead. In the mirror, I looked perpetually surprised by something, maybe my own face.

"Now hold still and try not to furrow," she said, so I sat back and stretched my legs. Since the photo would only be chest high, I was still wearing jeans and high-top sneakers under my dress.

"Here, before I forget." Claire was restuffing her backpack. "I grabbed your mail."

"Thanks," I said. She had my spare set of keys. It was mostly bills of course, and a few letters for Sibylline forwarded from the publisher. Pangstrom and Johnson got some too, but less often. I answered them all, though my mother, and now Claire, signed Sibylline's, since I believe, perhaps foolishly, that one can tell gender from handwriting. Then, on the bottom of the stack, there was another letter, with several of those yellow forwarding stickers attached, recording all the places I'd lived in my increasingly frantic wanderings through the shrinking bits of cheap New York.

"What's that one?" Claire asked. "I didn't recognize it."

It was addressed to Tom Stanks, c/o *Raunchy* magazine. And the return address was Sing Sing Penitentiary.

6

A few years back, when Jane and I split up, or rather (who am I kidding?) when she dumped me, the only possessions we fought over were the books. We'd spent eight or nine years together (even this was in dispute), and one could trace the epochs of our shared life in the shelves that lined our, soon to be her, apartment as if they were geological strata: first the two lonely his and her libraries that came shyly together, my Dylan Thomas rubbing against her Sylvia Plath, my Barthes kissing her Wilson, my Borges squeezed under her Waugh, with all our cute twinned stepvolumes: two *Franny*s and two *Zooey*s, two very *Pale Fire*s, and for some reason three *Ask the Dust*s. These were easy to dismantle, of course, and even a bit tender, as we pulled them apart and laid mine to rest in boxes, where they now remain, come to think of it, in my mother's storage room in the basement. Also easy were the new books, the bedside and desktop stacks—her review and advance copies of story collections by the young and promising, my complimentary issues of *Hot Asians #7* and *Best of Big Buns* piled on Henry James, who slumped half-read and prostrate, as if unable to face our breakup. The hard part of undoing our library came with that layer I call the Middle Ages, when for about four years we were eternally joined and not only buying but reading the same things, sometimes, forgive me, even out loud together in bed.

"Didn't I buy this?"

She was holding up Cortázar's *Hopscotch*.

"Yes," I said. "You bought it for me, remember?" She frowned, unsure. But I remembered. She brought it to read on the bus that time we used her uncle's time-share in the Poconos, back when she still thought being poor and unknown together was just perfect. Dazzlingly, dizzyingly, diamondly brilliant—that book made me carsick on the lurching ride up, then seasick all weekend in the waterbed, bobbing together and switching off, chapter by chapter, as we followed those other, cooler, maté-sipping fifties bohemians through Paris and Buenos Aires. All Jane wanted then was to die beautifully for art by my side, ideally in eccentrically titled chapters. As I stared at my face in the mirrored ceiling, pale and sweaty, like a drowning man going down in a wave of nausea, she offered me a fizzing Alka-Seltzer and asked me to ask her to marry me.

"Are you sure?" I asked, and tried to embrace her, though my sudden move set off a lurching roll that sent me bouncing off her chest. Our heads knocked. "Shit," I muttered. "I think your uncle overfilled this."

"We love each other," she declared. "What else matters?"

"Lots of things. What if I'm always poor and struggling?"

"I don't care."

"And you don't mind waiting till my first novel comes out to have the wedding? You know I can't get distracted now."

"I don't mind."

"And you understand," I said—and feel free to laugh at what an ass I was, as I have on many bitter nights since—"you understand that even if we are married, my work will always come first?"

Oh, how she loved that. The sweetly sad grandeur of it filled her to the brim. She clutched at my hands, as if I were a cramped swimmer getting pulled out by the tide, and we floated into each other's arms. "I understand," she told me. "I wouldn't want it any other way."

"I guess that changed," I told her, seven (?) years later, still poor and unknown, sitting on a box marked Russian Fic while she ruffled the dog-eared pages of the Cortázar and found the one red maple leaf we'd laid in the book as a mark. She held it up to me now like a tiny, brittle flag, captured in my defeat.

"Yes, yes, I admit it," she said. "I changed. I'm sorry. I'm thirty-one now. I want a husband and a house and a kid. Forgive me." And I tried to. I said:

"If I tell you, let's do it, let's get married and get pregnant right now, then you'll stay with me?"

The anger went out of her. She slumped. "No," she whispered, turning her head from me, as if an invisible hand had wrapped around her throat. "Not anymore. Not with you."

I was silent. She began to sob. Why is it that while she was breaking my heart, she was also the one who cried, and I was the one who watched, stony and unmoved like the heartbreaker? A big tear fell into *Hopscotch*. Page forty-nine. I know because when it dried it shriveled the paper, and I've gone back to review it many times.

"I'm sorry," she said. "But you're the one who changed. You used to be so passionate about everything. Writing. Life. Everything. Just taking a walk. Now I can't live with you. It's too sad. When was the last time you even wrote a poem?" Then she shut the book and crushed the leaf.

7

Yes, I admit I was a poet once. No, I wasn't much good. I'm not claiming to be some thwarted, tragic genius. This isn't that kind of story. The fact is, like many a socially awkward man-child, good with words but bad with people, I broke out in poetry, like acne, somewhere in preadolescence, and by the time I met Jane, versifying had already become one of those vestigial gifts, like card tricks or making crepes, that we trot out only on request. I wrote one poem a year, for Jane's birthday, because I couldn't afford a real gift, and offered it up the way others glue glittered macaroni onto coffee cans. And they probably ended up the same way, buried in a basement in Brooklyn.

After my mother died, I found in her night table an envelope containing copies of the very first poems I wrote, back in my golden age, which lasted from eight to nineteen. Creased and bent and stained, handwritten or typed on a typewriter, they were, I realized, the only works of mine she'd ever really liked and even read out loud to her cousin Sadie on the phone. I looked them over. They were, of course, thoroughly mediocre, about Fall or Time or Vacant Lots, or in one particularly wincing case, the Miracle of Hanukkah. So much for my poems, and their only two readers, both lost.

But still—like the former would-be anarchist whose subversion is now reduced to muttering under his breath after you order your lunch from him, like the meek bank teller who behind her smile is always plotting how to blow the vault, like the author of scathing, unsent op-ed pieces, or the sex outlaw who ravishes only with a glance— I have remained a secret poet in my heart, carving there the lines that no eye will ever trace, nor lips speak. And here, in my own true story, in my own name, I will invoke the rights of a poet and not, if I don't care to, go into all that endless fucking prosaic detail about the weather and how couches looked. And I won't pretend to know what everyone is thinking either, even me, or why we all do what we do. Like a poet I will simply say what I have to say, straight to the point. Because that's what poetry really is, the most information in the least words. We poets say what we mean, in the only way it can be said. And so if I say, just for example, *Her heart was as black as a spider*, that is just what I mean. Black. As a spider. Her heart.

8

I guess, before going any further, I should stop and explain about Claire.

Since, despite the blizzard of paper I've produced in what I'll call my career, there's never been more than a flurry of green, I've resorted to many other jobs along the way, including tutor. It was not very lucrative, ten or twenty bucks an hour helping variously hyphenated Americans get up to speed in written English or coaching public school kids who were "special," "alternatively gifted," or just plain extraordinary. But armed with my Ivy League credentials (I know, I know, whatever) and the 800 that by some weird fluke I got on the verbal GRE (don't be too impressed, I got a 350 in math), I solicited tutoring work with the posh uptown private schools as well, schools that, as a product of Queens' finest, I only knew from the movies. Most just ignored my emails. A few responded, then ignored my calls. Only one, the Bradley School, called me in for a depressing interview, where some administrator held forth on how great their students were, how they mostly went to what she insisted on calling "the Ivies," and how they didn't need much outside tutoring because the faculty "loved helping kids." I didn't, I admitted to myself while nodding my approval. I don't even like kids. I just love paying rent.

"We take an individual approach here. Does the thought of developing your own curriculum excite you?"

"Yes," I said. "Very much. It excites me a lot."

So by the time I left I had pretty much written it off and had completely forgotten the whole thing when, a few months later, I got a call from someone named Peter Nash.

"This Harry Bloch?"

"Yes it is. How can I—"

"Yeah, my daughter's not testing as well as she should."

"Um." It took me a minute to think of what he meant.

"You know Sally Sherman?"

"Um . . ." For some reason the name came back to me. "The lady from the Bradley School?"

"Right. You have some time this week?"

"I'll check my schedule," I said. I was in the kitchen about to eat lunch. I glanced down at my bowl of tomato soup. It was dead winter. My calendar was wide open for the next thirty years. "Let's see. How about Thursday at five?"

"And how much do you charge?"

My head swam. I'd never made more than twenty bucks an hour for anything. I gulped a big drink of air. "Fifty?" I croaked. "My usual fee is fifty, but if . . ." Luckily he stopped me before I talked myself out of it.

"OK, as long as that's not the unusual fee, ha! Look, I'll have Claire call you about the schedule. I handle the big things and she handles the little things. Ha!"

"Don't worry, I'll assess her individual strengths and weaknesses and develop an exciting core curriculum . . ." I rambled on a while before realizing he'd hung up.

A few hours later I got a message from Claire. If she hadn't introduced herself I would have thought she was her mom. Her voice was perfectly poised, with no teenage uncertainty. She confirmed the random time I'd suggested and gave her address, on the Upper East Side. I realized that she'd neglected to give her apartment number but decided to just wing it and look at the mailboxes. Fifty dollars! I was so amazed at my good fortune that I was afraid to call back and ruin it.

That Thursday, when I showed up, huddling in a wind so icy that it seemed to scissor right through to my underwear, I saw the reason she hadn't told me which buzzer to push: there was only one. It was all theirs, the whole five-story building. I was early, and as I paced back and forth, shivering, under the glowing lights of their house, the ridiculousness of my worries over charging a piddly fifty bucks made me blush. Although it's hardly news, it still never ceases to stupefy and amaze me: how rich other people are compared to me.

I buzzed, and a few frigid minutes later, Claire answered wearing a string bikini. She had very straight, very blond hair, very blue eyes, a microscopic nose that barely made a bump between her freckled cheeks, and a small round mouth. Her body, under or perhaps I should say around the bikini, since it covered only what was absolutely necessary with its three small triangles, was, well, it was fourteen: without fat, without wrinkles, without wear of any sort. She was like a doll never taken from the box. She was mint.

"Hi, come in. Sorry, I was under the sunlamp." She was not, by the by, tan at all. In fact her skin was so white that her veins looked blue. And I could see them all since she was so thin that I think I could have wrapped a hand around her thigh. She led me out of the burning cold into the soothing warmth of her home. "I've got sad."

"I'm sorry to hear that. What about?" I asked as I struggled with my scarf and hat and coat.

"Seasonal affective disorder."

"Oh."

"The sunlamp is supposed to help with it. Anyway, that's what they say."

"Oh." We were in a marble entrance hall with a grand staircase leading up and away and mail laid out like hors d'oeuvres on a silver platter. I dropped my glove and when I stooped to pick it up, I noticed four rubber bands on the floor, where they'd probably fallen off bundles of cash. Instinctively I picked them up.

"Here," I said, absurdly. "These rubber bands fell." I held them out and she accepted them, reluctantly.

"Thanks." She gestured at a double door on her left. "That's the study. I'll be right in as soon as I put these away. Do you want a cappuccino or anything?"

"No thanks," I said, though I really did.

The study, as you'd expect, was like the gentleman's club in a Bond film: towering shelves full of leather-bound books, a huge roaring fireplace, those wingback chairs with the buttons, a snooker table. After a dramatic pause, Claire entered. She was now dressed in a short wool tartan skirt, white tights, black patent leather shoes, a collared white blouse under a red sweater. Her hair was up in a ponytail. She wore glasses and was carrying a stack of books and a handful of dangerously sharp pencils. In other words, the perfect study look. She sat at the desk beside me, back straight, knees together, opened her books, got out a fresh sheet of paper and raised her pencil, fixing me with rapt attention.

It was hopeless. She had a paper on *The Scarlet Letter*, ten pages with quotes and three examples to support her thesis, due the next day, and she had nothing. Nothing. No rough draft. No notes. I wasn't even sure she'd read the book.

"Let's see," I said, floundering, sweating, as if I were the one with the paper due, while she sat there, utterly composed, listening politely, tapping her white teeth with her pencil's pink eraser and blinking her pretty blue eyes. "Do you know how to do an outline?" I asked.

"It rings a bell," she said. "How much are you charging my dad?"

"Excuse me?"

"How much are you charging an hour?"

"Fifty?"

She sighed and rolled her eyes. "You have two degrees from Columbia, don't you? You got an eight hundred on the GRE?"

"Yes."

"You're a published author?"

"Well . . . yes."

"Do you know what the agencies would bill for someone with your resume? One fifty at least."

"Really?"

"You should charge at least a hundred."

"Sorry."

"Look, I'm going to be frank," she said. "I have no problem with reading or writing papers in principle. But with school, field hockey, ballet, yearbook and all the volunteering I have to do to get into a decent college these days, I just don't think it's practical for me to write a paper on *The Scarlet Letter*, which will probably only be so-so anyway, when I'm sure you could write a totally awesome one in your sleep."

"Well, maybe not totally awesome."

"We'll tell my dad it's a hundred bucks an hour, he won't even remember, and that you need to come twice a week. And who knows, if this goes well, I'll refer you to all my friends."

"But I don't know if I can do that. It's cheating."

"I agree. In principle. But let's look at the situation realistically. The paper's due tomorrow. I've read the book. Or some of it anyway. I have the feel of it. I could write it if I had to. But there's only so many hours in the day and I can't exactly hire you to play field hockey for me, can I?"

"Ha. No, I guess not." She had a point.

"And to be perfectly frank, I already found a way to buy this paper on the Internet for less than I'm offering you, but I prefer to do business face to face, and besides, you seem . . . well, kind of sad."

"S-A-D?"

"No, just regular. In a sweet way. No offense."

"How could you tell?"

"The way you got here early and waited outside shivering till it was exactly five."

"You saw me?"

"From the sunroom. You kept staring up with this lost puppy expression on your face. Forlorn, like."

"Oh," I said. "I see."

What can I say? I did it. Not right away. It took some more charming and a double cappuccino, but somehow she talked me into it, and I spent half the night writing her paper, then met her behind a bush during her field hockey practice to deliver it. Before I knew it I was writing all her papers and also "tutoring" several of her classmates. It was a seamless scam: the kids raved about me to the parents, who happily paid my increasingly exorbitant rate when their children's grades went up.

Not that it was easy. Good work never is, and simplicity, if it is to seem natural, takes true craftsmanship. Think about Hemingway, sharpening his pencils with a knife, or Flaubert in his nightgown, hunting for a just word. That was me, tackling "What Would I Do If I Were Macbeth (or Mrs. Macbeth)?" The trick is hitting that sweet spot, B plus, say: good enough to please the parents but not so good that the teachers got suspicious when a lacrosse-playing knucklehead or stoned trust-core skate punk suddenly jumped to the head of the class.

Hence, under my stewardship, Chad Hicksley III finally learned what an adverb was but couldn't seem to get his past, present and perfect tenses straight, due to too many bong hits, while Dakota Steinberg, whose dad I think owned my neighborhood, showed huge improvement in Organization and Examples and figured out the difference between *its* and *it's*, but still tended toward the overly vernacular, as in her piece entitled, "Final Paper With At Least Three Sources Besides the Internet," in which she referred to works cited as "totally awesome" *(Fahrenheit 451)*, "kind of random" *(1984)* and, "bites" *(Brave New World)*. Claire managed everything, for a mere fifteen percent, and soon "tutoring" was providing a large part of my income. Certainly, if I figured my per-word rate, it was the most profitable writing I had ever done.

Since there was nothing to do now during our actual tutoring sessions, Claire and I became pals, lying around and chatting about "whatever." When she heard about all the books I was writing, and how little I made for them, she was aghast. At that point I was just about to renew for two more Zorgs and three Mordechais, and I was getting ready to pitch the first of what would become the Sibyllines.

"Have you signed?" Claire asked, leaning back in the wing chair with her feet over the arm, sipping a Diet Coke through a bendy straw.

"Well, not officially. They're in the mail."

"Why don't you let me look the papers over for you?"

"I don't know, Claire. I mean, these are grown-up publishers, not kids. And anyway, I already agreed. It wouldn't be right to go back on that, would it?"

She smiled, kindly, as if I were back out on her doorstep, shivering SADly. "Just let me worry about that. You get to work on my personal response for *To Kill a Mockingbird*. And leave that jacket here when you go. I'll get my housekeeper to fix the zipper."

And so, one way or another, Claire ended up costarring in almost every episode of my so-called life. She just kept popping up and making herself essential. Why? I can't rightly say. She didn't seem to care for her peers much more than I did. Her mom was MIA. Her dad was an ass. So I guess I filled some gap. As for the gap she filled in my world . . . well, I preferred not to probe too deeply into that wound. But I had to admit, now that she was going to be starting her junior year, I was already beginning to panic about what would happen when she inevitably flew the coop.

9

Meanwhile, back at the photo shoot, I left the letter from Sing Sing for last. After all, I hadn't been Tom Stanks, the Slut Whisperer, for years, and back when I was, correspondence from "wrongly incarcerated" prisoners was hardly a special event. Porn, like athlete's foot, thrives wherever there are men without women—prison, the military, comic book stores, dank math labs at MIT—and convicts had the time to not only read the magazine but respond to it, engage it you might say, something that in general only the lonely, crazy or dumb bothered to do. The fact that it was years out of date wasn't a big deal either. In prison nothing was out of date, and a porn mag was a treasure to be hoarded and passed and traded. Finally, I was in no rush to open the prisoner's letter because there was nothing in it for me. My other correspondents, the alien sex or urban violence fans, if encouraged with a signed photo or what have you, would at least buy more books. And the Sibylline Lorindo-Gold readers—not only was she my top earner, but some of those vampire babes were pretty cute.

This was a sore point between Claire and me, and even as I sliced the latest vampire mail open, breaking the seal with my middle (satanic) finger, I could see her frowning suspiciously. It wasn't jealousy of course. Her worry was strictly business: "One pissed-off chick on a website," she said, "blabbing about how Sibylline is really a creepy middle-aged horndog, and it's all over."

She was right of course. She was right. But still, I'd followed the links to the sweet little herspaces and facebooklets these girls directed me to in their emails and found the graphics of lace and blood, the clanging or sighing music, the preposterous poetry, all doomy-gloomy. I'd seen the red and purple hair, pierced postpubertal nipples, snarling, sneering pouts and, peeking through the raccoon ghost makeup, the wide eyes of scared children, as if in this underland, one could be both the sleepless victim and the creature under the bed. How does a nineteen-year-old girl decide she is into flogging, bondage, vampyrism and "extreme anal," whatever that is? Why would she want somebody to lock her in a steel belt or bite her neck with fake fangs and let her real blood drip into a silver chalice? What forces, socio, psycho, sexo, could twist otherwise healthy young women into such radical forms? I had no idea, but I would've liked to find out.

Claire forbade it. "Don't get mixed up with freaks," she counseled, like someone on her third divorce. "They'll freak out on you in the end." Which seemed reasonable, but sitting in the photo studio, waiting under the lights and sweating through my dress and wig while the photographer rethought me, it also felt a bit irrelevant: how much more freaked could I get? While Claire stepped behind the camera to consult, I considered my image in the mirror. I reflected, as it were. It was a disturbing view.

Hopefully, by the time the photos were lit and Photoshopped and colored and printed, they would look passable—a nice if somewhat severe older lady. But in the raw form, under these glaring white bulbs, I looked frightening. We are all, of course, genetic combos of our parents, but here I appeared as the Dr. Frankenstein version, some mad cloning experiment gone wrong. My mother had been quite attractive and, even when she grew older and rounder, always had a sweet face. Now I was she, but with my father's big nose, sharp chin and troublesome eyebrows slapped on like a cheap gag. Or else—worse perhaps, since I barely remembered him and knew him only as a dream and a photo—I was my father, aged past his own early death and back now in a nightmare, wearing my mother's hair, eyes, mouth and breasts. I was, it seemed, not so much my parents' offspring as their medium: in my flesh their ghosts now came and went and mingled their vaporous souls. Sometimes, even without my drag, just walking as myself past a mirror or shop window, I saw it, and it made me catch my breath: my mother's face in those final months, hardened by illness, when the cancer had eaten away her femininity and she looked like me. I was my dying mother. I was my father, if he had lived to grow old.

"Hey, what's going on over there?" I asked, reeling myself back from the abyss of the mirror.

"Just a minute," Claire said. "There's a shadow on your nose we're trying to fix."

"Good luck," I said, and to avoid looking at myself again (having already seen both my parents' ghosts, who knows what I'd see this time?), I dug out that last fan letter and tore it along the seam. It was short, written in blue ink on looseleaf paper, in the hand of a clever fourth grader, the floppy script wandering over the lines.

"Holy fuck," I announced, standing up.

"Harry," Claire scolded, since the lights were all arranged and this could only aggravate the nose problem.

"Holy fuck," I repeated, waving the letter. "Look at this."

She took the page and read. Here's what it said:

Dear Mr. Thomas Stanks,
    I am a big reader of "Raunchy" and I think you're writings and magazine is great. I have a "business" "proposition" for you. I have many offers to sell my story to the medias, but never have told the real story, the whole truth that really

happened to anyone. I mean EVERYTHING!! Maybe you can write this book with me? It will sell a lot for sure. Come see me if you want to discuss. I have some conditions.

Sincerely,

Darian Clay

"Darian Clay?" Her mind traced the name. Then her eyes widened. "Not the dude with the heads?"

"That's the one."

The photographer shouted, "OK, I'm ready," but Claire ignored him.

"I completely remember this," she said.

"How could you? You were five."

"My dad was married to this model for about twelve minutes, and I remember her being all freaked out and him going to pick her up after night shoots." She looked down at the letter in her hands. "I can't believe I'm touching something he touched. And you're going to write his book." She grinned at me. "That is awesome."

"I didn't say that. Who knows if it's even for real? We'll see."

The photographer came over and lit a cigarette. "Excuse me, Claire? Madam Lorindo-Gold? In case either of you care, the shot is now ruined. And we are back to square one with the nose."

Claire handed him the letter. "Check it out. Darian Clay."

"Oh my God, the photo guy?" He scanned the letter, puffing smoke. "I remember exactly where I was when the news said they caught him. In my ex's loft, cooking leek and potato soup. My friend even knew someone who saw the pictures. Well, he said he did, anyway." He handed back the page. "This is too sick though. You can't do it."

"Of course he can," Claire said. "He has to."

"Well, if he does," he asked her, as if I weren't there, "can I take the author photo?"

10

For those of you who, like Claire, were born yesterday or just got to town or, like my mother, prefer not to know about such things, Darian Clay, aka the Shutterbug, aka the Photo Killer, abducted, tortured and brutally murdered four women in New York City from 1996 to 1997. A demented wannabe artist, Clay forced the women to pose for photos before killing them, dismembering their corpses, and disposing of the parts, or most of them, in Dumpsters around Queens and Long Island. All except the heads.

The photos were sent, perhaps mockingly, perhaps hopefully, to the police during the manhunt, showing up as each girl's severed remains were found. Although never released to the public, the images were described by the press as "ghastly tableaux," "terrifying mise-en-scenes" and other terms of high aesthetic horror. I remember the mood of mounting hysteria that gripped the city during those months, as each new murder cranked up the fear and outrage. There were screaming red headlines on the tabloids and police sketches on TV, warning women to beware of a lightly penciled fellow who could be anyone white under fifty. A hotline was set up to intensify the panic with a rash of false sightings, false accusations and false confessions. There were angry town meetings with Police Commissioner Safir and Mayor Giuliani, who put his foot in it by reassuring the public that only a few women—young, beautiful models—really had anything to worry about. There were shrill panel discussions about the objectification of women, and of course we in the porn world were fingered as accessories, along with fashion and advertising, since we somehow made chopping up women "acceptable." I admit, at the time, the thought did creep me out. I kept imagining a stack of blood-smeared *Raunchy*'s with my name on them. But as Jane reminded me when I couldn't sleep, in truth our average reader was far more likely to be a lonely security guard atop the midnight toilet or a cop sitting up in a parked car, eating doughnuts and watching out for the killer. Now, all these years later, I had to wonder.

Clay was finally captured when a fifth woman, Noreen Velanopolis, called the police and reported a suspicious man trying to coax her into modeling for him. At the trial, he pled not guilty. He insisted, to the disgust of the jury and the denial of the victims' loved ones, that all of the murdered women were willing models whom he had paid and who left his basement studio happy and intact. However, DNA evidence (hair or blood) found in his basement linked him to the victims, and witnesses placed him, or a man answering his description, in the vicinity of two of the abductions. Clay had been taken into custody without incident, denied bail, and after a long and grueling trial, found guilty on all counts and sentenced to death. He had spent the last ten years on death row, exhausting his appeals and sitting alone in a cell, where, it now appeared, he spent a lot of his "free" time reading my alter ego's pornographic prose.

Clay had never confessed. The heads were never found.

11

Right after we got back from the photo shoot, Claire did some research and came back even more enthused. Clearly there was money to be made.

"If he confesses, exclusive to you, we're talking six figures," she said. "And that's just the advance. There's paperback, major on a supermarket book like this. There's excerpts in the tabs. Who knows? Maybe we can go serial."

"Don't call it that."

"What?"

"Going serial."

"Oh yeah right." She was very excited, squirming and tapping in a way that was much more childish than her normally cool demeanor, but she was also flushed and her eyes were wide and dilated. She seemed almost turned on, which I tried my best not to notice. "And then there's movie rights. DVDs. Cable. TV." She sang these words like an incantation and even seemed to view me with slightly more respect, as if the very fact that I had attracted this kind of potential wealth and cultural currency, even if only by chance, endowed me with a different aura: if the real forces and powers of the culture could draw toward me, then I must be interesting in some other, deeper, though admittedly invisible way.

"What's all this *we* business?" I asked.

"Come on," she said. "The tutoring season's almost over. Let me work this one with you."

"We'll see." I tried to assert myself. "Maybe you can observe me. If it even happens."

"Cool," she said. "I'll run some numbers." Whatever that meant. What difference did it make? She never listened to me anyway.

Next, I had to go through a whole rigmarole with the Bureau of Prisons, get my fingerprints taken and my background checked. I was given a list of instructions about what not to bring or do. The most chilling was Do Not Wear Denim. It was what the convicts wore, and in case of a riot or other disturbance, the guards would try to avoid shooting the guy in cords.

I also met with Clay's attorney, Carol Flosky. Her office was down near the courts on Park Row, in a building that I would describe as decrepit yet lawyerly: creaky elevator, dark hallway, the missing black and white octagonal tiles in the once-fancy hall replaced, indifferently, with off-green bathroom squares. Her office had books and files stacked from the floor to the ceiling, and leaks pinging into pans, but it was a big room full of big furniture, all leather and wood, and it held a big view of the courthouse from across a plaza, as well as an impressive young woman who answered the door.

Black-haired, shapely and sleekly petite under glasses, hairpins and a dark wool suit, she introduced herself as Theresa Trio, legal aide, before showing me to Ms. Flosky, who was disheveled, blond and fiftysomething, in a cardigan with glasses perched on her hair. She stood behind her desk, smoking, and waved me in. I put my hand out for a shake.

"Nice to meet you," I began.

"Fuck no!" she screeched.

"Sorry?" I froze, smile drying on my face, hand still limply in midair.

"Yes, yes," she added while shaking her head no. I realized she wasn't speaking to me, just staring while she talked on her phone's headset. She waved impatiently at a chair heaped with files. I lifted the stack and sat, holding them in my lap and pretending to be fascinated with the only artwork in the room, a trite black-and-white photo of some leafless trees poking out of some snow. There was an ashtray the size of a dinner plate stuffed with butts and the room had that deep, sour smoke smell, as if they cured hams in there at night.

"Total dog crap!" she yelled right in my face.

I smiled and nodded.

"That's right, you douche!"

It was making me feel a bit odd to sit there blankly while she looked straight at me and barked, "Yes! No! Bullshit! Fuck!" so I turned to the window and watched the courthouse steps. It was a gusty day, which seemed to heighten the sense of being behind glass, as if I were watching a silent film. People pushed uphill, their bodies strained and wavering, hair and trousers flapping in the wind. Dresses and skirts clung deliriously to their mistresses' curves. A hat rolled down. A plastic deli bag took off in a giddy spiral.

"OK, let's get something straight right now," Flosky said. "I think this whole thing stinks."

Not sure whom she meant, I pointed curiously at myself.

"Yeah, you," she said, and aimed a nail at me. "El stinko."

"Huh," I said, trying to be noncommittal. "I see."

"But Darian wants this, so there you go." She waved her cigarette, drawing a little daisy of smoke in the air, then sat and took a long, thoughtful drag. "Let's be clear. I'm not privy to the substance of what he wants to discuss with you. Nor will I be if this goes forward. It's totally between you two."

"OK."

"But!" I flinched as she stood back up. "There are a few items we need to discuss. One!" She held up a thumb. "He's offering you a fifty-fifty split, which I assume is all right with you."

"Yes, certainly." Fifty percent was very generous. Claire had urged me to push for thirty-five and settle for twenty-five. On the other hand, she explained, Clay's share would go to settling debts, including what had to be enormous legal bills, and then right into a victim's fund, since he wasn't allowed to profit from his crimes. I suppose it was easy to be extravagant with money you'd never see. Still I said, "Thank you very much."

"Don't thank me," Flosky answered. "It's not my money." Not yet, I thought. She held up two fingers.

"Which brings me to item B. Not one word of what he tells you, not one thing that you learn, nothing what-so-fucking-ever is to be published, released, given out in an interview, leaked or in any manner disseminated until after Mr. Clay's death, natural or not. Which means, if I have my way, you won't see squat for a long, long time." She smiled. "And neither will I."

I tried to smile back, but her face went blank on me. "Hello?" she said. "Hello?" She tapped her headphones. "Jack, you bastard, what the fuck are you trying to pull?"

Waving and nodding, I backed away. Theresa Trio, clattering away on a keyboard, with plugs in her own ears, didn't speak or look up either, so I showed myself out and reported back to Claire.

"Damn it," she said, when I told her my tale. "I knew there had to be a catch." She liked the fifty-fifty part all right, pronouncing it "sweet." But if Clay got his death sentence overturned, or commuted, or indefinitely delayed, then I got nothing. However, the lawyers Claire consulted calmed her down. Clay, they assured her, was a dead man. His case had run its course, and his execution was set, for three months hence, when he would most certainly die. The only things that could save him now were a stay from the governor, which was politically unthinkable, or a new appeal, for which there was no legal basis. Perhaps this was why he had decided to speak, to unburden his heart, if he had one, and leave it all behind when he passed from this world, leave it behind with me.

12

I took an evening train upstate. I had to be at the prison early to go through the extensive entry process and decided it was better to head up the night before and stay in a nearby hotel. Then, after being frisked and cleared, I'd meet Darian Clay.

It was only then, on the train to Sing Sing, when the nervousness and excitement of the last week faded away, that the other, deeper nervousness, and excitement, began to surface: I was on my way to meet a multiple murderer. I was on my way to meet, and possibly even work for, an evil man. And not evil like the mean health food store owner I worked for when I was fourteen who made me scrub out the gluten press. Clay was truly evil, in a way almost no one really is. He was not just someone who had done wrong, out of selfishness or stupidity, fear or hate, characteristics which are all too typically human and easy to understand. Clay was different, alien and apart. Whatever the root of his crimes, he had crossed a line and obliterated his own humanity: he had become a monster.

And I was scared to meet the monster. I admit it. I was squirming in my seat. Absurdly frightened, like a child touching a haunted house on a dare, scared of nothing in broad daylight, or like when, eyeing a shark in a glass tank, we step back, just in case. Frightened also of setting foot in the prison for any reason, even as a guest. Wasn't there always a small chance of not being let out? And then there was the deeper fear—contamination: superstitious, primitive, but for that very reason unshakable, the fear that evil could somehow be infectious, that contact with the monster could damage me, do something weird to my "soul."

Frankly, I was feeling like I wouldn't have minded being back home, in my old bedroom, which I'd turned into a study, sitting at the same desk where I'd composed my boyish poems, dreaming of a journey from Zorg to a warm, moist planet where the inhabitants wore masks over their heads and identified each other by their genitals, or else plotting the race to stop the biggest shipment of tainted crack ever to hit Harlem and expose the corrupt white politicians who were secretly backing it. Only one man stood in their way. Mordechai Jones.

Outside the window, as darkness fell, and the train sped north, and the city faded into country, we also seemed to be climbing back into winter. There was still snow up there, on the dead fields and silent buildings, and along the phone wires and fence posts. The spare trees were empty, except for the pines, which were black clumps now in the dark. Up top, where the mountains were iced, the sky was very clear and there were an uncountable number of stars. And sitting across from me, riding backward through space, which I couldn't stand because it made me sick, was Theresa Trio, legal aide.

Trio had some papers for Clay to sign and would also act as my escort, showing me the way to the hotel and prison and walking me through the process, although our meetings with Clay would be separate. She was dressed for travel now, not business, in jeans and a parka that she removed in the overheated train to reveal a baggy ACLU sweatshirt. A button on her backpack urged me to Spread Peace In the MidEast. I noticed something else too: she wasn't afraid.

"You're not scared?" I asked, with a smile. "Making this trip?"

"No," she said. "If you try anything, I have pepper spray."

I laughed. "You know what I mean. Going into the prison. Meeting with a killer."

"Wrongly convicted man, you mean. I work for his lawyer."

"Right. Sorry. Anyway, all I meant . . ." The conversation was getting away from me and I regretted starting it. I was tempted to just shut my eyes and pretend to fall asleep. Start snoring maybe. "All I meant was that it must be interesting. I mean being a lawyer, you have to deal with a lot of criminals and just unsavory types."

"Like porn writers?"

"Ha." I laughed again. "Good one. That's two in a row. I'm an ass, I know. I can't help it. Maybe as a lawyer you can relate."

She smiled a bit now, despite herself. A narrow, grudging smile.

"Anyway," I said, shrugging. "Whatever. Never mind." I turned and stared out the window. Trees. Snow. Stars. As far as I could see it looked exactly the same, as if we hadn't moved at all.

"Actually I'm not a lawyer yet," she said. "I'm doing an internship. I'm a volunteer aide."

"Oh yeah? And why with Flosky?"

"Because I think capital punishment is barbaric. Because even if Clay, or anyone else on death row, were guilty, then fine, they are murderers, but it would be criminal too for us to kill them. There's no way, as a society, we can do that and be civilized."

"Since when were we civilized?" I asked. "Is that even up for debate? Not that I disagree," I quickly added. "I oppose it too. I don't feel comfortable with the state having that power. Not many rich white guys on death row."

"Exactly!" she declared, sitting forward, and finally seeming to warm a bit.

"But still," I couldn't help adding, "I can't help thinking, someone killed those girls, someone did those things, and that person is evil, and doesn't that evil bastard deserve to die?"

"Well, if you feel that way, if he's evil and deserves to die, how could you as a good person, as a civilized man, be doing this job right now?"

"You keep saying that. Who says I'm such a good person?" I asked. "I'm just a writer. Don't worry, once you're a lawyer, you'll understand."

She rolled her eyes, the smile vanished, and she withdrew the slight offer of goodwill she'd extended. The conversation was over. She reached into her purse, put on her glasses, and settled in to read *Crimson Darkness Falls* by Sibylline Lorindo-Gold.

I had never seen anyone reading one of my books before. I assumed of course that someone somewhere must read them, and early on, I admit, I even went to bookshops to see my false names on the shelf, and lurk around like a bird-watcher waiting to see that elusive species, the reader, flit in and pick on me. But it never happened, not once, and my image of the person for whom I wrote remained a vague smudge, less real than my own characters.

My first impulse was to tell her. But then I realized it could be a bad move to let her or her boss or Clay know who I was, or who else I was. Besides, she'd probably never believe me anyway. And what if she did but thought I sucked?

I cleared my throat. "Any good?" I asked, as casually as I could manage.

"What?" She looked annoyed.

"That book. Is it any good?"

She nodded. I guess that was better than a no, but hardly satisfying.

"What's it about?"

"Sorry?" I was clearly bugging her now.

"What's it about?"

She gave me a withering glance and sighed. "Vampires, OK?"

"Huh, interesting."

"Look, don't give me any shit about my taste in books, Mr. Slut Talker."

"I wasn't. I wouldn't. I heard her books were pretty good actually."

She looked up and met my eyes, to judge if I was teasing or not.

"I think she's great," she said.

I think I may have blushed. I know I had to look down. She's a fan, I thought, a real fan. Of mine. And then, because I can't leave well enough alone, any more than I could stop flipping ahead in books, I had to have that next thought, the one I shouldn't be thinking. I can't help it. It's part of being a writer, or a poet, even a bad one. Although I was joking with Theresa, in fact we poets are indeed savages: civilization depends on repression, and we always think that next thing, however unthinkable, and however unspeakable, we speak it too, if only silently, in writing, to ourselves. And so I looked at Theresa Trio and wondered if, under that loose sweatshirt and jeans, anything soft and pink had been pierced. If anything tender needed a little bite.

As she read on, I tried to follow the story with her in my mind, guessing what she might be smiling or frowning over. In the early chapters, my heroine, Sasha, a college student majoring in archaeology, is offered a summer internship in New York, cataloging the collection of a wealthy, reclusive couple. I'm happy to report that Theresa read that part with rapt attention, furrowing her brow, twisting her hair, even, once, chewing her plump lower lip in dramatic sympathy when, on her first night in New York, Sasha takes a walk and is nearly raped in Central Park, only to be rescued by a wolf that mauls her attacker. But then, just as we (Theresa, Sasha, and I) got to the steps of the mysterious couple's elegant townhouse, when the mounting suspense should have been nigh on unbearable, she abruptly shut the book and went to sleep, closing her dark lashes, and leaving behind one slender finger trapped between the pages to hold her place until we got to Ossining, where there was fresh snow on the ground.

13

From *Crimson Darkness Falls* by Sibylline Lorindo-Gold, chapter 3:

I arrived as instructed, just after sundown. A light rain was beginning to fall. As I stood there, clutching my suitcase on the steps of the townhouse, everything around me—the fog-haloed lampposts of hallowed Sutton Place, the dark skyline, the raindrops disappearing soundlessly into the river—seemed beautiful and unreal. I, Sasha Burns, a small town girl, was being invited to inspect the private collection of Aram and Ivy Vane. Schenectady had never seemed so far. A sudden wave of fear went through me and I wanted to run, to race back to Penn Station and catch the first train home. It's only nerves, I told myself, but it felt like something more, a primitive animal reaction, like when one of Dad's hunting dogs smelled mountain lion. Then, before I had a chance to ring the bell, the lock clicked and the massive door swung open. Cautiously, I stepped inside.

"Welcome," a deep, vaguely foreign voice reached me unseen. "Please do come in."

It was a magnificent room, a long, high-ceilinged chamber with fireplaces roaring at both ends. A chandelier glowered from above. Floor-to-ceiling shelves held rare volumes in old tongues. There was little furniture—a few Persian rugs and some beautifully preserved antiques—but a grand piano dominated one corner, a violin resting on its lid. Then a man emerged from the shadows. He was tall and whip-thin, dressed all in black, his hair prematurely gray, I thought, since his strong, handsome face didn't seem older than midthirties. Wide forehead, dark skin, straight, noble nose. The only irregularities were his full, almost feminine lips, the scar that ran from his left temple to his jaw, and his deeply green eyes, eyes that seemed to glow in their sockets like jewels sleeping in a mine where light had never reached.

"I am Aram," he said, taking my hand in his. "I am so pleased you could come. Allow me to present my wife."

He gestured and I gasped. Somehow a woman had appeared beside me without my noticing, as if out of the fog and smoke. And not just any woman. The most beautiful creature I had ever seen. People say I'm cute—thin, blond, blue-eyed and fastest on my track team—but I'd never thought of myself as glamorous or sexy and this woman made me feel like a tomboy. She was tall and voluptuous, with a filmy black dress hugging her ripe curves, jet-black hair falling to her hips, and a pale, perfect oval of a face with blood-red lips and the saddest, most beautiful eyes, like two black tears about to fall.

"Good evening," she said, "I'm Ivy. You must be exhausted after your trip. Let me show you to your room."

The next few days passed in a blur. A wonderful blur. During the day, I was alone in the library, helping to catalog the magnificent collection. I had never seen such artifacts: not only Sumerian, Egyptian, Aramaic, Hebrew and African, but Chinese, Japanese and Indian as well. This sounds nerdy, but unpacking those treasures and cleaning the dust from them with a tiny sable-haired brush was heaven. Only two thoughts bothered me: One, why had such priceless pieces never before been seen or recorded? And two, why me? True, I majored in archaeology at a pretty good state school, but the closest I'd come to a project like this was weighing Iroquois arrowheads at camp.

Aram explained that they wanted to maintain their privacy and prevent any word of their holdings from leaking out. Also, they claimed to find my youthful naiveté refreshing. They were bored with life, they told me, as they sat before huge feasts, watching me pig out on truffles and caviar but never swallowing a mouthful themselves and only touching the wine to their lips. I, certainly, was the furthest thing from bored. They were fascinating: they spoke a dozen languages, played championship-level chess together, and accompanied each other on piano and violin, switching off as the mood changed, from Bach to Schoenberg. They competed to see who could recite the most Shakespeare but gave up just before dawn, with a draw.

I admit, I'd had a crush on Aram from the beginning, though I never in a thousand lifetimes thought he'd take notice of me. My feelings about Ivy were more complicated. I'd never even considered romance with a fellow girl, but she was so beautiful, so graceful, so brilliant, and in some mysterious way so tragic, while at the same time seeming so strong and dominating, almost more like a man. It was confusing.

Then one night she came to my room with a bottle of wine, explaining that Aram was out. Neither of them ever seemed to leave the house, so I asked where.

"Hunting," she said and laughed in a deep-throated way that made me drop the subject. Hunting? In New York? Did she mean for other girls? Was this what made her so sad? If such was his pleasure, I could not imagine too many resisting. Could I? Would I want to? For a second, I remembered the wolf who had ravaged my attacker in the park. Didn't that beast, too, have green eyes?

"Won't you invite me in?" Ivy asked, interrupting my reverie. I laughed and shook off the image.

"Of course!" I held the door back, and she floated over the threshold.

That night, we talked and laughed and listened to music and drank, or I did, and the next thing I knew I must have fallen asleep, because I woke up in the dark. Then, as my senses adjusted, I realized someone was there. I felt strong hands touching my face. I felt breath on my lips. Aram? I thought. Knowing it was wrong, but unable to resist, I let my mouth part to accept the devouring kiss. I put my arms out . . . and felt long hair and the warm body of a beautiful woman. It was Ivy!

Even as we embraced, I told myself I was only dreaming, and the next morning I doubted that it had really happened. But it went on: days spent among books and dusty relics, nights of squab and Schubert, and then Ivy slipping silently into my bed, a finger pressed to my lips to keep me from asking questions.

"Not tonight, sweetness, I beg of you," she would whisper. "Not while we have tonight." I guess I was too dazzled to think straight. It was like I was under a spell. I had never met anyone like them. But I didn't realize exactly how unique they were until the night that I found them fencing in the parlor.

That's right, fencing, as in dueling with swords. I came downstairs, expecting an evening of Mozart, and there they were, hair flying, sweat pouring, swinging these blades at each other. They darted and lunged and jumped over couches. They thrust and parried and broke chairs. It crossed my mind that perhaps they were fighting over me, but they didn't even seem to care that I was there. Finally, with a brutal grunt, Aram sprang forward like a panther and, to my utter horror, sank his foil deep into Ivy's chest, right between her snow-pale breasts, the lovely breasts I'd been kissing just hours before. She staggered about, tearing her dress open and moaning, with the foil stuck in her body, while Aram watched, impassive, his mouth twisted into a cruel smile. I was too shocked to move. She crashed into a small Second Empire end table and collapsed.

"Ivy," I cried, and ran to her. But then, with her last breath, she pulled a huge handgun from the drawer of the table and fired, hitting Aram right in the heart. I saw a hole blow open in his chest and he went down, just as Ivy sighed and died on the priceless carpet before me. I fell on my knees. I wept. Then suddenly, Ivy reached up and gave me a kiss. A big wet one, smack on the lips. I gasped and the dead woman beneath me laughed.

"Ivy, you're alive?"

"Of course," she said, sitting up, the sword still stuck in her cleavage. "Although this does sting." She pulled it out and rubbed the wound, which seemed to be shrinking, healing before my eyes.

"But you shot Aram," I said. "You killed him."

"He deserves it," she said.

"Sour grapes," Aram said, sitting up, fingering his bullet hole. "You can never just lose gracefully." He stood, smiling, and came forward. "But don't worry, I'll get my revenge." I stared in shock, unable to believe my eyes. Was this some trick? An illusion? But how?

"So sorry to scare you," Ivy said. "But you see we are a bit jaded, and in marriages as long as ours, you need to relieve the tension. You'll understand when you're older. How long have we been together, darling?"

He shrugged. "It feels like forever, but it's only nine hundred years." He coughed. "Excuse me," he said, and cleared his throat, then spit into his hand. Smiling, he held it out to me. There was a bullet resting in his palm. My eyes widened in amazement. I couldn't breathe. For a second I thought I was losing my mind. Suddenly, they both began laughing madly, like wild children, embracing with maniacal glee.

It was then that I first saw the fangs.

14

"You Tom Stanks, the Slut Whisperer?" His voice was mild, deep, and a little hoarse, and he spoke the Queens English like me. I walked across the visiting room, polite smile set on my face, the tie Claire had picked and pre-tied for me tight across my throat, and I jumped only a little when the guard shut the door behind me. There were no bars or squeaky gates, just a normal door with a small window. And we weren't in a cell, just a cement room painted an ugly green and furnished with a table and chairs.

I said, "My name is Bloch, actually. Harry."

"Yeah, that's right. I keep forgetting. I'm Darian."

"Nice to meet you." I held out my hand and he chuckled.

"It's been a while since anyone's said that." He held up his arms to show that they were cuffed. "Have a seat."

I reached to pull back a chair but it wouldn't budge.

"Everything's nailed down here," he said. "Including me."

"Right." I sat.

"So," he asked, "do I look like you expected?"

I shrugged nonchalantly. "I didn't really think about it." The truth of course was that I had been thinking about it nonstop. It's a question many writers must sooner or later face: what exactly should a homicidal maniac look like? Do we make him a monster, hugely obese for example, like poor old Sade himself, wallowing in his prison of flesh? How about a shriveled creature in a wheelchair? An evil dwarf, so beloved of David Lynch? A mad scientist with wild hair and crazy glasses, flipping a giant switch? How about all the suavely devilish geniuses and demonic pretty boys, from Lecter back through Dracula to Lucifer himself? Or perhaps you prefer the quiet creep, the insignificant worm who wouldn't hurt a fly?

But the challenge of coming up with a fresh look for one's psycho is really just a cover for a deeper dilemma: evil has no face, except perhaps in the mirror. Let's say, for example, that you're reading this book on the train to work. Now look around. Who among you is the liar, the adulterer, the thief? What about the arsonist, the psychopath, the cannibal? Really, it could be anyone. History is full of ordinary folks doing horrible things for no good reason. In stories, however, this homely truth strikes us as unconvincing. We don't buy it. At least not in trade paperback. So fiction is left with a paradoxical task, one that religion, psychology, and the daily news all fail to achieve: to make reality believable.

So I'll just report the facts as I found them and you take them as you will: he looked fine. He was not an ogre and he didn't look like Brad Pitt (though I'd be happy to sell him the movie rights). He looked like someone's good-looking uncle, the one who keeps fit, playing tennis and ordering the fish. Prison had been good to him. He'd been working out, and even in the bulky jumpsuit I could see that every muscle of his arms, neck and shoulders jumped like a plucked wire. Before prison, he had been good-looking but weaselly, in skinny black suits and shirts at his trial, with his long, greasy hair in a ponytail for court and a couple of rotten teeth. But the state had fixed his teeth and cut his hair. Time had grayed his temples and refined his face. His wrinkles crinkled. His brown eyes twinkled. He looked ready to pose for the thermal underwear ads in a Christmas catalog, gazing into the eyes of a blond wife, beside a roaring fire.

Sitting with him, two feet from evil, I knew the awful truth, but I still couldn't quite grasp it. I was meeting with an ordinary man, nice enough, if not overly bright. You wouldn't fear him. You might even like him. Until you found out that he had chopped off girls' heads and then thrown their bodies in the trash.

"Well, you sure don't look like I pictured," he announced, looking me up and down, frowning like a diner who regretted ordering the special.

"Oh?"

"Younger. Much younger. Smaller too. Shorter and skinnier. You are the Slut Whisperer, right?"

"Well yeah, I wrote that column among—"

"You just don't seem like the instinctually dominant type is all. But you are experienced?"

"Sure."

He searched my eyes, as if he could peek inside, and asked, "So then you have worked extensively, training bitches?"

"Well, I'm a writer," I began, trying to scoot back in the bolted chair. I crossed my legs and arms instead. "Which you know, of course. And as a writer, needless to say, a certain amount of the research that I do is in the form of research per se, as well as actual reporting and speculative writing, as such. I wrote a lot of things, over the years, which as I work with you, projecting forward, this ability I'm sure you'll appreciate, is the ability to project. As such."

Smiling dismally, I imagined myself trying to slip a collar around Jane. Would she bite my hand? Or punch my nose, like that time she accidentally elbowed me in bed and gave me a nosebleed? No. She would laugh. And she wouldn't try to hide it either, like she did when she was helping stuff the toilet paper into my nostrils.

"Yeah well, the reason I ask." Clay sounded dubious. "This project is a two-way street."

"Oh yes." I was glad to change the subject. "I think your letter mentioned conditions?"

"Yeah. Take a look at this." He pushed across a manila folder and I flipped it open.

"These look like letters."

"Fan mail. Love letters from my groupies."

"Groupies?"

"All these girls are in love with me," he explained with a vague wave. "Some nice ones there too. Different ages. A few are even married. I get them from all over, though of course I'm more famous locally, I mean down in New York, not up here in the woods. Go on, read one out loud." He sat back and prepared to listen.

There were a lot of them, written in different hands, or typed on colored stationery. A few thick bundles seemed to stretch back for years, while others were just holiday cards with murky Polaroids and lewd scrawls inside. I selected a mauve letter with a scalloped edge and read from the round, loping script.

" 'I'm not usually like this. So passionate about a man. Just the normal girl . . . next store?' " I cleared my throat. Why was I reading this? " 'But I can't stop thinking about what it would be like to be with you, serving your every pleasure as you wish, at your command, sir. I am five foot two, 127 with a 36 C and big sensible nipples . . . ' " I paused there, reluctant to turn the page.

"So what do you think?" Clay asked.

"She must mean *sensitive*," I suggested.

"About the girl."

"Great. I'm sure you must be psyched."

He snorted dismissively and jangled his chain above his head. "Hell of a lot of good it does me. I'll never touch hair nor hide of them."

"Oh right. That sucks."

Clay shrugged. "Simple twist of fate. Here I am locked up and suddenly every girl wants me. Not that I had any problems with that in the past but it's different when you're famous."

"Right. Right."

"You get that a lot? Being a writer?"

"Not that much," I admitted.

"But I bet you got some stories."

"Sure. Some."

"There's pictures in the back."

"Sorry?"

"A lot of the girls send me pictures. Nothing like what I'd do my-self of course. Just amateur stuff." He winked. I shut the folder and pushed it back.

"Listen, Mr. Clay. Darian. I'm not sure what you want me to do here."

He smiled and I noticed that his state-sponsored teeth were weirdly white. "I want you to write. You're a writer, aren't you?"

"Yes . . ."

"Look," he said. "I'm never getting out of here. I know that. I'll never be allowed to touch another girl or take another picture. All I have now is my mind." He tapped his temple, three times, like knock-ing on a door. "Up here I'm free."

"I see," I said, though I still didn't. I was just noticing how close and hot the air was in there and how much I hated that tie around my neck. How the weird thing was the way I kept forgetting I was talking to a killer and not just the inappropriate, sleazy guy from work who cornered you, suggesting you cruise chicks together, maybe suggest-ing more. Some everyday creep you shrugged off and then brooded about when he scooped up the hottest girl in the office. He leaned toward me and laid his cuffs on the folder. His nails were chewed to the purplish underflesh, the cuticles bitten and raw, red as the gums around his too-white teeth.

"I want you to go see these girls for me, that I can't," he said. "I got a list of ones close by that I asked and they're willing. You talk to them, interview them, and write about me and them, doing what I tell you but in your own style."

"My style?"

He fixed me with his eyes, described in the dumber papers as co-bralike, but to me they were puppy eyes, wet and warm, brimming with earnest soulfulness. "That's what I picked you for," he said. "I dig your voice."

For a moment I said nothing, but I managed to keep a straight face, like I was swallowing something rotten at a dinner party. He waited patiently.

"Let me get this straight," I said. "You want me to go see these women and then write stories about you having sex with them, acting out your fantasies?"

"Exactly."

"Like a porn magazine but just for you?"

"Right. For me to read in my cell."

"Huh."

"And masturbate," he added.

"Got it," I said. "Thanks."

"But"—he pointed a finger at me—"it's got to be quid pro quo. You know what that means?"

"More or less."

"Each story you write for me you get a chapter for the book about my life. And not all the good stuff right away. We'll start at the beginning, when I was a kid and whatnot, but don't worry, you'll get your book. A best seller. Guaranteed."

"Wow," I said, sneaking a look at my watch, wondering what time the train left. "I don't know. To be honest, I'm going to have to think about this."

"Sure, think all you want. Take your time. I have eighty-eight days."

15

I felt sick. The whole time leaving the prison—passing through the checkpoints, signing for my cell phone and keys, desperately untying my tie—I was afraid I was going to throw up, but when I got back to the hotel it had passed. I immediately packed and checked out. I didn't wait for Theresa Trio, although her meeting with Clay was after mine and we had planned to return together. I was also supposed to call Claire and let her know how it went, but I didn't do that either. I just asked the desk clerk to call me a cab and waited for it outside, in my too-light jacket. It helped to fill my lungs with clear air and feel the wind in my face. It was cold but it smelled like spring: damp soil and melting ice. I got to the station early, with an hour to kill before the next train to the city. I bought my ticket and tossed the schedule in the trash. I wasn't planning on coming back.

I went to the men's room, splashed water in my face, dried my hands under the blower. I went back out to the empty waiting room and paced. Then I saw a car pull up and park in the loading zone. Four people got out and entered the station, cold air rushing in the automatic doors with them, as if it had been waiting for the chance. Their hats and bundled coats made them look formless and indistinct, but there was an older man with glasses helping a woman with a cane, another older guy with a trimmed gray beard, and a guy in his forties, clean-shaven. They walked right toward me, and when I stepped aside to let them pass, the younger man called my name.

"You Mr. Bloch?"

"Yes."

He was good-looking and fit, if unremarkable: short gelled hair and a winter tan, carefully manicured hands. I would have guessed dentist or commodities trader. "I'm John Toner."

"Sorry?"

"Sandy Toner's husband."

"Oh," I said. "I see."

"This is Mr. and Mrs. Jarrel. And that's Mr. Hicks. Do you know who we are?"

"Yes," I said. "I do."

They were the survivors, the families of the girls Clay killed. I invited them to the station coffee shop, but they declined and we sat on the plastic waiting area chairs. This was awkward, as they were bolted in a row, so I ended up standing in front of them as if facing a panel. Mr. Hicks spoke first. His gray hair stuck up crazily when he removed his hat.

"We've learned, and I won't say how, about this book project you've got going and we wanted to speak to you in person and let you know that we, as the families of the victims, are strongly opposed to it. Couldn't be more strongly. We're here to appeal to you personally. To let that animal—"

The Jarrels had settled into their seats, like puffy birds, and seemed content to listen calmly to Hicks, but Toner could barely contain himself, squirming and sighing, twisting the dial on his expensive dive watch. He cut Hicks off almost immediately.

"Appeal's got nothing to do with it. We already have a lawyer ready to slap an injunction on this anytime. A top lawyer, believe me." He pointed a finger at my chest, and I noticed he had a wedding band on. It was either the ring he'd exchanged with his dead wife or he had remarried. "Money's no object. This is fair warning, that's all. Look at these poor people. You want to open old wounds?"

The Jarrels blinked calmly at me, as if we were talking about the cold. They were holding hands. Hicks looked down at his own empty palms. He seemed embarrassed.

"Look, Mr. Bloch," he said. "I'm sure you mean well. You've got a job to do."

Toner burst in again. "That's got nothing—"

"Jack, please," Hicks said. "Let me say this."

"Bloodsucker," Toner muttered and turned away.

Hicks leaned toward me. His eyes were a watery blue under his glasses, like rocks at the bottom of a goldfish bowl. "We all deal with things in our own way," he said. "But you can imagine what it's like. My wife couldn't handle it. It broke her. She lost her will to live. She's buried next to Janet now. So I'm asking. For all of our sakes. For our girls too. Please let us rest in peace."

I agreed, more or less. I told them that this was just a first meeting between Clay and me. I said that I wasn't planning on doing the book and their wishes would definitely weigh in. I didn't bother to address the legal issue because I knew, from Claire's attorney, that we were on firm ground, regardless. I also knew that Toner was rich (the top lawyer was no doubt his), that Clay had once worked for him at the factory he owned, and that this was how Clay had met his wife, adding a measure of guilt, a sense of being the connection between killer and victim, that I knew was surely the true source of Toner's rage. I even knew that Mrs. Hicks had died of heart disease and cirrhosis of the liver. I knew all about them from my research, but I wondered, seeing them in person, if you encountered these people randomly, would you know? Not the exact truth of course, but would you know, when you met them, that something was wrong, that something terrible had happened? Did tragedy show, any more than evil? And I wondered, also, why only three of the dead girls were represented. Where was the family of the fourth?

16

When I got home there were five messages on my voice mail. Two from Claire that I skipped. She'd already left one on my cell. One from Morris wanting to get a drink. One from Jane. Isn't it strange how, no matter how long it's been, certain voices stay recognizable, after one word, one breath?

There was a party in two days to celebrate the spring issue of *The Torn Plaid Coat* and she was inviting me, last minute. She had hesitated because of the potential awkwardness, but now she realized that she did really want to see me, she said. If I wanted to come. If it wasn't too difficult for me. Of course it was too difficult. But of course I couldn't stand to let her know it. So of course I had to go. False pride and foolishness, I know, but sometimes that's all we have left.

The last message on my phone was a voice and a name that I didn't know.

"Hello, Mr. Bloch. This is Dani Giancarlo. Daniella, I mean. I'm sorry for bothering you at home. I hope you don't mind, but I'm wondering if I could meet with you anytime tomorrow. Thanks."

She gave a number, then, "Oh, I'm Dora Giancarlo's sister. OK, thanks."

Dora Giancarlo was Clay's other victim: Nancy Jarrel. Janet Hicks. Sandy Toner. Dora Giancarlo. I called her back. When she answered, there was a roar of voices in the background, like she was at a party. I told her not to worry, I'd spoken to the others. She insisted on meeting me anyway.

"But I'm not writing the book," I repeated, louder. "I agreed."

"No," she yelled into the phone. "No, please. Don't."

17

"Of course you're doing the book." Claire was perched on my desk chair, in a plaid miniskirt, black tights and turtleneck, poking at her BlackBerry while I paced and wrung my hands. "Not to sound insensitive, but so what if the victims' families don't want it? You're a writer. You're supposed to tell the story, not be influenced by that."

"But what about this deal with Clay?" I asked. "Going to see these fucked-up groupies and writing little porn stories for him? How creepy is that?"

She shrugged. "It's like in your book *Born to the Game*, when Mordechai agreed to bust the King Pimp out of prison for the greater good of catching the crooked white warden."

"No, it's not like that at all. Here's the difference. I made that up. This is real. And totally fucking twisted. I'll be scarred for life."

"But you're already scarred for life. You were a porn editor. You ghostwrite term papers for high school kids. You dress up like your dead mother and write soft-core S&M vampire books and meanwhile you haven't even had a real, human girlfriend in how long?"

I shrugged. I'd lost track.

"You're a mess. No offense. This is your big break. Maybe your last. Focus on that. Forget about meeting this sister. Let me meet her for you."

"No, that's OK. I feel like I owe it to her."

"Whatever." She sighed. "And what about Jane's party?"

"How do you even know about it?"

"I checked your messages while you were gone. What if there was a business call? Go to the party and schmooze. The relationship is ancient history. But let me cut your hair first. And wear your other black sweater."

"It itches," I said. "What's wrong with this one?"

"It has a hole in the armpit."

I went and checked my armpit in the bathroom mirror. She was right.

"Harry?" She appeared in the door. "Can I crash here tonight?"

"Won't your dad care?"

"He's in St. Bart's with the girlfriend. I told him have fun but you better not marry her."

"OK, make up the sofa and I'll order Chinese."

"Great," she said. "And take that sweater off. I'll try to sew it."

I'd first learned that Jane was seeing her now husband Ryan when I ran into them at a Christmas party, our old Columbia professor's annual open house. It wasn't the sort of event I frequented, but Claire and my mother had both urged me to go, and I wasn't worried about seeing Jane there, since I'd heard she was on a writer's cleansing retreat in the Himalayas. But as soon as I walked in and took off my coat, I saw her, clear chakras aglow, a Tibetan shawl around her shoulders. At first, we were both stunned, as if we'd seen each other's ghosts. Then we fake laughed and half-hugged. She introduced me to Ryan, whom I pretended not to know. I hadn't made it past page three of his tediously clever novel, but his face and name were everywhere just then. They told me how they'd met, or their eyes had, at the mountaintop monastery during a throat-singing concert.

"We'd taken a vow of silence for the week," Ryan eagerly explained, assuming like most happy folks that I couldn't wait to know all about it. "So I had to slip her a note during meditation."

"We went back and forth like that all week." Jane laughed. "*MacSweeney's* is publishing the notes!"

"Ha," I said. "That's great."

Ryan beamed. "When we could finally speak, at the airport, I didn't say a word. I just kissed her." He tried to demonstrate, but Jane looked away, blushing, and he landed one in her hair.

"It's like that story I wrote, remember?" I asked Jane, just saying something so I wouldn't scream. "About the two female sherpas and the mountaineer who get trapped in an ice storm and have to share body warmth?" I'd published it in *Raunchy* under the title "Mighty Him-a-Lay-Hers," and back then, she'd laughed herself purple.

Now she said, "Not really," in a pinched voice and squeezed Ryan's hand, as if sending a signal pulse. "Let's all get a drink. I hear the wine punch rocks."

"It's awesome," I agreed. "You should try it. But I'm just on my way out. My mom's sick," I added, unforgivably.

"Send her my love."

Jane called me later to smooth things out and tell me they were engaged. No one knew yet except for the families and me. When I reported back to my mother, she merely shrugged and, as usual, crushed my few remaining ego crumbs under her colossal support.

"Good. You're better off."

"But you always loved Jane. You said she was smart, beautiful."

"Smart, yes. Beautiful, yes. Also successful. And very sexy with a great figure. But all wrong for you."

"I see."

Claire was equally sensitive. "She's a starfucker. Believe me, I know. My dad married at least three of them, including my mom.

She dropped you like a bad stock, cut her losses, then saw her opening with what's his face. Why don't you date a porn girl? That will at least get you some press."

In any case, that was the last I'd heard from Jane, except for after my mother died, when she wrote a very kind note. And my mother's parting advice for me? "Wait a few years," she'd told me. "Then marry Claire."

18

That night, while Claire slumbered on my couch, I had a dream. It wasn't really a nightmare. It wasn't even about meeting Clay. It was about me. I was watching myself, in my apartment, but it was like it used to look, back when my mother was alive. In fact, she was alive in the dream, though sick and in her bed. I was making her soup and talking to her by yelling back and forth down the hall, which was how she preferred to communicate. The dream was like a movie with the sound turned off. I could see everything, as if I were there, watching our mouths move, but unable to hear what we were saying.

Then I noticed something strange. I was stirring the soup with my right hand. Big deal, I know, but I am a lefty, a severe lefty, and I don't do anything with my right hand. But there I was, stirring soup, adding salt, grinding pepper, all with my usually useless right hand. It's like in a mirror, I thought, still sleeping, and began to wonder, did I ever stir soup with my right? It's possible, isn't it? But then I noticed that in the dream I was also wearing my watch on my left, like righties do, and that was definitely wrong. Then it seemed to me that the backs of my hands, in the dream, were hairier than normal, only a bit, but still, I started to get a weird feeling, like the thin edge of a rising panic pushing its way into my chest. Then I saw that in the dream I was wearing blue socks, navy blue, and that's definitely impossible since I only ever owned white or black. And these looked like wool, also impossible since wool makes my feet sweat. I looked closely, as if zooming in, and my face in the dream had different lines than my waking face. The forehead creases were missing and there were deep verticals by the mouth. And there, sneaking across the right temple, snaking through the hair, was a thin blue vein that was not mine. It's not me, I realized. That man isn't me.

But by then it was too late. He was already heading down the hall toward my mother's room, balancing the bowl of soup on a plate, with the spoon and napkin tucked under one arm and the salt under the other since she always wanted more, no matter how much you added, and whistling soundlessly as he went. And suddenly I knew that he was death, coming for my mother, and I started to scream, to warn her, but it was a silent world and, as if underwater, my screams fell empty from my mouth and rolled away, and no one could hear them, except me, apparently, since I woke up, sweating, in my mother's bed, and ran to the mirror and for a crazy moment, before I was really awake and my eyes adjusted to the light, and before I remembered mirrors were backward anyway, I touched my own right temple and thought I saw the blue vein.

19

The following afternoon, I met Dani Giancarlo at a coffee shop in Soho. When she walked in, a chill went through me, and although she was beautiful and smiling at the world, I felt sad. She wore jeans tucked into high boots and a white cable-knit sweater and was hauling an enormous leather shoulder bag along with her backpack and purse. Her hair was long and straight and blond. That was the only difference. Otherwise she was a dead ringer for her sister with the long brown hair. I stood.

"Ms. Giancarlo? Over here."

She looked momentarily startled, then smiled, waved shyly, and came over. I noticed her dark red nail polish, a weird contrast with the rest of her appearance.

"Hi," she said, and shook my hand before piling her luggage onto the other chair at our table. "Sorry. I have no time to go home between school and work."

"What are you studying?"

"Psychology. I think." The waitress came by and she ordered a decaf soy cappuccino.

"And you work at a bar or a club?"

"Yes." She looked surprised. "How did you know?"

"It was loud on the phone when I spoke to you. Like a party. And just now you were exceedingly polite to our waitress, like someone who knows what it's like. And that bag makes me think you have to change for work, and dress up too, since your hair and makeup are done."

"Wow." She laughed. "You should be a detective. Although I guess it makes sense that a writer is observant too."

"Actually, I mostly write fiction. And not very realistic fiction either."

She smiled shyly again. "And you worked for *Raunchy*. They told me."

"They?"

"Toner and the others."

"Ah well, then I guess you know they came to see me too. And they're adamant about me not writing the book."

"I know."

"And frankly, after meeting him, I'm more than a little queasy about it myself."

"I'm sure. He's disgusting." She reflexively reached into her purse for a pack of Marlboro Lights, which she then left untouched. She sipped her pseudo-coffee, frowned, then added sugar, stirred, and sipped it from the spoon, like soup. I raised my own cup and realized it was empty. Awkwardly, I put it back down.

"Well then," I said. "Not to be rude, but why did you want to see me?"

She stopped fidgeting and looked me in the eye.

"Because I'm still hoping you'll write it. I wanted to tell you that in person."

"I have to say I'm surprised to hear that. Can I ask why?"

She took a minute to think, slowly restirring her gross beverage, but when she spoke it was in a calm, even tone. "My sister and I were close as children. But by the time she died we had drifted apart. Or I had drifted. She was the golden child. Smart, pretty, wanted to be an actress. She was going to college. I had already run away by then and gotten caught up in my own thing. Drugs and whatever. It's a long boring story. Then after my sister died, my mother fell into a depression and two years later she killed herself. Or as my dad said, accidentally took an overdose of sleeping pills. Now he lives in Arizona. He's got a new wife and two kids. He's OK, I mean he helps me with school and stuff, but he doesn't want to talk about anything. But I feel like I owe it to Dora. To find out what happened. What her last hours were like. To find her, you know, remains and to give her a real burial. I can't blame the other families or even my dad. I guess some people are just the type who don't want to know."

"But not you."

She shook her head.

"Dora was your twin," I said.

"Yes." She smiled. "Of course. That's how you recognized me."

"Yes. It's interesting that you said she was the pretty one. You look identical. Except for the hair. You dyed it?"

"Yeah." She ran a hand through it, and it glittered as it fell. "I don't like it. I did it for work."

"Bigger tips?"

"Yeah. But I refuse to get a boob job." She laughed again. "I guess I can tell you, since you probably won't be shocked. I'm actually a stripper not a waitress."

I laughed too. "To be honest, stripper was my first guess. I was being polite."

I put her in a cab and found the subway. As usual the train to Queens took forever, and while I sat on the platform I thought about Dani. There was something familiar that nagged at me, because really I did not know anyone remotely like her, too beautiful and too haunted. Even as she smiled and giggled blondly, she was her own dark sister's ghost. Then later, at my desk, I got it: she was not the kind of girl I ever really met; she was the kind of girl I dreamed up and put into my books, where she either stabbed the hero in his sleep or slipped from his grip on a rooftop and fell to her death.

20

The *Torn Plaid Coat* party was in a bar in Williamsburg. I had to take three trains to get there, but still, when I reached the door, where a few dozen bikes were chained, and peeked in at that convention of expensive jeans, ironic vintage T-shirts and interesting glasses, my knees buckled and I almost turned around. Luckily the reading was in progress and I was able to slip in quickly and duck to the back. At the podium, a freckled young poetess with long red ringlets was holding forth, chanting in that whiny up-and-down singsong I think of as the generic poetic.

> *I recall:*
> *the morning light*
> *was clear and firm*
> *the sheets were crisp.*
> *Chau-bak brought breadfruit*
> *from the garden*
> *and opened it with*

a knife.
You, too, opened me.
Parting like any ripe breadfruit does.
In a way no man ever had.
Sweet summer sister.
I recall.

This got a warm round of applause and then Jane stepped up.

"Thanks, Margaret, that was lovely. And you can read more of her work in the new issue of *Coat*. Not to be too pushy, ha." There were a few chuckles. Jane laughed nervously at her little joke and pushed a strand of hair behind her ear. She looked more beautiful than ever, in a blue dress, awkward and happy. "Our next reader, who is also appearing—well, not appearing, his work is appearing in our spring issue—is fictionist Michael Branborn, whose short story collection *Impossible Tribes* is due out this fall. Michael?"

A tousled young man, younger than me anyway, in thick black eyeglass frames, and wearing a leather jacket over a vintage *Happy Days* T-shirt, got up and hugged Jane chastely before acknowledging the hearty applause. Clearly he was a local favorite. In the front row, I recognized the shaved head of Ryan, Jane's husband. He wore plastic red eyeglass frames and a Gumby T-shirt and sat with a woman whom I recognized as important from somewhere. Maybe on Charlie Rose.

"Thanks," the young writer began. "This story is from my book. It's called, 'The Alien Invasion of Scarsdale.'" There was a lot of overly enthusiastic laughter at this. Branborn laughed too. "I used to really dig these toys called Transformers. Does anybody here remember Transformers?" More whoops and howls. "Cool. Well this takes place in the summer of 1990, which, as you might remember, was the last year for the original Japanese line of Transformers."

"Yes!" someone shouted, and Michael laughed again.

"All right. Cool. Ha. OK so anyway, here's the story." He took a sip of Brooklyn Beer from the bottle. " 'Josh racing down the driveway, skidding to a stop on his Schwinn Racer five-speed. I had envied that bike ever since he got it for his birthday. Chrome handle bars and banana seat."

This got a nice laugh too, and unable to swallow anymore, I got up and went downstairs, where, like some guilt-stricken perv, I loitered about in the restroom, pretending to wash my hands. I searched my bloodshot eyes in the mirror, counted my gray hairs, and by the time I climbed back up, Branborn had reached his climax.

" 'And so . . . , '" he was now intoning, beer raised, manuscript aloft, " 'we fall at last into the arms of our own lawn, which was, that summer, the greenest green in all of Scarsdale.' "

Jubilant applause. The tattooed pixie sitting in front of me whispered to her multipierced friend: "I love that, 'greenest green.' "

I fled once more, this time to the bar. I was about to order a shot of Pepto-Bismol and split when I felt a tap on my arm.

"Hi, Jane." We exchanged an awkward cheek kiss and shoulder-level hug. "How are you?"

"Super. Everything's excellent," she said. "How are you?"

"Fantastically superb."

She laughed. "Did you like the reading?"

"Absolutely incredible."

"OK, OK. I get it. Here, take this anyway." She handed me a copy of *The Torn Plaid Coat*. The cover of course was a plaid, this time drawn in what looked like crayon, with a ragged tear actually die-cut into the paper, exposing part of the contents page.

"Thanks," I said. By then a small herd of writers and artists had gathered around us, or around her, as I was quickly closed out of the circle. "Ted, Kylie, Jeremy, Sloane," she sang. "This is Harry. A friend." I winced at that.

"Hi, everyone." I waved roundly, searching for a way out. There was a lull as the group regarded me. Jane pointed to a tall fuzzy man. "Ted's novel just got picked up."

"Great," I said.

He put his palms together and dipped his beard.

"Actually, you might be interested," Jane went on. "It's about coming of age, really, in an eccentric family in Ann Arbor in the nineties."

"Great," I said again. "That does sound interesting."

"Don't congratulate me too much," Ted said. "Selling it was the easy part. Now I have to write it." He mock whispered, "I'm sentencing myself to Yaddo."

We all chuckled.

"God, don't do that," drawled Kylie, blowing smoke through her bangs. She'd written an anorexic memoir called *Skintight*. I recognized her from the naked picture on the cover, which I'd ogled in the store, without buying it, of course. "I wrote my book sitting alone in a room at the Chelsea."

"Yeah, the bathroom," snapped Jeremy, a hooded and baggy-jeaned fellow, who'd written a memoir about growing up rich and misunderstood in Connecticut as the son of a famous writer. He turned to me. "I never even leave Brooklyn anymore. What do you do?"

"Podiatrist," I said. "In Queens. I have to get back, actually. Emergency. Poor kid might lose a toe. Excuse me." But I found my retreat blocked by Ryan, pale ale in hand. Why had I ever left my room? In my life, I mean.

"Hey, Bloch. How are you?"

"Ryan, hi, what's up?" We shook hands heartily.

"So Harry, what are you working on?" he asked with a smile.

"Oh, Ryan, the usual bullshit," I said, and laughed shrilly.

"Seriously," he said, "when are you going to write something real, with your real name on it?"

"I am, I am," I told him. "It's a coming-of-age novel. *Only the Lame Know Queens*."

"Seriously, Harry," he said again, in a warmer tone, and behind their twin windows, his eyes blinked kindly at me.

And then, I don't know why, for no good reason, maybe to chase away that look, too close to pity, or to squash the slightly human feeling I was almost having near someone I couldn't afford to like, I said, "Actually, Ryan, I'm cowriting a book with Darian Clay, the serial killer."

"Really?" he said, stepping back. "You don't say?"

"Holy shit," Jeremy broke in, bumping into Ryan. "The one they're about to execute?"

"He took those pictures, I remember," Kylie said, joining the circle. "He chopped up those girls."

"They never found the heads," Ted added through his beard.

"Did you really meet him?" blond Sloane, the spoken word artist, asked as she sidled up. "That is so creepy," she added, standing a bit too close.

"Yeah, of course," I told her, with a casual smile. "I'm going back to interview him. They're going to execute him in like eightysomething days."

A brief silence descended, though this time I was not the uneasy one. I felt at peace. Perhaps the angel of death passed over. Perhaps each reflected on his or her own proud project and the dust it would one day become. Jane stared at the faux-torn copy of *Coat* in her hand. Ryan raised his beer bottle to his lips. They all shut up for a moment and looked at the ceiling or the floor, as if in acknowledgment of what I myself had suddenly decided: I was going to write this book. Finally, there was a real writer in the room.

As I nodded good-bye and turned to go, I heard Jeremy whisper to Jane. "He's also a podiatrist."

Walking to the train, I left Dani a message telling her I was going ahead with the book. When I emerged in Flushing, there was a response on my voice mail. She was at work, and again noise drowned her out, but I could hear that she was excited. "Come in for a free drink if you want," she shouted, and then giggled. "Unless that's totally weird and inappropriate."

As opposed to what? I thought, although I didn't call back. I ate some *bibimbop* at a Korean place and went home, to bed, alone. But I was smiling.

PART TWO

April 16, 2009 — May 5, 2009

21

From *Crimson Darkness Falls*, chapter 6:

I have decided. I am ready to give myself to Aram. I am ready to be turned. As if there was ever really any doubt, any choice. I know full well that either he or Ivy could have taken me any time, by force, if they so wished. But the truth it has taken me longer to admit is that I would not have resisted. I was waiting for them. I was yearning.

Still they did not take me. Cruelly, they gave me my freedom, my choice. Why cruelly? Because in the end it is so much more humiliating to make me beg. Is that not the ultimate demonstration of the hunter's power, when the prey surrenders, offers her throat to the fang? The spider, the cobra, the flame that calls the moth: are they killers or lovers who know us better than ourselves? After all, the vampire must be invited in.

You might as well know, I was still a virgin. Snicker if you want, my friends all did, leaving condoms in my locker at the swimming pool and signing me up for creepy online dating sites as a prank. But the truth is that I was not a prude, not scared, at least not in the way they all thought. I was scared of myself. Here is my true secret, which I'd never whispered to anyone: a virgin, I longed for defilement. My purity cried out for darkness. My dad always told me not to give away my "precious flower" to anyone unworthy, but the whole time, my heart was silently beseeching, Daddy, don't you see? I long for the cruel stranger who will pluck my tender blossom and fling it in the muck!

For weeks, after I learned the truth about Ivy and Aram, they made not the slightest move or threat. Ivy even ceased her nocturnal visits to my room. Instead, they seemed to be tutoring me in their history, as if helping me to decide.

Aram is more than nine hundred years old, though he appears to be even younger than forty-three, the age at which he was turned by Ivy, who must be over a thousand, though she looks like she's twenty-five. Ivy is vampire royalty, the descendant of a bloodline, a House, they call it, that goes back to ancient times. She is a pure, born vampire, which makes her extremely powerful and rare. Still, when she met Aram, she fell hopelessly in love. He was a knight then, a Crusader journeying to the Holy Land. In Egypt he visited the brothel Ivy was running, where the women were actually all vampiresses. Infatuated with the handsome, charming knight, she turned him. They were married in Jerusalem and he carried his bride back to Europe like the plague.

They built a fortune, as mercenaries, brigands and pirates. They learned Greek and Latin, mathematics and philosophy, studying with scholars and monks who never suspected they were the ones harvesting children from the villagers, who blamed it on Gypsies and Jews. They attended conservatory in Vienna. They traveled through India and across China, learning Sanskrit and meditating in caves for years, then spent a decade in Japan learning calligraphy, flower arranging and swordsmanship.

They went everywhere—Africa, South America, even the Arctic, with a cargo of live victims chained below decks for food. They fought in both world wars, on both sides. They'd been in New York for decades and had amassed yet another fortune in real estate, buying up property just after the Depression. Through a web of false names and companies, they controlled nightclubs, drug dens, bars, trendy restaurants and a famous art gallery. They wore the best clothes, owned the finest of everything, and feasted on the most beautiful boys and girls in the world.

Yet they were bored. Eternally and exquisitely bored. Ivy, who had experienced every sensual pleasure possible, and found every man and woman she encountered at her feet, spent most days in her room, reading poetry. Aram was sick to death of his own hunger, his bloodlust, and felt like a junkie when, with nightfall, he once again needed to seek his prey and bring his trophies home to his beloved. They loved each other utterly, divinely and satanically, to the point of despair, but for two such passionate souls to be together so long inevitably led to epic fights that those of us who break up every six months can't imagine. That was when the games of killing each other began: shooting, stabbing, hanging, drowning. It amused their jaded senses and relieved the tension, while hiding a darker truth: the only thing that still thrilled and frightened them, that made their pulse quicken, was the thought of dying together.

I think this is the reason they gave me the choice. To let me see far down that path before I took the first step, the one with no return. I think this is why Aram spent so many hours working with me, going through the artifacts and telling me about his life. Why he let me see him when he returned from the hunt, hair wild, clothes torn and dirty, blood on his teeth and the look of a victorious predator in his blazing green eyes. But why me? Why did they deign to grant me the decision at all, when they'd left a trail of empty bodies behind them? All I knew was that my own hunger was growing stronger and stronger. The more Aram warned me away, the more I wanted him, and to be his. Although in so many ways, without saying it, he seemed to be urging me to flee while I still could, another force, deeper than fear, was drawing me, hopelessly, helplessly closer.

Finally, the night before my twenty-first birthday, I couldn't stand any more. Aram was showing me a battle-ax, circa 1400. As he hoisted the weapon in his hands, those hands that could caress a violin or crush a windpipe, I saw that distant look in his eyes.

"I took many lives with this," he mused.

I reached out and touched him, the tips of my fingers kissing his wrist. "Take mine."

He looked at me curiously. I let my fingers circle his strong but surprisingly thin and delicate wrist. "Not with your weapon. With your lips. Your arms. Your fangs. Take my life. Take me." Summoning all my courage, I looked up and met his eyes. "Please."

He said nothing. He held my gaze. He set down the ax and took me in his arms. Then he bent his face to mine and let his lips brush my lips before settling his mouth on my throat. I gasped as he entered. How can I describe this feeling? Pain filled with pleasure, sweetness sharpened with fear. And then the fear melted as he drank from me, and I lost myself, feeling his presence everywhere within me, every nerve, every vein . . .

"Aram!" It was Ivy, there before us. Aram pulled away, smiling, my blood oozing through his lips. He pulled Ivy close. He pressed his mouth to hers. He fed her my blood from his lips. While she sucked on his mouth her eyes fixed, wildly, on mine.

I held my breath. I waited for the change. For something. Nothing came.

"What happened?" I asked. "What's wrong?"

Smiling and licking his lips, Aram turned to Ivy. "Would you like to explain?"

Ivy leaned toward me. "What is your mother's real name?" she asked.

"My mother?" My mother died giving birth to me. I am named after her. "Her name was Sasha Smith, why? She was an orphan. She never knew her real name."

"Your mother's name," Ivy said, "was Sasha Divina Diamonedes de Troth, Princess of the Royal House of Troth. She was my cousin."

"What?" I felt like I was dreaming. I wanted to laugh.

"We played and hunted together as children. She fell in love with a mortal as I did. But instead of turning your father, as I turned Aram, she attempted to turn herself, and live as humans lived. It killed her."

"But what are you saying?" I asked. "That I'm some kind of vampire?"

"You are a half-breed. Very rare. Few survive. And to carry royal blood, that is unique. We searched the world for you. Watched and protected you from afar. And brought you here when the time was right."

"But why? Why now?"

Aram put his hand on mine. "The reason my bite didn't turn you is that your own vampire blood makes you impervious. You are inoculated. But from the day you turn twenty-one, you will begin to grow and change. To develop new powers, unique to a half-breed. If you train with us you will be even stronger. And then . . ." He hesitated. Ivy took my other hand.

"Then when you are ready, dear cousin, we will let you feed on us. Drink our blood. And then you will be as we are. Forever."

22

The first woman on Clay's list was Morgan Chase. She lived in a quaint little building on Horatio Street, in the West Village, and worked in corporate banking, which is what it takes to live like a bohemian in the Village these days. She was in her thirties, tall and slim, with fashionably cut dark hair, and dressed in a perfectly fitting but very subdued suit. Prada, I think, or Jil Sander. Her living room, when I met her, was tastefully decorated and immaculate, with a lot of well-worn old friends on the shelves: the darkly tressed Brontë sisters were there, weeping together, beside fat *Pamela* and *Clarissa*, promiscuous, sprawling Trollope, and even Walpole and Radcliffe, the original moody Gothics, with their crypts and dungeons and moss. No doubt if I peeked behind Pamela's skirt I'd find *The Story of O*. Her coffee was good and she used real cream. In other words, Morgan was highly educated, attractive and stylish. Really, under different circumstances, I would have been happy to take her out myself, but then I'd never ask. She was clearly out of my league.

Perhaps you are surprised to learn that this is the kind of woman who writes love letters to a murderer of women. Let's pause here and consider this fact, because it's a question that will come up again, and honestly, I don't want to waste too much time thinking about it. I'm not that big on character motivation, frankly, with my vampires and wizards, my hit men and nymphomaniacs. I'm really not even that interested in motivation as a person, though perhaps I should be. Why anyone, myself included, did what we did was a hopeless mystery to me.

So when I met Morgan Chase, I was surprised and I wasn't. Remember, I put in a lot of time pounding out the porn. I spent countless hours staring through a loupe at proof sheets that, however delusional, were indeed proof of one thing: someone will do anything. And when you add in the letters to the editor, the amateur photos, the drunken confidences at parties, you realize that perversity might reside in anybody, if anything in inverse proportion to outward appearance. Of course the postcolonial, postmodern, postfeminist of color yearns to be spanked by old white men, while the fiftyish WASP CEO longs to feel a three-hundred-pound black woman's high heels stabbing his back. At best, there is a vague, even contrary, relationship between who we are variously as workers, citizens, friends, lovers, strangers and by ourselves. These different sides are like the many faces of a theoretical quantum coin, and though they may overlap or connect along a seam or even cross planes, they will never be seen all at once, at least not in this universe. And for the multidimensional coin to see itself: that's a thought beyond the mind of even the High Lord Wizard of Zorg.

23

Transcript of a letter, dated September 6, 2008, from Morgan Chase[*] to Darian Clay, written in purple ink (from a fountain pen) on thick pale rose paper:

Dear Sir,

I know, lying here in my bed, while you lie in your cell, that we are together. I know, though the courts say you are a killer, that you are innocent. I know, though the newspapers say that you will be put to death in—I can't say it, a very short time—I know you will be free, and that you will hold me in your arms, and then I will give myself to you, My Love, completely, totally, like no woman ever gave

---

[*] In several instances, throughout this book, names and identifying characteristics have been altered.

herself to a Man, no lover to her Beloved, no slave to her Master. Please, please, write to me. Tell me what You will do to me when that day comes. Tell me what You will have me do for You.

Yours forever,

Morgan

24

"Hi. I'm Harry Bloch."

"Morgan Chase."

"Thanks for seeing me like this."

"Of course, my pleasure. Thank you."

"Sure."

"Would you like some coffee or tea?"

"I don't want you to go to any trouble."

"No trouble. I just brewed a fresh pot of coffee."

"OK then, sure, that sounds great."

"Cream and sugar?"

"Just cream please, thanks."

"Unless you'd rather have tea?"

"No, coffee is great."

"Be right back."

"OK."

I sat at the table. I had just arrived, but already I was socially exhausted and my face felt stiff from smiling. I wanted to slip out the door while she was in the kitchen. I felt that mixture of defeat and panic that we feel five minutes into what we know will be a disastrous first date, what the rabbit must feel just as he steps into the trap.

But it was too late to run, so I took out my minirecorder and mic, my pad and pens, my manila file of notes, and got ready to work. Morgan Chase came back with two steaming mugs of coffee and set them down on two coasters. I thanked her and took an appreciative sip. I double-checked my notes.

"OK," I said, "let's say you're with Darian, and he has you tied to the bed—"

She tremored so badly that her cup skipped and coffee jumped across the table at me. I pulled my belongings back from the spreading tide. There were a few starry spots on my files.

"Sorry," she blurted and ran away, returning with a sponge and paper towels. "I'm really very sorry," she said again, violently swabbing the table. "I feel terrible about this."

"Don't mention it." It was her table, after all.

"No, I mean, I'm sorry, but I don't think I can do this." Her eyes were on the sponge. "I just can't."

I stood. "Please don't be sorry," I said, perhaps a bit too eagerly. "I understand completely. I don't want to embarrass you."

"I feel terrible to have wasted your time."

"Not at all. This was a bad idea."

Immensely relieved, I stuffed my gear in my bag and hurried out, thumping down the creaky steps and out into the fresh air. No doubt Clay would fire me. The book would perish. Claire would be furious. I would stay broke and unloved. So what? I could breathe. Leaves were nearly open and the river smelled close, mingling with car fumes and the herbal sweetener of someone smoking pot.

"Wait." A hand at my elbow stopped me. It was she. "Please. Come back."

Her front door was open behind her. She was breathless and still holding a sponge in one hand.

"Are you sure?"

She nodded, just barely able to look me in the eye. I followed her back in, resignedly, as if I were the one being tormented. We sat back down at the table. She poured more coffee, slowly this time, and reset her mug, on its coaster, directly in front of her, halfway across her side of the table. I realized that the big white throw pillow was set precisely in the middle of the white couch. Over the fireplace, a square white porcelain vase was placed in the exact center of the mantle. She herself was now recentered, sitting perfectly straight on the edge of her chair, and looking right at me.

I rearranged my things to make them a bit neater and lined up my piles with the table edge. I drank from my cup and put it down right across from hers.

"Let me be frank," I said. "You seem like a nice lady. Smart. Attractive." She colored slightly. "And reserved. Why are you doing this?"

She smiled, girlishly, and when her nose crinkled I noticed the freckles hidden under her powder. Her eyes jumped to mine and then away. "Why Mr. Bloch," she asked me, like a heroine in one of the books on her shelf, "haven't you ever been in love?"

Morgan was in college during the murders and the trial. English major of course. Growing up in the Midwest and attending school in Chicago, she remembered the case only vaguely, but she did recall the manhunt, the shivers of fear she felt watching the news with her sorority sisters, and of course, the handsome defendant. It was only years later, after she had dropped the books and earned an MBA in New York, that she again ran across the story in the local papers, now centered on the endless appeals. Meanwhile, her personal life had not gone well. An early marriage to a depressive Byron scholar had ended badly and was followed by years of successful workaholism, boring dates with colleagues, and a fertile fantasy life that grew tangled and wild within the walls of that pristine apartment.

The more Morgan spoke, the more relaxed she seemed, and as coffee proceeded to wine and cheese, and we proceeded to the white-on-white living space, she became more voluble, in that way we sometimes are with strangers. I'd experienced this before with interviewees, who often said extraordinary things, even on tape, simply because I sat there nodding and let them fill up the silence. Morgan was attractive, as noted above (she even reminded me a bit of Jane, if only in her bookishly clumsy grace), but I was careful not to mistake her gradually loosening tongue for real intimacy. If anything, the opposite forces were at play: wine and anonymity. Not only were her name and reputation safe with me but, as Clay's errand boy, I was even less threatening than a therapist or priest, since I would offer no judgment or diagnosis at all. Who cares what I thought? I was just the ghost.

"Even when I was married," she said, pouring more wine, "there was always something missing for me, sexually." She sat in the overstuffed chair, bare feet folded beneath her thighs, pointy black heels leaning together on the floor, while I sank slowly into the couch. "I had a hard time, you know, having orgasms."

She glanced at me, as if to gauge my reaction. I looked at the piece of Brie in my hand and nodded sagely. "I see," I said.

"I even thought that maybe I was gay, but that wasn't it. I had no attraction to women. Then I thought it was organic, you know, like a hormone thing or I just had a low sex drive." She dated men from work, some very handsome, some very rich, but never felt any real erotic passion, except in her own imagination, creating elaborate fantasies about the dominant, dangerous men she read about or saw on TV, Darian Clay included.

"The truth is, I've always had these fantasies. I would imagine scenarios when I was by myself. But I never discussed them with anyone. I thought there was just something wrong with me. Then I discovered the whole Internet world."

"Porn?" I asked, trying to sound nonchalant as I dunked my cheese in my wine. "Oops." I chuckled suavely and popped it in my mouth. "You were talking, I think, about porn?"

"Yes. I went to those websites. The worst I could find. And to those forums and rooms. It's awful the things I look at online. I've even called some of those phone lines and had men say terrible things to me, call me a pig and a slut, while I, you know. I was horribly ashamed of course, but I couldn't help myself. It was all I thought about. But I never did anything or told anyone and I never expected to. Until I met Darian. Somehow he sensed it in me."

She wrote Clay a letter of support expressing belief in his innocence. He answered, and a correspondence developed, becoming more romantic, more passionate, more erotic. He asked for photos, perfumed paper, pubic hair folded into letters. He told her what to do.

In many ways Clay was the perfect boyfriend, especially for a shy woman who'd been hurt before. He had unlimited time and energy to focus on her. He was passionate, interested, devoted. There was (she thought) no competition from other women, and little risk of real life ruining the fantasy. This was one man who would never leave the toilet seat up or snore or fart or disappoint her in bed. He would never be commitment-phobic or emotionally unavailable or have intimacy issues. Based on what I'd seen, she was far more intelligent than he was, but wasn't this the case for lots of women? And if she was largely projecting her fantasies onto him, didn't plenty of men do this, and not at a distance either, but with the women right beside them every day? Even the kinkiness becomes easier to understand. Of course she could let her fantasies run further, and into darker places, than the average woman: there was no chance they would ever come true.

"But you can't ever be together," I said, trying to press her. "I mean, not really."

She smiled, swirling the wine in her glass, watching it slip down the sides. "I feel closer to him than to anyone I ever met. And I believe he will be free one day. Lots of couples have endured long separations."

"Sure, if they were together and then something happened, a war or whatever. But you've never once really been alone. Or had sex."

She smiled again. Clearly, her look seemed to say, you have never truly loved, nor has any woman truly loved you.

"In the end, sex is all in the mind," she told me. "Bodies don't matter."

25

From *The Taming of the Slut* by Tom Stanks:

> Morgan felt him before she saw him. She looked up from her magazine and there he was, standing by the door of the subway car, a tall man, dark-haired, brutally handsome, dressed all in black—black suit, black overcoat, black boots. He didn't look away like most men did when she caught them staring. He met her eyes with his deep, dark eyes. Piercingly intelligent and soulful, in a strong masculine way, they seemed to burn right into her, to see the secrets of her heart. She blushed and looked down, and pressed her long, slender legs together more tightly under the dress that suddenly felt too short. But the shudder of fear that went through her well-toned body, and even the flash of anger, did nothing to stop the sudden spring of desire she felt between her shapely legs. She peeked again. He was still staring. Now she felt sure that he knew she was aroused and could see the hard nipples on her full,

ripe breasts thrusting against the thin jersey fabric. She was ashamed. It was like she had no control over her own body. It was like he was in control.

When they got to her stop she fled, clacking on her high spiked heels up the steps, down her dark street and home, afraid to look back, but thinking, fearing, perhaps hoping that he was there behind her like a shadow. A shadow cast by the night.

By the time Morgan pushed into her tastefully decorated apartment on Horatio Street, she could barely contain herself. The juice was running down her inner thighs like sap from a split maple tree in high season. She ran to the bedroom and got her vibrator out of its hiding place. Her breathing was crazy. She closed her eyes. She moaned. And then she heard it. Demonic laughter. She looked up. It was him, the dark stranger from the train. She had forgotten to lock the door. Or had she purposely left it unlocked, for him?

"I knew it," he said. "I always know. I can smell when a woman wants me."

"Who, who are you?"

"My name is Darian," he said, stepping in. "But you will call me Master."

26

"Pretty good," Darian said, when I stopped reading. "But why's it take so long to get to the good stuff? Like that part where he cuts her panties off with his pocketknife? I would have done that right on the train."

"This seemed more realistic," I explained. "It builds the tension. You track her, getting closer, knowing all along."

"Yeah, that is true," he allowed. "I can always tell. I like how he knew from just a sniff that she wanted it."

"Thanks."

"But what about later when he slaps her? You said she almost came. Why almost? She should just come right there." He snapped his fingers.

"Well, if that happens right on page one, there's no story," I argued, as if I were back in school, defending myself against a writing workshop. Who did this guy think he was, anyway? At least I could spell. "You need something to work up to. Writingwise."

He nodded noncommitally. "What's the rest?"

"Look, I can't read the whole thing to you. We only have an hour." Now that he was starting to bug me, I was no longer frightened. I foresaw a long, annoying sentence for myself if I didn't get this interview going. I put the pages back in their manila envelope. "You can take it back to your cell, after, and read the rest."

"OK, OK," he said. "Let's do it. Get out your little recorder."

Which I did. It took me a minute to get it going and to find my questions. Clay waited patiently, a vague smile on his lips.

"You were abandoned by your mother, right?" I asked.

"Wrong." He snapped the word off and then stared at me, motionless.

"Sorry, I was just going by what I read."

"You read wrong," he snapped again.

"Well, this is your chance to set it right."

"Why don't you tell me about *your* mother?"

"My mother's dead," I told him.

"Sorry." He frowned, at himself, it seemed. "No offense."

"It's all right." I paused the tape. "Look, we don't have to discuss it if you don't want to. But you said we would start at the beginning."

"You're right. Deal's a deal." He nodded at the recorder and I started it rolling again. He took a breath. "My mother. For one thing she didn't abandon me. The cops took my mother from me. And then the state kept me from her. That's who ruined my childhood. The government. Same people as got me now. People say I hate women? I hate cops. If they find a chopped-up social worker from child services, come talk to me. But no one loves girls more than me. That's my life's work."

"Let's get back to your mother," I said. "Maybe it's not true. I'm just asking about what I read, but the papers also say that she was . . . that she worked . . ."

"A whore?" He leaned forward, grinning, cuffed hands between his knees. "Is that the word you're looking for? Sure, my mother was a whore. I'll say it. So what? We had to eat. How many women around this country last night spread their legs for some guy they don't want so they can eat? It's called marriage. So my dad, whoever the fuck he was, took off. He's the bastard, not me. So she didn't fuck him for her rent. She fucked some other guy. So what? She was a whore. She was a waitress. She worked in a factory sewing doll clothes. Probably no one does that anymore, huh? Here, I mean. This was out in Brooklyn. I remember she brought me home some and I put them on my GI Joe. She sewed my clothes there too. I guess they let her."

"She sewed you clothes?" I asked. "Like pants? That's hard, I think."

"No, I mean sewed them up, you know. With patches. Because we were poor."

"Right, right."

"She was a good mom is my point. We had breakfast together every morning. Cereal. I remember I loved the taste of coffee, even when I was just a little kid—"

"Me too," I chimed in without thinking.

"So she used to put just a little in my milk."

"With a lot of sugar, me too!"

"I still get the craving for that sometimes," he said.

"You can get that here?"

"What? Coffee and milk? Sure. I mean I only feel like it once in a while."

"Oh yeah. Of course." I laughed. "I wasn't thinking. I pictured you like ordering it."

"Yeah right, from the CO." Clay laughed too, showing those choppers, which reminded me again where I was. I felt a sudden wave of self-disgust, of shame before my own eyes, giggling with the killer. But it worked, or seemed to; the connection was made and he relaxed, leaning back in his chair as he went on without my prompting.

"Then one day she left and never came back. The whole night went by. I had a neighbor who used to look after me, but this was after we moved out from there. A hotel in Corona, I think. Or Ozone Park, maybe? I can't remember exactly."

"I can check that."

"I was alone the whole night through. No food in the house. Just some Cap'n Crunch at the bottom of the box, I remember, like the crumbs. No milk."

"You were scared."

"Fuck yeah. I was five. So I hid in the closet. I guess I felt safer. And then, the next morning, I had to use the bathroom really bad, I remember that, but it seemed so far to cross the room. I remember, it must have been pretty early, cause the TV was on the whole time, it was the *Today* show and I knew the cartoons would start soon and I could peek out and see them."

He stared into space now as he spoke, leaning forward, perfectly still, brown eyes on nothing. I held still too, in the windowless room that smelled like ammonia, like hospitals and men's rooms, and heard the fluorescent strip above us softly hum. It cast our shadows down flat: the pencil in my hand on the notebook, the shape of his shoulders and head unfolded, like a blank map, across the table and floor. What is the name for that color? Not gray, not black, but a darker tone of whatever the shadow touches—fake wood, gray linoleum, tan paper, pink skin.

"And then suddenly the door opened and it wasn't my mom, it was the cops. Just suddenly cops were all over. Or it seemed that way, maybe it was only two cops, but you know, they seemed huge with their uniforms and guns and belts. And social services was with them. And they took me. And that was it."

He stopped. I waited. And then: "You never saw your mother again?"

"No. Never again. That was it."

27

When I came out of the visitors' room, Flosky and Theresa were there, waiting in the outer room with the benches and vending machines.

"Hi," I said, smiling. Flosky turned away, smoking furiously despite the large No Smoking sign on the wall above her head. Theresa looked tired and pale, her black hair pulled back from her face. She drew a folder from her briefcase.

"Here's the signed copy of your contract."

"Thanks. Is something wrong?"

Theresa lowered her voice. "Our last appeal was denied." She glanced over her shoulder at Flosky, who was ashing her cigarette in the water fountain. It was Theresa who actually looked sad. Flosky just looked slightly more pissed off than usual.

"Sorry." I wasn't sure what to say. Was I sorry, now that I had gotten to know him, that Darian was going to die? Not particularly. "So it's over then?" I asked Theresa.

"Nothing's over," Flosky broke in. "Don't worry about that."

"No," I fumphered. "I didn't mean it like that."

She turned on the water fountain and doused her cigarette, then fed a dollar into the soda machine and pressed the button for Diet Coke. The dollar spat back out.

"Fucking thing." She flailed at the machine, kicking and punching, then stumbled as her pointy-toed shoe caught an edge. "Fuck," she repeated, hopping on one heel. "That's a brand-new shoe."

"Here, let me try," I said. I pulled out my money and slid a smoother bill into the machine. I could see from its scarred face that it had borne the blows of many frustrated visitors. The soda can dropped as the guard entered the room.

"Carol Flosky?" he called out.

"Yeah?"

"Your client's ready."

"OK." She grabbed her case and, hobbling with remarkable dignity, proceeded through the door toward her client. I noticed too, as she passed, that when she'd punched the soda machine, the thick ring on her finger had cut the flesh, revealing a slim line of blood. She hadn't so much as flinched. If I ever get in trouble, I thought, I want her as my lawyer. The guard sniffed.

"You been smoking in here?" he asked me.

"Me? No. I don't smoke."

He frowned at me and left me alone with Theresa and a large, awkward silence.

"You want a soda?" I asked lamely. "I don't like diet."

She shook her head. "He doesn't know yet," she said. "She's going to tell him now."

"I know. He was fine when I saw him. The interview went really well."

Theresa sat down and took out a fat law book bristling with yellow Post-its. She snapped open her glasses case and put them on. Is it any wonder that I've always had a little thing for the sexy librarian type? What could be hotter than a girl who reads?

"Hey," I said. "You know that writer, the vampire one you told me about? I checked her out. Looks pretty good."

"I think so," Theresa said without looking up.

"I saw where she has a new book coming out soon."

"It's just out. I got it."

"Really?" This was news to me. "I'll have to check it out. So you got it already, huh? You're really a fan?"

She ignored me and bent into her work. Where her shirt lifted in back, I saw an inch of pale skin, and the tendrils of a black tattoo, creeping up, or down. My inner vampire felt his fangs.

"Well, just if you're interested," I went on, "I saw where the author's doing this online thing too." It was a gimmick my publisher had come up with. In truth, I barely understood the concept, but Claire had promised to help. "She's going to be inside a chat room," I explained, trying not to look too alarmed.

"Yes," she said into her law book. "I already know."

28

On the train I started transcribing the interview, typing into my laptop while listening to the tape on headphones, always the worst part. It's amazing how long-winded people seem when you have to type it all out, myself included. It took me a while, when I began doing interviews, to learn to stop interrupting my interviewees so that I could talk. Then later I'd have to listen to myself on tape, telling my own tired anecdotes. And the sound of my own voice grated, a nasally Queens whine even worse than I'd imagined. Even now, listening to myself with Clay, I winced every time I heard one of my annoying tics, like endlessly saying "Right, right." The truth is that the writers and filmmakers most admired for their natural-sounding dialogue are completely stylized, while most real, unedited transcriptions of actual conversations soon grow unbearably boring.

And so it was with Clay. He went on and on, in a monologue both chilling and numbing, through the litany of horrors that was his journey in the child welfare system, shunted from foster home to foster home, neglected, bullied, beaten and quite possibly molested.

One of his former foster parents was later arrested for molesting boys, although Clay was not specifically named as a victim and when I brought it up he denied it. But his statements differed from the record in many ways, especially about his mother.

Geraldine Clay was a nightmare. The pathological nature of her mothering went far beyond the poverty and neglect Clay described. She was a prostitute with a long record of arrests, including many for theft, drug possession and public drunkenness. According to the child welfare case notes, introduced into the record during the sentencing phase of his trial, she not only left him alone for extended periods but also kept little Darian locked in the closet while she entertained clients. At first he cried, so she gagged him until he learned to remain silent. If he wet himself during his incarcerations, he was beaten. Although it's true that social services took him that morning after her arrest, when she informed an officer in the station her child was still home alone, he became a ward of the state only by default. Even after her release from jail, after doing sixty days for misdemeanor soliciting, she never showed up at any of her son's custody hearings. She just left him behind as she continued to accumulate arrests in various cities—San Francisco, Los Angeles, Detroit. Then maybe she cleaned up her act, because after 1996 there is nothing. She would have been around forty or forty-five by then and it's possible that, like many chronic recidivists, she just aged out, got too old and tired for the extremely stressful life of a full-time criminal. Or maybe she got killed.

29

Finally I fell asleep on the train, wearing my headphones, with the tape running. I had some weird dreams I couldn't recall, woke up choking on the cord, and reached home exhausted. But the day wasn't over yet. As I came down the street from the subway, a guy who looked like an undercover cop got out of an undercover cop car. The car was a black Chevy. The guy wore a black overcoat over a navy suit with a white shirt and a red tie. He didn't seem like the tough type though. He looked smart—unframed spectacles, a tight mouth, lined face. His graying black hair was brushed back, kind of long for a cop. I felt a rush of irrational fear, the fear that, despite my constant insistence that nothing is my fault, I am somehow, deep down, obscurely but irredeemably guilty.

"Bloch?" he asked.

"Yes?" I said in a quiet voice.

"Special Agent Townes."

"Yes?" He showed me ID but I just glanced at it. I knew his name from my research on the Internet, and now his face looked vaguely familiar as well: he was the FBI agent who caught Clay.

"I need a minute," he said.

"Sure." I forced a deeper tone into my voice. "Come on up for a cup of coffee."

"No time. I have to fly to Memphis tonight. If you don't mind we can sit in my car." He opened the back door without waiting to see if I minded. I did mind, but I got in anyway, and as he slid in beside me, the fed behind the wheel got out, to give us our privacy, or maybe to avoid witnessing my torture.

"How's the book coming?" he asked. We were both staring straight ahead, as if parked in a drive-in movie.

"Good," I said. "Thanks for asking."

"I thought you promised the families of the victims that you wouldn't write it?"

"I never promised anything. And not all the relatives feel that way."

"Daniella Giancarlo? She's a mess. Junkie, stripper. She's one step from the can herself. I'm talking here about the other families. The Jarrels. The Hicks. Good honest people who just want to suffer in peace. Mr. Toner got a lawyer. He owns a factory around here. A big spread out on the Island too."

"What's he make?"

"Huh?"

"The factory."

"Polybags. Those rolls of plastic bags that the dry cleaners put over your clothes."

"Darian Clay worked there?"

"Yeah. That's right. And how do you think he feels? Knowing that sick fuck spotted his wife at his factory? You should respect their wishes. It's the least you can do."

I shrugged. I kept my tone steady. "Daniella Giancarlo may not own a garbage bag factory, but her sister is just as dead."

Townes turned and regarded the side of my face. I wasn't the author of *Hot-blooded Killer, Cold-hearted Pimp*, a Mordechai Jones Mystery for nothing.

"Look," he said. "Of course she's obsessed with the case, she was in a fog when it happened. She's got guilt, whatever, plus she's twins. Issues up the yin-yang. Ever think you're taking advantage of her?"

"Ever think it's none of your business?" I asked, and immediately regretted it. I braced for a punch, and my right eye, closer to him, squinted involuntarily. This is the other side of that irrational fear I mentioned, equally irrational outbursts of stubborn rebelliousness.

But Townes didn't even blink. "Catching killers is my business," he said. "Feeding like a parasite on the corpses of the victims is yours."

Then he put his hand out and I shook it. He didn't even squeeze that hard. Still, as I got out, waving jauntily, and headed toward the door of my building, I kept a guiding hand on the wall: my knees were shaking so bad, I was afraid I'd fall.

But when I told Claire, in a rush of panic mixed with pride, about how I'd been leaned on by the feds, she laughed. She was wearing a leotard and leg warmers, doing some kind of yoga in my living room, with her cell phone headset on.

"Townes? Townes can suck my left tit," she said, while bending herself in two. "Of course he wants you out. I've been checking up on him. He just signed a deal to write his memoirs, but he has to wait till he retires. If he quits early, he gives up his full pension, dental, everything. Meanwhile, you're going to beat him to the punch, the movie, the whole megillah." She smiled at me from under an arm, or leg. "It's a tough one all right, but it's his balls caught in the zipper, not yours."

"Really? A memoir?" I asked, sitting on the couch, trying not to watch her tiny prelegal bottom rise and fall. "Who's ghosting his book?"

30

Crimson Night and Fog was published, to little or no fanfare. Even my ceremonial trip to the Barnes & Noble in the Roosevelt Field Mall was a bust. The book was nowhere in sight, although I found a few scrambled copies of my others misplaced about and quietly reshelved them. Finally I asked a young sales associate if that new, eagerly awaited novel by Sibylline Lorindo-Gold wasn't due out today. He shrugged and checked the computer, which said there were four copies on the shelf. I insisted, and he dragged his heels into the back, emerging with a book much like the one I already had at home: a plump trade paperback, with a cover image of a crimson sky bleeding into a black mountain range. I had wanted the blood streaks to be embossed so they would pop out and look more like actual drops, but it wasn't cost effective. I thanked the associate, who shrugged again, and once he'd wandered off, I set the book in a prominent place on the Horror/ Urban Paranormal shelf, before slinking off to the bus.

Luckily, I did have a few readers out there somewhere, if not in my home borough. That night I prepared to meet the handful of souls who would gather, in a far corner of the Web, to chat about the new book with the author.

Claire and I had joked about my donning my Sibylline wig for the session, or lighting black candles and sipping claret, but instead I opted for my usual writing gear: sweatpants, T-shirt, terry-cloth bathrobe, glass of ice and one-liter bottle of Coke. Why not a two-liter? Here's a writing tip: I find that the big bottles lose their gas too quickly. I can't compose on flat soda. And don't forget to recap the bottle or the whole thing's moot.

I signed on as crimson1, and for ten sickening minutes, I hung there in cyberspace alone. It was dark and cold. Then, one by one, a small constellation of lights blinked on: darklilangel and burningangel23, bloodlover78, bleed4U, satangirl and demonatrix. Claire made me nervous, standing behind me as I typed, so I promised to read the exchanges out loud to her while she reclined on the couch.

"Oy," I groaned. "Satangirl wants to know where I get my ideas? Jesus. Where do you think? Out of my ass."

"You wrote that?"

"No. I wrote, 'Dreams, Fears and my Daily Life. Though I won't say which is which.'"

"Good. OK. What else?"

"Bloodkidz asks if Mistress Clio and Baron Charlus von Faubourg St. Germaine will finally do it in this volume."

"Read it and see, you cheap bastard."

"Right," I said, and typed just the first part. Claire grabbed the can of nuts I'd put out for my energy snack.

"Who's next?" she asked, picking out the cashews.

And on we went, me reading and typing, Claire shouting out answers, until a screen name came up that made me pause and keep it to myself. Someone called vampT3 popped on but said nothing, as if standing in the doorway, while the others grilled me on vampyre arcana and the fates of characters whom I'd forgotten I ever made up. I read those aloud to Claire, meanwhile keeping one secret eye on that silent name, as if flirting behind my girlfriend's back with the vamp at another table, and asking myself, did or did not those three little *t*s belong to Theresa Trio? Was that my legal aide peeking at me from behind a screen somewhere in the city? Was she wearing those sexy glasses?

Then vampT3 cyber-spoke: Did it bother me as, no offense, a nice-seeming older lady, to know that so many readers found my work so erotic? She, as a woman who by the way was straight, nevertheless felt that I, a fellow woman but older and wiser and more experienced, had somehow touched on her deepest, darkest desires, the fantasies she never told anyone and thought belonged to her alone. How did that make me feel? As a writer? As a woman?

"What're they saying?" Claire demanded, now lying flat on her back, staring at the ceiling in boredom as she dropped peanuts into her mouth.

"Nothing, same baloney. Darkchild asks can I really taste the difference between type A blood and type AB, because he or she can't. Blood4U on the other hand is eager to donate."

"Skip the sickos."

"Hey, watch it," I said. "The sickos paid for those nuts."

31

The second woman on Clay's list was Marie Fontaine. She lived in Ridgefield Park, New Jersey, in an apartment that I realized, when the bus let me off at the corner, was most likely over her parents' garage. The house was a split-level, weather-beaten, with black streaks along the seams in the white siding and some raw spots in the thin, early lawn. As you may remember, it was a strange spring. After a warm winter that was both kind (how could one not be thrilled to be walking in a T-shirt in December?) and troubling (how could this weather not be the final verdict—we have broken the earth?), April was gripped by a sudden cold snap that sent snow flurries swirling through a bright afternoon. On the Fontaines' lawn, a pink and white dogwood had bloomed too soon, probably during a day of false spring, and now it dropped its petals in the mud. Following Marie's directions, I went up the stairs beside the garage, to a thin wooden door, behind which I heard the throb of industrial pop.

I knocked loudly, and she must have been waiting, because the volume turned down immediately, and a moment later, she opened the door—a short, thick girl with big eyes, big lips and a big bust. Her coloring was dark Mediterranean. Her clothing was gothic mall.

"Hi, I'm Marie." She put out a small hand. We shook.

"Harry Bloch. Thanks for meeting me."

We went in. It was a studio with a sleeping alcove and kitchenette, rather like Fonzie's but with a lot more black lace and candles. Along with the posters of the Cure, Nine Inch Nails and Marilyn Manson, there were pictures of Charlie, the original Manson, as well as those celebrated serial-killing couples the Honeymoon Killers and the Moors Murderers. On the bureau was a small shrine dedicated to Clay: some bones tied in hexes, a squirrel skull, dripped-down black candles and incense, news photos taped to the mirror. I spotted the letters, Clay's letters to her, the mates of the ones from her to him in my file. Hers were tied with red ribbon and tucked into a shell-decorated box. It made me sad, this one touch of girlishness in the midst of all the willed, overweening Evil. I wondered how she'd feel if she knew how Clay had snickered, handing over her love letters, along with the naked Polaroids, which I had with me now, in a manila envelope in my shoulder bag.

Then again, perhaps she wouldn't mind at all. Where Morgan Chase had been reluctant to open up, putting me in the embarrassing position of reluctant seducer, Marie opened up all too easily, embarrassing me even more with her instant intimacy and putting me in the place of the equally reluctant seduced. She was not beautiful, or particularly graceful or charming or bright. But she had the attractiveness of youth, of eager young flesh at its ripest, and she was certainly a good deal cuter than either of her homicidal poster girls: the 250-pound Martha Beck, female half (or three-quarters) of the Honeymoon Killers, whose execution had to be delayed because she was too fat for the electric chair, or Myra Hindley, of the Moors Murderers, whose dyed blond hair and Nazi chic made her an arch-ironic sex symbol but who, plain, mannish-looking, and with an IQ of 107, would have been utterly unremarkable without her notoriety. Nevertheless it was clearly these couples who formed her ideal of doomed, high romantic love: outsiders beyond good and evil or, depending on your point of view, stunted runts so weak they could only lift themselves up by preying on children and old women.

This is where the clever reader stops me and says, But aren't you, harmless Harry, feeding on these very fantasies? Why else would your books be crammed so full of gratuitous you-know-what? Why needs must you be so explicit? Well, I'll tell you. First and foremost, it's a living, and as any waiter or stripper can attest, one man's gratuity is another girl's rent. But there's another more important, if paradoxical reason: I suspect the push toward explicitness actually originates not in my pulpy lizard brain but in the high art cortex itself. Let me explain.

To those of you who read for dark thrills and secret chills: Don't worry, it's all coming. And I don't judge you. And to those squeamish souls who, sighting blood on the page, flinch and look away, I say, You're not the only ones, believe me. If you think it's hard to read that stuff, try writing it with one hand over your eyes. But it's also right there that the sleeping poet in me stirs and licks his chops. Because if there's one commandment I'd preach to every scribbler sharpening a pencil for the hunt, it's this: when you hit a nerve in the reader, or better yet yourself, write harder.

32

Interview Transcript: Marie Fontaine, 4/22/09

MF: Am I afraid to be in love with a man who they say has murdered? Not at all. He's beyond your judgment. After all, they want to kill him, don't they? And not even in person, but at a distance. At least he did it with his own hand. If he did it, I mean. To me it's the ultimate erotic act. Death and eroticism are linked. It's a thin line though most people are too afraid. Great sex takes us to the edge of the abyss and orgasm pushes us over. It's like a taste of death. Sex with a killer doesn't scare me. It turns me on.

HB: Really?

MF: Yes. Does that shock you?

HB: No.

MF: I want to fuck him.

HB: Right.

MF: In the ass.

HB: Right.

MF: I mean him in my ass.

HB: Got it. And if he asked you to help kill someone? To help him lure someone into a trap or hold them down, you'd do it?

MF: Of course. I'd do anything.

HB: You'd commit murder yourself?

MF: Yes. Yes, I would.

HB: Anyone? A friend? A family member?

MF: Of course. What difference does it make? Those are just abstract concepts. He is my only true family. He is friend, brother, lover. We create our own morality, like Nietzsche. That's why you can't understand me or him. We're outside your morality. Society's values. Consumerism. My supposed family just sit there and watch TV. They obey and just chew the slop they feed them like cattle, so who's the prisoner, if you really think about it? What about Iraq? If I wake up and see through it all, then I'm free, even if they lock me up. See what I mean? He's free. Because he set himself free in his mind. Job, house, school, family, this shitty town in this shitty state. I despise it. But you have only to awaken from this too-troubled dream. Then nothing is real. And everything is permitted. Do what thou wilt is the whole of my law.

HB: Crowley.

MF: Yes. You've read him?

HB: Sure. A long time ago. When I was your age, maybe. A teenager. Are you in school?

MF: No. I'm twenty-two.

HB: You work at a job?

MF: Office work. Nonsecretarial.

HB: You follow Crowley?

MF: I read him often.

HB: You're a satanist?

MF: Maybe. Maybe not.

HB: What about a child? Could you murder a child with your own hands if Darian asked you to?

MF: Let me try to put this in terms you can understand. So you can see how depraved I am. Want to know my ultimate fantasy?

HB: Sure.

MF: I want to see him kill someone, disembowel them, and then fuck me in the blood.

HB: Really? You'd really do it?

MF: It turns me on. The blood, the sweat, like a sacrificial ordeal. Ritualized. I get aroused just thinking about it. I'll show you, if you want. I don't care.

HB: That's cool. I believe you.

MF: Here. Look up my skirt. Go ahead. I don't give a damn what anybody thinks.

HB: Actually I have to get going . . .

MF: See? Go ahead and look. I don't care.

33

I got out of there as soon as I could. Gentle reader, what is the etiquette in such a case? Even the ol' Slut Whisperer's not sure. Like the time I got caught in an improv comedy club or front row at my cousin's bris, I stayed grimly till the end of Marie's performance, smiling like wood as she rooted under her skirt, but I averted my burning eyes from the finale. Not that she was so evil or vile. Not at all. Despite her best efforts, she was normal enough. That's what made it unbearable. Trapped in her life, in her family. No friends probably. Lousy job. Hating how she looked. The oddly shaped, awkward shy girl. If she'd been smarter or richer, she would have escaped into art school. But as it was she saw no way out, besides Darian.

I also have to admit that if she stirred no erotic interest, she did arouse the sadist in me. I wanted to give her a rude awakening. I had always hated that poseur, wannabe evil bullshit. I wanted to show her true suffering: child abuse, political torture, cancer, genocide, the real horrors of the real world. I wanted to laugh in her face and spit on her pretentious little Satan. To tell her that her lover was vermin, semiliterate scum, and that even to him she was nothing, a joke. I wanted to rub her nose in shit.

I didn't, of course, though who knows, it might have done her some good. And as for trying to be kind or understanding—showing that I pitied her would've been truly cruel. What else did she have, alone in her room, except her evil dreams? So I left, letting her think I was shocked. I said a quick good-bye and hurried out, her big crude laugh chasing me from behind the door, and waited for my bus in the cold rather than stay any longer.

On the bus I was forlorn. I sat behind the driver, forehead to the glass, and the brakes sighed and snorted. It was wet out and everything gleamed. Leaves jumped into the wind and pressed themselves to my window, as if sneaking a ride out of town. Beads of water stood like gooseflesh on the brightly finished cars. I saw toys, bikes, gnomes, an abandoned Rudolph toppled in the grass. A swing set dappled in rust. Black and green plastic garbage cans lined up at the curb. An umbrella lay gutted, showing its silver bones. Was everyone everywhere as unhappy as poor Marie and I? When we entered the tunnel, I leaned back and shut my eyes.

By the time I got out to Queens I was in a truly foul mood, and when I walked by the flower shop and saw Morris, my J. Duke Johnson photo model, I stopped in to get cheered up. It turned out he'd had a fight with his boyfriend and was even grimmer than I.

"Let's go out for a drink or six," Morris suggested. "I need to dull my senses."

"OK, where? Jacqui's?" This was the corner bar.

"God no. No place around here, I don't want to have to discuss anything with anyone I know. And no place gay either. No place with anyone who I care what they think."

"Gee, thanks."

"You know what I mean."

"Yeah. I think I know a place."

"No one we know will be there?"

"Highly doubtful."

"And homo-free?"

"That I can almost guarantee."

34

RSVP's, the strip club where Daniella worked, was somewhere out by the airport. I called her cell and a few minutes later I got a text. Yes, she was dancing that night. She'd leave my name plus one and some drink tickets at the door. Morris was thrilled.

"I want a real trashy blonde with big tits to straddle me and rub them in my face," he declared as we rode over in a cab. "But huge, ginormous tits. With big, pink nipples."

The building was a concrete bunker: no windows and a neon sign, long and low on an industrial block (forlorn!) with orange street-lamps and the occasional plane roaring overhead. We pushed through a turnstile, from the brightly lit night into darkness, and waited for our eyes to adjust.

At first, Morris seemed stunned by all the female flesh, but he warmed right up once he got a few drinks in him. He was ordering saki, or "sah-kay," as he called it, and by the second little bottle he was on his feet, throwing money on the runway and tucking it into G-strings like a drunken salaryman. Even so, no one was about to mistake him for a frat boy. He howled, "You go, girl," at the dancers, demanded to know where a black girl got her extensions, and when invited to smack a bottom, cooed, "Damn. You do Pilates, bitch?" They were thrilled, of course, and our booth quickly became a locus of attention, with two or three girls bouncing and giggling around us, including a big, boobular blonde.

"Are these real?" he asked, weighing and prodding her breasts like they were capons he was thinking of stuffing.

"Honey, haven't you ever felt a fake tit? Some of your boys must have them."

"Yes, but these are much better. The nipple is so stiff."

"That's 'cause you're tugging on it."

A nubile young redhead squeezed in beside them. "Mine are real. Feel them." Her breasts were small and pert and freckled. Morris gave a thoughtful squeeze. "Tender," he decided. The girls squealed as he asked them each to rub a breast on his cheek.

Then I noticed that we had another visitor. A huge black guy, almost as big as Morris, dressed in fatigues and sporting an afro and goatee, was standing over our table holding hands with a tiny Asian girl in her bra and panties.

"Yo, excuse me," he said.

"Yes?" I asked, wondering if Morris was as useless in a fight as I am.

He pointed at Morris. "That dude there. He's J. Duke Johnson, the author, isn't he?"

"No. But I know what you mean. It's a weird resemblance."

"Ha. Got it. Keeping it cool, right?" He shook my hand in his huge mitt, then reached across me and tapped Morris. "Excuse me, Mr. Johnson. Mr. Johnson!"

Morris looked around, smiling, as if also curiously searching for Mr. Johnson. Our visitor leaned into him, blocking the stage. The girls stepped back and covered their boobs. "I just want to say I'm a big fan of your work. It's an inspiration."

"Well, thanks . . . ," Morris said vaguely, confused but drunkenly pleased to meet a fan of flower arranging. "It's all about shape and color."

I kicked him under the table.

"He's a fan of your books," I added. "Mordechai Jones."

"Right. Right! Well, thank you so much. That's sweet." Morris shook his hand.

"Can I buy you a drink?"

"Certainly," Morris snapped. "Hot sah-kay!"

The new guy ordered a Courvoisier for himself, and I asked for a Coke.

"Can't drink," I said, nervously. "I'm his bodyguard." We all laughed at that one, I the loudest.

"Why don't you and your little friend join us?" Morris suggested, and they squeezed in. I was now between the two men, with the girls along the perimeter.

"This here's May Ling," the guy said.

"Well, aren't you cute?" Morris said, and shook her hand.

"And I'm RX738."

"Sorry?" Morris asked.

"RX738." He took out a couple of business cards and gave them to us. Sure enough, they said RX738, along with a phone number and email address.

"Would you look at that?" Morris wondered.

"I'm a DJ and producer," he explained. "I do some rapping. And I build beats."

"Good for you."

"But it's in my lyrics that you really influenced me the most."

"Why thank you. I love your hair. Like a whole revolutionary vibe."

"Exactly. That's my tip. And I know that's what Mordechai preaches. Black unity. Turn the guns from each other and aim them at the true enemy: Whitey. No offense," he said to me.

"That's OK," I said quickly and sipped my Coke.

"You know what would be fucking tight?" he asked.

"Tell me." Morris sipped his sake.

"If you would rap on my record. Just swing by the studio and lay down a track."

"Sure!" Morris said. "I'd love to."

I saw my life flashing before my eyes, and it ended with Morris in a soundbooth, trying to rap. I whispered in his ear, "Shut the fuck up. You're going to get us killed."

But Morris wasn't listening. His eyes were on the stage. "Look at her," he muttered.

It was Daniella. I had almost missed her. Her song was "Tainted Love" and she was hanging upside down from the pole. Legs wrapped like the doubled snakes on the doctor's staff, long blond hair trailing through the lights, she floated there above us, turning slowly, eyes shut, as if dancing for herself alone, then slithered down to the filthy stage and crawled to the men in the loosened ties and wedding rings who held out money like bait.

"Go, you hot bitch," Morris yelled, splashing sake.

"Hell yes," RX738 concurred.

Daniella peered in our direction, shielding her eyes from the glare. She smiled and waved. I waved back.

"RX!" she called. "RX!"

Fifteen minutes later, Dani was happily seated on RX's lap, sipping tequila, while the Asian girl held his hand in both of hers, stroking it, and the blonde and the redhead cuddled with Morris and sipped champagne. I sat in the middle again, with my Coke, trying not to gawk at Dani's mostly naked body. She was drawn from all long lines—arms, legs, smooth belly—with high little breasts and the miraculous ass of a ballerina. She lit a Marlboro light and looked around to make sure no one was watching.

"How's the book coming?" she asked.

"OK," I said. "Slow. To be honest, it's pretty depressing."

"You a writer too?" RX asked me.

"Yeah," I said, uneasily.

"Too?" she asked. I shrugged. "He's interviewing Darian Clay," she told him. "He's going to find out the truth about my sister."

"Fuck! Really? That's some hard-core shit, for real."

"Thanks," I said.

"I'm not for real," Morris blurted. "I'm bullshit." While I wasn't watching, he had floated across the line from ecstatic to morose. He stood abruptly, toppling the girls. Tears ran down his cheeks. "I'm not Doc Marten. I'm a florist. And I'm in love."

"What the fuck?" RX said.

"Who's Doc Marten?" Dani asked.

"Duke," I said. "Duke, sit down. You're drunk, Duke."

Morris dropped heavily into the seat beside me. "Duke?" he asked, loudly. "Who's Doc Marten then?"

"You're Duke Johnson," I whispered frantically, sweat crawling down my back. "Doc Martens makes the boots."

"Oh yeah," he said, then bellowed, "Duke Johnson!"

"What the fuck?" RX wondered again. "You Duke Johnson or you ain't?"

"Ain't! Ain't!" Morris tried to stand again but I held him back. "I'm Morris. I own Heavenly Arrangements. I'm fucked up. Fucked! Up!"

"But if you ain't motherfucking Duke Johnson, who the fuck is?"

"Him. Him." Morris pointed at me. "He is."

"You?"

"Afraid so," I said, and held my breath.

"He's an awesome writer," Dani said. "He wrote porn too."

"Damn. Duke Johnson's white." I waited for a blow, but he seemed more disheartened than angry.

"Sorry," I said. "I didn't mean to hurt anyone." I couldn't think of what to say.

"Damn. White," he muttered as he pondered this revelation. Morris was now weeping into the blonde's enormous boobs while the redhead stroked his head. RX738 finished his drink.

"Well, you did write some good shit," he said finally, then laughed and play-slapped my arm so that it only bruised lightly. "What the fuck, we all got secrets. I'll tell you some shit." He leaned forward. "I'm from the burbs. Long Island. I went to Great Neck South High."

"Me too," Dani said. "I moved there from Hollis junior year. My parents wanted me in a better school. That's how we know each other."

"Course I dealt reefer and blow there. Got mixed up with the Bloods."

"Sure," I said quickly. "Right."

"Damn," he said again. "Duke Johnson. I still want to shake your hand."

We shook. "Thanks RX738," I said. I don't think I've ever been prouder.

35

From *Double Down on the Deuce* by J. Duke Johnson, chapter 1:

"Mordechai Jones? Funny, you don't look Jewish."

She smiled slyly at her own joke as she stepped into my office. I'd heard it before. I am six-two, 200 pounds on a good day, and a deep dark brown every day, good or bad. Which was today? That remained to be seen, after the witty blonde with the hot body and the cold blue eyes told me what she wanted.

"My mother was an Ethiopian Jew," I explained. "Traditionally, Judaism passes through the mother's side, so yeah, technically I am Jewish." I held out my hand. "Though I don't keep strictly kosher anymore, Miss . . . ?"

"Cherry Blaze. I dance at the Player's Club. Jorges the bartender told me about you." She shook out a Marlboro Light 100, which I felt revealed an ambivalent nature. "I want you to find a missing person. My daddy. Juniper Blaze." She fumbled in her purse for a light.

"When was the last time you saw him?" I asked, getting out a match.

"Ten years ago," she said.

I leaned across and lit her. "Not easy, but doable," I said. "Where was he then?"

She looked me in the eye and exhaled between pursed red lips. "In his coffin."

Down at the Hi-Lo, two drinks later (whiskey sours for her, Chivas rocks for me), Cherry Blaze tried to clarify her story. It was clear all right, clear that this girl was either crazy or lying. Or she was telling the truth. In which case I'd be a crazy fool to go near it.

Her pops was a trumpet player, Juniper "Honky" Blaze, so-named for both his sound and his color, making the scene in the fifties and sixties as the one white dude who could hang. He had the chops, they said, and could hit that high, sweet spot, but by the time Cherry came along, that day was long past. Now Daddy was a junkie, playing dives and raising little Blaze out of a suitcase. On the old Forty-deuce you grew up fast, so at eighteen, when Daddy died behind one shot too many, she didn't cry. She hit the pole. Today she was twenty-eight and still looked mighty fine. As long as you didn't stare into her eyes, the way I was doing now.

"Let's cut to the twist," I said, and lit her next 100. "Why come to me?"

"I had a dream about him."

"A dream?" I'd heard a lot of tales in my day, and even more in my nights, but that was a first. I laughed. "All right, I'll bite. Let's hear it." I ordered us two more.

She didn't laugh or look angry either. She sipped her drink. She smoked her smoke. She looked me in the eye. She spoke:

"About a month ago, I had this dream, where my dad was in my room, playing a song. 'Goodbye Pork Pie Hat.' One of his favorites. But in the dream he wasn't playing it through the horn. I mean it was his trumpet sound for sure, but it was just coming from his lips, pursed up like a kiss. Anyway, in the dream he took my hand and led me into the closet, the same closet I have now, but it turned into a long hallway that opened into our old hotel room, down by Times Square. Then he got excited, playing wilder and higher, and pointing under the bed. Finally I looked, and there was his old trumpet case, full of blood. Now my dad was screaming, trumpet-screaming. So I put my hand in the blood. And there was a knife inside. That's when I woke up."

"Creepy," I allowed. "I had a crazy one myself last night. My grandma was riding an elephant up Broadway. Always happens when I eat Popeye's chicken after midnight."

"I know." She waved her smoke. "Everyone has weird dreams. So what. But I kept having it. And I found myself humming that song. I couldn't get it out of my head. In the shower. On the train. At work. It was driving me nuts."

"So you got issues. But I still don't think you need a detective. More like a week at the beach."

"That's what I thought."

"OK then." I reached for my wallet.

"Until my dad started sending me emails."

"What?" For the first time, my ears twitched a little, and my nose opened up, like a hound catching the scent of something new in the air.

"Yeah. Little notes. About things only he would know. How we used to get hot fudge sundaes at the Howard Johnson after his gig. About pawning his horn to buy me school shoes. How I could dance but couldn't sing." She finished her drink. "So what do you think? Do I need a detective now?"

I helped myself to a smoke from her pack, broke off the filter. "And where would you suggest this detective start looking?"

She picked up the matches and lit my cigarette. "The graveyard, of course."

36

The next time I went to interview Darian Clay, the weather was cool and clear. You could see a long way and even the trees on the farthest ridges seemed distinct. Inside the visiting room, of course, there was no weather, and the time was always the same: midnight or noon under the flat fluorescent glare. I sat in my bolted chair at the bolted table. The cement floor had just been cleaned and the pine scent stung my nose.

"Good. That story was pretty good." Clay grinned as he offered his critique of my Marie Fontaine piece. "You really captured her character. It's the little details. Like her chomping the bit in that scene where I brand her."

"Thanks," I said, uneasily flattered, and then sneezed.

"God bless," Clay said. "You got to watch it this time of year. I take vitamins."

"I'm fine. Thanks."

He sat back, thoughtfully stroking his chin. He was unshaven and the whiskers were coming in black and gray, like mine. "That Marie's a little chubster though, huh?"

"No." I shrugged. "Well, just a little."

"I don't mind that."

"No, she's cute . . . ," I agreed, seeing her again in my head, hearing that mocking laugh. I ruffled my notes, as if to hide her memory from Clay. I started the tape. "So you wanted to talk about going to school, you said?"

"Well, art school yeah, but I didn't go."

"Why not?"

He chuckled. "They rejected me. That's why not. Who knows what I could have been? A famous artist."

"Sure. Well, let's talk about that. How did you begin making art? When did you know that you wanted to be a photographer?"

"You know, I'll tell you. It was at my foster mom's, Mrs. Gretchen, who I hated." He stretched his legs, easing into the story, revealing the thick white gym socks stuffed into his prison slippers. "A real cunt and a half. Used to beat me with this old car antenna. Right across the thighs, that stung like hell. She ought to be the one in prison instead of sitting on her ass in that old house watching TV. Her boyfriend used to strip me, push me in a cold shower, and then throw me out on the porch naked so that the neighbors could see. For humiliation."

"Why?"

"Wetting the bed," he said amiably, looking me right in the eye.

"Oh right, right."

"But he had a camera, see? An old Nikon. He used to shoot a lot of just regular stuff. Her around the yard. His car. Squirrels and such. The leaves. He'd let me look through the eyepiece, when he had it set up on the tripod, but I better not press the trigger, man. Waste his film. Ha. So I'd keep my hands behind my back and just take like pretend pictures." He smiled and made a play camera out of his cuffed hands, hard-bitten fingers bracketing his face. "Click. Pick the moment. Click."

He paused and I fought the urge to jump in, as I would at a dinner party during an awkward silence. Clay knit his fingers together and folded his hands in his lap and went on:

"He had a darkroom down in the basement and he'd let me help out. Sometimes I'd sneak down there too when he wasn't around. I liked the smell of the chemicals and that earthy basement kind of smell. It was small, dark. I don't know, I felt safe there. And I liked seeing the prints form in the developer. Coming to life like underwater in the tray. Anyway." He sat back, crossing his legs. "I couldn't wait to get my own camera. I just scraped up every dime I could, working odd jobs, stealing change. Then finally I got a used Canon. I was fifteen. I was thrilled. The thing leaked so bad, I had to cover it with tape every time I reloaded, but fuck it. I was a photographer. Except I still had to pretend, because I couldn't afford film."

On the tape you can hear us both laugh.

"But then," he said, "I started shooting for real. I shot a lot of stuff. I don't know where the hell it went. I bet it's worth some bucks now. Collector's item."

"What kind of stuff?"

"Anything. Trees. Dogs. Other kids. The neighbors. I carried it everywhere, crept around like a scout or whatever. Learned patience. You know. Waiting. That's what it is. Like a hunter. Waiting for the thing to show itself, the thing you're seeking." He crouched forward and made his hands into a rifle, sighting along the thumb at me. I smiled.

"But you shot mostly models, right? I mean posed photos."

"Same thing. It's the same thing. That's the relationship between you and the subject. Waiting, working, coaxing, looking, waiting for something to emerge. That mysterious thing or whatever. That's the hardest part."

"Waiting?"

"Yeah. That and getting them to hold still." He chuckled again, lightly, and chewed a finger. I uncapped my pen and made a pointless checkmark on my notes.

"So when did you decide to make it a career?" I asked.

He spit something invisible from his tongue and shrugged. "As soon as I knew it was one. Like at first I wanted to take the news photos, you know, like wars and fires and whatnot. Like a foreign correspondent. Escape. Then later I realized, hey, someone took the pictures in the magazines too, ha. Like posters, billboards, everything. There's pictures everywhere and someone's taking them, right?"

"But you wanted to do fine art."

"Yeah, this one teacher I had. Mr. Barnsworth. He lent me books, well, they were from the library, but anyway he saw me tramping around the fields near school with my camera and showed me books: Stieglitz, Brassai, Walker Evans, Diane Arbus. She was my favorite. That's when I realized, a photographer could be an artist just like a painter or whatever. He could create an image. Like express something and not just record it. It could be a picture of his mind." He slowed again, following a thought in the air above me. Tiny flares, reflections of the plastic light fixture, moved inside his eyes.

"So you applied to art school," I prompted.

"Yeah, to a bunch." For the first time maybe, he seemed visibly annoyed. He ran his hands through his hair, brushing his head with the chain. "They didn't want me. Poor kid from nowhere. Shit schools. Bad grades, so I couldn't get a scholarship. I mean there was no way I could go otherwise. Anyway, that's all art school is. A big clusterfuck for rich poseurs. Who the fuck needs it? But it's a system, right? You have to go to the art schools to get into the galleries, to learn how to talk that bullshit. That's what they're learning, to talk shit."

"You did take a class though?"

"Yeah, at the community center, with some jerk-off. Supposedly a professional fine art photographer. Two shows in Baltimore, big deal. He told me I was underdeveloped like I was a retard or some shit. That I needed seasoning like a bowl of soup. After that I just worked on my own. But that's the thing about art. No one can say, right? Who can judge it? Only the future. Maybe a hundred years from now, I'll be hanging in a museum. Maybe my work will be worth a fortune. Hell, they say it always goes up when the artist dies. Who knows? Maybe your books about mummies and elves from Mars will sell a million too, after we're dead."

He laughed again, softly to himself, and fell silent. Again I held my tongue. Shut up, I told myself. Let the fucker talk.

"That's what art is too," he said, finally. "Revenge. Ha. And justice. A photograph's like evidence. It's like a message in a bottle for the future. Something I saw in my dreams but that won't come to pass for a long time yet. I have faith in this. I'm not afraid to die. I know my work will be there after I'm gone, one hundred, two hundred years. You live forever in the mind of others. And those you touch. I don't need religion or anybody's god. Art is my heaven."

37

When I got home the apartment was empty. Claire's mom was in town, on a shopping layover between Palm Springs and Europe, and Claire had to meet her for some "family bondage." So I went down to the Peking duck place on Main Street and got on line, communicating with hand signals when my turn came at the window. Behind the steamed glass, a man in a tall white hat laid golden ducks on a thick round of wood and slashed them to glistening bits with a cleaver. Another man tucked the slices into open pockets of dough, added cucumber and scallion, a dribble of brown sauce. I sat at a long table of loners, across from a middle-aged guy with paint on his coveralls, next to a young woman in hospital scrubs and a raincoat, all of us staring into the blank space between us as we chewed. Everyone was speaking Chinese, if they spoke at all. It was a relief not to understand.

Then I went home, cruised through my email, my regular mail, my voice mail, the *Times*. I took a shower, clipped my nails, swabbed my ears out. Then when I couldn't restrain my curiosity any longer, I went online. And like a spider sitting in my corner of the Web, I watched for vampT3. Was this cyber-stalking or merely cyber-lurking? Lying in wait for a woman, or not even, a mere name, a blip that might or might not be Theresa Trio, I was embarrassed, in front of myself. This was a new low, combining the perverse and the pathetic. Perthetic!

vampT3: Hey . . .

crimson1: Hi

vampT3: hows it going?

crimson1: Good . . . you?

vampT3: good . . . i still can't believe im really talking to you. Sibylline!

crimson1: me either . . . neither, I mean.

vampT3: you cant believe your talking to ME???

crimson1: I mean I don't usually speak to fans. Not that you are I mean necessarily.

vampT3: but I am ur fan. lol

crimson1: lol? Lolly?

vampT3: No that means laughing out loud! Sorry

crimson1: I'm sorry . . . just not used to this text thing

vampT3: IM . . . lol

crimson1: right, ha.

vampT3: so can i ask you . . . what i said last time . . . did it seem strange to you?

crimson1: No . . . what?

vampT3: about your books . . .

crimson1: right

vampT3: but i felt like, reading your work, i keep thinking how does she know how i feel?

crimson1: just a hunch

vampT3: haha. But you really don't think it's weird?

crimson1: well if it is I wrote it so I guess then I'm a total weirdo

vampT3: good me too

crimson1: lol

vampT3: Is it too forward to suggest that we meet? If it is im sorry.

crimson1: no its not that, I'd love too. But with the book just out, I'm traveling a lot, you know . . .

vampT3: oh you're out of town?

crimson1: yes

vampT3: i didn't think you did readings or book tour stuff. They say you're a recluse

vampT3: are you there?

crimson1: yes sorry . . . ha . . . you got me . . . I forgot you knew so much . . . it's true . . . I don't know if I'd use the word recluse but I don't often see people or go out . . . tho I am out of town now . . . in seclusion.

vampT3: sorry if I hit a nerve

crimson1: no its fine . . . maybe I'll get over it one day and we'll meet.

vampT3: i hope so . . . but i understand . . . we can talk again like this tho?

crimson1: yes of course I'd like that

vampT3: good

vampT3: hey!

crimson1: yes?

vampT3: not that you care but if you want to check this out . . . goodnight!

She sent me a link, then quickly signed off, and her little light went out. I clicked the link and was led to a secluded site where vampire lovers gathered for vampire business. Here was a review of my new book, posted by one vampT3:

> *Crimson Night and Fog* is Sibylline's greatest work yet. While the plot revolves around trying to recover the Holy Sword of Mithras from the evil Baron Charlus von Faubourg St. Germaine, and is plenty thrilling, the real heart of the story is Sasha's struggle between her desire for Aram and Ivy, her bisexual vampire lovers, with whom she shares a wild, erotic passion, and her growing feelings for Jack Silver, the war correspondent/fashion photographer and vampire hunter, for whom she feels a deeper and more mature love. This situation is further complicated by the fact that Ivy once tried to turn Jack after a night of wild sex. Jack refused, trying instead to slice off Ivy's head. She has hated him bitterly ever since. This complex love triangle/square/trapezoid? reflects Sasha's own duality. She is half vampire and half human, and is constantly struggling between these two sides. It is not a clear-cut good/evil battle, for as Aram explains to Sasha:
>
> "Vampires are no different than tigers or wolves. It is only humans who kill for hate, bigotry, greed or lust. A vampire Holocaust or mob lynching is as unthinkable as one done

by lions. Humans have been lulled into complacency by be-
lieving themselves at the top of the food chain and have, in
their madness, turned on each other. The human race would
be better off, with less war and disease, if vampires did even
more to cull their ranks, like jaguars and leopards do with
antelopes."

Theresa, assuming it was Theresa, went on to elucidate these themes
and the recurring imagery that expressed them. It was all news to
me, a review of a book that sounded pretty good but that someone
else had written. Someone like her, for example. Reading her writing
(about my writing) filled me with a strange elation close to panic or
vertigo. I felt myself swelling into a genius. I was also certain I'd be
exposed as a talentless fraud. I was like a balloon, pumped full of hot
air, flying higher and terrified of bursting. Isn't this the deepest wish
of every little scribbler? To be loved, not for ourselves, but for the
beauty of our work. Except I hated my work. I squeezed it out and
sliced it like baloney, page by page, and despising what I wrote, it was
hard not to despise those who read it. Unless they were right about
me and I was all wrong.

Why do we read? In the beginning, as children, why do we love the
books we love? For most, I think, it's travel, a flight into adventure,
into a dream that feels like our own. But for a few it is also escape,
flight from boredom, unhappiness, loneliness, from where or who we
can no longer bear to be. When I read, the words on the page replace
the voice in my head and I cease, for a little while, to be me, or at least
to be so painfully aware of being me. These are the real readers, the
maniacs, the ones who dose themselves with fiction the way junkies
get high, the way lovers adore the beloved: beyond reason.

This kind of reading, ironically, precedes all judgment. Objective
criteria don't enter in, any more than with love. (I say ironically because it is these very readers who, having fallen for books, become
scholars, critics, editors—in other words, snobs—while maintaining
their secret vice.) Genre fans—vampire lovers, sci-fi geeks, mystery

addicts—are a kind of atavistic species, a pure but anomalous breed. They still read like children, foolish and grave, or like teenagers, desperate and courageous. They read because they need to.

Of course, the other reader who fits this profile is the porn fan. He (or she!) is a prisoner trapped in a finite body and an unaccommodating world that will never fulfill desire's impossible demands. Seeking ecstasy, they escape into language, which goes everywhere, touches everyone, and never ends. What love poem, what manifesto, what high cry of art has ever done what the lowest, dumbest scratch of dirty words can do to a lonely soul late at night?

And isn't that why we write? (We writers, the worst readers of all.) To send our secret message out and reach that stranger we will never know? To meet undercover with the others, the ones who hide their faces in our books? Don't we write to them? To Theresa Trio? To Darian Clay?

Walking through the kitchen later, I noticed my cell phone glowing on the counter. I had been so distracted by the instant messaging that I hadn't heard its soft moan. There was a text message from Dani: "Thanks for coming the other night! You don't have to write book if you don't want. I understand. Call if you want."

I didn't call. It was too late.

38

The third name on Clay's list was Sandra Dawson. She lived in Brooklyn, on the cusp of Bushwick. I took the L train to Montrose and then walked a few blocks. It was a neighborhood of car repair shops, mattress warehouses and restaurants advertising Mexican, Dominican, or Ecuadoran food. She rented a railroad flat on the top floor of a three-story brick building, with a bodega downstairs and a metal grille over the street door. I knew from her letters that she was in her midtwenties and lived with a roommate, a girl who had no idea who Sandra "really was." Nor did her colleagues in the financial district, where she worked as "a word processor," while pursuing a degree in library science. In the photos Clay gave me she was little and sly, with thin blond hair and thin pale arms. Her body was like a young boy's, smooth, freckled and hairless. You could count the ribs. In person, when I hauled myself up her stairs, she looked more prosaic in glasses, a ponytail and a printed cotton dress with flip-flops. Her roommate was out, she said, but still, after a brief deliberation, she decided that she'd feel better talking in her own room.

Her bedroom was younger than the rest of the apartment, with a ruffle under the bed, a puffy white comforter, a beveled white dresser with a curvy mirror and pictures cut from magazines taped to the wall. Although there was a theme of dark glamour to the selection, the images were far softer than at Marie Fontaine's place and featured red roses, black skies cut by a slivered moon, and voluptuous women in lacy underwear, pouting beside still waters or crumbling walls of stone.

"I'm a subslut," she informed me, as if that were an official post, one rank below full slut, or perhaps she filled in for sluts who had the flu.

"What's that exactly?"

"I'm a submissive masochist by nature. I like the man to control me. I like pain and humiliation. I like to be abused."

"Huh, interesting." I put what I hoped was a calm, thoughtful expression on my face. She was completely matter-of-fact, sitting cross-legged on the bed while I squirmed in a white wicker chair. "When did you first realize you were like that?"

"I just always was. When I was little I liked testing myself, seeing how hard my cousin could bite down on my finger and stuff. I was always trying to get the other kids to tie me up."

"Like how? You mean for games?"

"Yeah, like tied to a tree, or if we played some fantasy game I'd always find a way to get taken prisoner with my hands tied behind my back or blindfolded. Most of the kids didn't tie very well, and I'm skinny so usually I could slip right out, but this one girl tied me really tight—she was into it, really serious, she bound me so I couldn't move at all—and the jump rope we were using, you know that white rope, really cut in, and it went between my legs and that was the first time I really remember being excited and I shifted around so the rope rubbed against my clit."

"Huh. Interesting," I repeated, sounding, I hoped, very professional. I crossed my legs without thinking, then realizing this looked like I was guarding my crotch, I uncrossed them.

"Then we started playing a lot, me and her. Her name was Clarissa. Always something like I was the slave or the captive. Sometimes we even played that I was her dog. We took my dog's real leash and bowl and put the leash on me and she made me fetch and then drink out of the bowl. Then she walked me in the backyard and I peed and my mom caught me." She laughed brightly and covered her mouth. I laughed too.

"What happened?"

"My poor parents were so clueless. My mom told my dad, who spanked me. Which just totally sealed the deal of course."

"What happened to Clarissa?"

"We drifted apart. She went to a different school. As far as I heard, she's vanilla. You know, like a straight regular girl. I think she's married."

"And you don't want that."

"You know my ultimate fantasy?" She tucked her legs under her and leaned forward confidentially.

"What?"

"To be sold into the white slave trade."

"Does that exist?" I asked, picturing a Technicolor harem movie with Jerry Lewis.

"I've heard about it."

"What, like you imagine being owned by one person or turned out at a brothel?"

"Usually a mix of both."

"And you like that? Do you think you'd really do it?"

"If my owner said I had to, of course."

"Your owner?"

"Master Darian." She smiled serenely.

"Oh, he's your owner? Officially."

"We made a contract. I belong to him. I'm registered as his slave on the Internet. That's why I'm with you now."

"He commanded you to talk to me?"

"Yes. Well, more than that."

"More?"

She hesitated. "He said he was lending me to you."

"Sorry?" I asked, pretending I didn't hear.

"As a gift. Because he likes what you wrote."

"Really? Huh. He didn't mention it. Like, how do you mean gift?" She moved toward me, palms out. I felt myself blushing, not the coolest look for a middle-aged man.

"As a slave," she said. "To use anyway you want."

"I, I don't know."

"Please." Her voice rose higher. "He'll be mad if I don't. He wants you to use me. He wants you to know how it feels, so that you can write about it."

"Oh, well, thanks. Thanks a lot. That's sweet, but-but." I began to stammer, as if reaching for fresh ways to express anxiety. "I can just, just imagine it all from here, or I mean later at home. Or. Or what I meant to say. It's all part of being a writer. Not really having to, to, to . . ." I swallowed. "To do anything."

"But I want to," she said. She dropped to her knees. "I'd be honored, sir, to receive your abuse." She leaned forward, chest on the floor and gazed up at me in the posture of a supplicant puppy. Her nose touched the tip of my shoe.

"Well!" I giggled and jerked as if she'd tickled me, clipping her with my toe. She squeaked in pain.

"Oh, sorry, sorry. I'm terribly sorry."

"That's OK," she mumbled, clutching her nose. "I like it."

"Right, right." Now I was no longer stuttering, but for some reason I had an English accent that I couldn't control. "Well, it's not that I'm not flattered. Because really I am. Quite." I shoveled my stuff into my bag and stood. She followed on knees, arms out, beseeching, as I prattled on.

"It's just rather bad timing. Do thank your master for me. And thank you as well. Good day." I jerked her cool hand in my sweaty grip and ran out, embarrassed, weirdly upset, and, I admit, with one small part of me hating myself for not seizing the chance to do something awful. What kind of lame writer was I?

Somewhere between lust and tears, I bolted downstairs and up the street, so rattled that I was through the subway turnstile before I realized I'd forgotten my tape recorder. Great. Now I had to go back. I was tempted to just leave it behind rather than march back up and face her. As a nice final touch, the train came rolling in just as I began reclimbing the stairs to the street. Perhaps the passengers would point at me and jeer as they rode by.

Cursing myself, I hurried back and again trudged up the two flights, trying to catch my breath and stifle the images that bloomed in my overheated brain: the kneeling girl, the pleading eyes. When was the last time anyone had called me sir?

The door was still open like I'd left it. "Sandra," I called. "It's me again. Sorry, I forgot my recorder." Huffing, I crossed to the bedroom and rapped the door frame with my knuckles, "Hello, hello," as I stepped through. Then I halted, as if I had accidentally entered the wrong room, the wrong apartment, the wrong world.

How many times have I written scenes of horror and mayhem? Hundreds. And often, I admit, out of laziness or just to squeeze time, I've described them as "indescribable" or "beyond words." But actually the words for violence are always simple and easy to find; a child knows them. It is the thoughts those words engender that seem impossible: Is this really the stuff we are made of? Is this all we are inside?

Once, on a sleepless night, I elaborated a whole theory of art predicated on simply reminding the ever-forgetful mind of the most basic truths: We float in water and revolve around the sun. We are born out of a woman's body and are made of meat and bone. One day, pretty soon, we will die.

And so, stepping through that door in Brooklyn, I was not only, as I would probably say in a book, speechless with fear, I was struck completely wordless, breathless, thoughtless, by one simple English sentence I could not understand: Sandra Dawson was dead.

She was nude and hanging upside down, though it was hard to tell at first glance because her head was gone. Her feet were bound together and tied to the ceiling fan. Her torso had been slit open, and the skin peeled back, attached somehow to her hands, like wings or like a cloak held open to expose the interior of her body. Her intestines dangled beneath her, reaching the floor, where they gathered in a pink coil. Her neck still dripped steadily, like a broken pipe.

Then, as if it really were just a story after all, Sandra's body began to turn. It rotated slowly, like an acrobat in the circus, picking up speed as the fan's blades spun. I realized what this meant—someone had hit the switch—and suddenly feeling the presence of another in the room, there behind me, in the door, I began, with what felt like excruciating slowness, to turn around. That was it.

I woke up on the floor. Probably fifteen or twenty minutes had elapsed. Before I was knocked out, I had been too scared to even feel my fear, as if my cowardly mind had jumped clear, abandoning my body, which closed like a fist to protect the fragile heart. Now all that delayed terror was waiting for me. As soon as my eyes opened, and I saw where I was, I leaped to my feet and fled, as if on fire, through the apartment, down the stairs and out into the middle of the street.

I kept running, in a blind, dumb panic, and it was only at the corner, out of breath, that I was able to force myself to glance back, as if afraid the building would explode. Then, as some oxygen returned to my brain, I called 911 on my cell phone and reported a murder. I gave Sandra's address and name. I gave my own name and number.

But when they told me to remain at the scene and wait for the police, I said I couldn't. I was already running down the street again, frantically scanning up and down each block for cabs. I tried as best I could to explain the new fear that was forming in my mind: I had to get to Manhattan, to an apartment on Horatio Street for which I didn't have the address, where another woman, whose phone number I didn't have on me, was, I feared, in mortal danger, for reasons far too weird and complex to explain. By the time I got to the subway I was panting, and seeing no cabs but already hearing distant sirens, I hung up on the cops and ran down to wait for the train into the city, to find Morgan Chase.

39

Pacing the L train platform, cell phone dead in my hand, I realized that my head was pounding. It turned out that the alarm bell that had been ringing in my skull since I came to wasn't just fear. It was pain as well. I touched the back of my head lightly and winced. There was dried blood in my hair and a sore place at the base of the skull. Was I mildly concussed? My thinking was both slow and madly racing, and as I paced the platform, craning my head over the tracks to squint down the tunnel for that dim light, I recalled the irrational thought I'd had as that body turned above me, just before the blow: Darian Clay had done this. Darian Clay is here. A primal terror had gripped me, and if I had not been knocked unconscious, I might have screamed. Now, as the shock wore off, and I felt the chills and tremors pass through my belly and my knees, another, quieter but more insidious fear began to spread. Whoever it was in that apartment with me, only one thing was sure: it was not Darian Clay. But then who?

The train came blasting into the station, and the shaking and screeching set off a major earthquake in my head. Maybe I did have a concussion after all. I hurried on board, took a seat, and immediately began psychically pushing the driver, as if I could will this one train to go faster, skip stops, to fly. I stood for no reason and sat back down. I ticked off the seconds at each stop. After the long passage under the river, we arrived at First Avenue. The train waited, it seemed forever, although no one got on. Third Avenue was next. A pointless stop, I decided, only two blocks away. We pulled into Union Square and I watched the people get on and off, staring at them in a rage. At last the door dinged and began to slide shut. Someone running late blocked it with an arm and I groaned out loud. Everyone looked. I smiled stiffly and turned away. I stared at the dark tunnel passing by and considered my pale reflection. I checked my cell phone, which I knew could not be working. And then, incredibly, through some combination of spent adrenaline, animal defense mechanism, psychic horror and head injury, I fell, briefly, asleep.

40

I woke up a minute later in the station. It was Eighth Avenue, my stop. I lurched to my feet and stumbled out the doors before they shut, then ran up the stairs and through the turnstile. As soon as I reached the street, my phone rang. It was the police.

"Hello?"

"Yes, we have a record of a 911 call placed from this phone?"

"Yes." The other line beeped. "Hold on, one second please." I switched over. It was also the police.

"Harry Bloch? Mr. Hairy Bloch?"

"Yes?" I tried crossing Fourteenth against the light and a bus chased me back to the curb.

"This is Detective Bronchovich of the New York Police Department. I'm at the scene of a crime reported from this phone."

"Yes. Sandra Dawson. I know."

"Do you know that leaving the scene of a crime is against the law?" There was another beep.

"Hold on, sorry . . ." I switched over. It was Claire.

"Harry, we need to talk. I just checked your mail."

"Later, Claire, please."

"They're trying to fuck us on *Bitch Goddess of Zorg*, Harry. This is serious."

"Not now."

"Well, Harry, now is when they're fucking us. I am sitting here in your office right now, getting fucked."

"Bye," I said, and switched back to the cops. "Hello? Detective Bronchitis?"

"Where are you? We need to speak to you immediately, sir." I was jogging down the avenue now, trying to remember the order and names of streets. There was the Biography bookstore. Where was that, too far or too soon?

"I know," I panted, turning around in circles. "But I'm afraid that there might be another victim, you see—"

"Where?"

"Horatio Street."

"Where?"

"Horatio Street, in the Village, you know."

"Sir, you're in Manhattan? You left the scene of a murder and went to Manhattan?"

"Yes, well, I'm afraid for this other woman, she lives here . . ."

"Where? What's the address?"

"I don't know. I just know Horatio, so I'm looking. Shit . . ." Distracted by the phone, I had walked too far and was no longer sure of the way. "Fuck. Fuck."

"What? What is it?" The detective was shouting now.

"I lost my way. You know how these streets in the Village get all twisty?" I ran back up Greenwich and turned onto Horatio. The cop on the phone kept berating me but I was breathing too hard to answer and looking too intently to listen. There it was. I remembered. Morgan Chase's building.

"I'll call you back," I said and hung up on Detective B.

Her building was easy to break into. It was one of those old Village buildings, crooked and charming and, as I had hoped, the door lock popped obligingly when I slid my metrocard in the crack. In the movies they use credit cards, but often they are too rigid. Or at least that's what I'd imagined for my protagonists, who were constantly breaking and entering, and what I'd discovered doing research on my own door, after which I changed the lock.

As for Morgan Chase's apartment door, I didn't have to try and break it—it was unlocked. Fear came surging back, in my veins, in my mouth, and my hand shook as I pushed the door open. Then I smelled that smell. Though I had described it in books without ever knowing it myself, I understood it immediately, as we all would: death.

Morgan Chase, at least I assumed it was she, was strapped to her bed, arms and legs spread wide. Her head, hands and feet had been severed and now wilted flowers decorated the bloody stumps. A hand extended from the truncated neck. Her two feet rested on either side of her body. The head was nowhere in sight. The bed itself was saturated with drying blood. Flies buzzed all over. I knew I was going to be sick and so, in order not to contaminate the evidence, I ran back downstairs and threw up in the gutter, in full view of several passersby, before calling 911 again.

41

This time I waited for the cops to arrive. A regular radio car showed up first with two uniformed officers, both young, a Latino man and a black woman. They had me wait, sitting on the steps while they went up. I felt sorry for them. They came down a minute later, visibly shaken, too distraught to realize they were clutching each other by the arm. By now the super and some neighbors had come out, and the cops held them at bay, calling in for help and blocking the door frame with that yellow tape. Next came another cop car with two more uniforms and after that a truck with crime scene technicians in windbreakers carrying cases of equipment. They looked extremely professional, pushed right by me without a word, and I assumed that, unlike the rookies, they'd seen a lot of awful things in their jobs, but I felt sorry for them too. We would all be having the same nightmares now for a while.

Then Detective Bronchovich showed up almost at the same time as two other detectives from the local precinct. He was a big ruddy guy with sandy hair, a brush mustache and a cheap blue suit. The two Manhattan detectives, a man and a woman, both wore black suits.

They all talked to each other first, with a few glances at me. Then Detective B. came over.

"You Bloch?"

"Yes."

He showed me his ID, and when I put my hand out he shook it, roughly. He had a lot of red hair on the backs of his hands and wore both wedding and school rings.

"Don't move. I need a statement as soon as I get back down."

"Right."

As he marched past me up the steps, I noticed his socks didn't match and I felt kind of bad for him too. He seemed pretty tough, and nice enough for a cop, but I sensed he wasn't that sharp and was about to step way out of his depth. About the Manhattan cops, I didn't care either way.

Then, while they were all upstairs, Special Agent Townes arrived. He didn't say anything. Just gave me a look, like it was all he could do not to kick me, and then went upstairs. Him I didn't like at all, but I knew he was the smartest. So when they all came back down as a group, silently, their shoes clumping on the old creaky steps, and gathered around me on the stoop, I addressed myself to him.

"I have a bad feeling we should go to New Jersey."

"Why's that?" he asked. His blue eyes narrowed at me.

"There might be another victim. A girl named Marie Fontaine. Her address is back at my place but I can find it if we drive. Elm Street in Ridgefield Park. I can explain why, but I think we should talk on the way."

His expression of disdain didn't change, but he only thought for a second before he nodded.

"Let's go."

The same agent was behind the wheel as last time, with another beside him. Townes and I rode in the back. We headed toward the tunnel, scattering traffic with short bursts from the siren. I filled him in, and when I told him about my deal with Darian Clay, the sneer on his face curled back into a growl.

"Jesus, I knew you writers were sleazebags but this is low even for a bottom-feeder like you. Talk about a deal with the devil."

"Talk about a mixed metaphor," I said. "You want to watch those in your book."

His eyes shot toward me, then slid away.

"How'd you hear about that?" he asked in a flat, menacing tone. But I didn't care. He couldn't scare me anymore. I was already completely terrified.

"Through the bottom-feeding network," I said. "Guess you want to protect the victims from being exploited by anyone but you."

I didn't see the punch. I guess I wasn't looking. Suddenly a star burst in my right eye and sent me left, banging my head on the window. When I looked over, Townes was sitting calmly with his hands in his lap. Neither of the agents up front had stirred. It was like nothing had happened except now my face hurt a lot. I suppose I was lucky I was sitting on his left. He spoke in the same flat tone, facing forward.

"When you've stomached as much gore as I have for twenty years, and caught as many killers, then you can think about earning something off of it."

"Right," I said. "Good point. I take back everything I said."

"You OK?" he asked.

"Fine. Just a headache. Allergies, I guess. It's spring."

With the agents in front using the GPS and radioing in for guidance, we found the right highway exit. Local police met us, one in front and one behind, top lights turning as we rolled through the neighborhood streets. We passed the bus stop. The rusting swings. I searched my scattered memories for the house: white siding leaking black, a spotty lawn, the dogwood.

"That's it," I said. "On the right."

"There," Townes told the driver. "White house on the right."

The agent pulled into the driveway while his partner alerted the cops, who screeched to a halt in front of Marie's.

"Wait here," Townes told me. All three doors slammed and I was sealed in the silent car, watching as cops hurried to the door of the main house. A big woman in stretch pants and a pink sweater answered and I assumed she was Marie's mother. I learned later that she and her husband had been away on vacation, visiting the grandmother in Florida. They hadn't been concerned when their daughter didn't answer her door, or no more than usual. She often disappeared for days or weeks or simply went a while without speaking to them. They did notice an odd smell emanating from her room, but that wasn't unusual either.

While one female cop urged the mother back inside, Townes, his agents and the other cops sprinted around the house and up the stairs that led to Marie's studio above the garage. From the backseat of the car, with the window up, the lawn looked like a stage set just before the drama begins: two cops guarding the white house trimmed in faded blue, spinning lights tinting the scene rose. The wind pushed small clouds from the sky. It shook the dogwood, and pink flakes flew diagonally over the ground. Two or three landed softly on the hood of the car, or stuck to the window before me like melting snow.

A minute later, two cops emerged, holding hankies over their mouths. One slipped on the stairs and his friend grabbed him. The sole of his shoe left a smear of blood. They helped each other down to the lawn, where one fell to his knees, retching, while the other hugged him. The agents came next, their black raincoats fluttering around them. They swooped over the lawn, muttering into their radios. One big, buzz-cut agent stopped and reached up under his mirrored sunglasses to wipe the tears from his cheeks. Townes descended slowly. He opened the car door, and the sound, scent and touch of the outside flowed back in.

"Come on," he said. "You saw the others. You might as well see this."

Keeping my sore mouth shut, I got out and reluctantly followed him across the lawn. Halfway there I heard a wail come through the screen door to the house. Someone had told the mother. I floated for a second, as if a wave had hit me, lifting my feet, but when Townes looked back I kept a straight face and climbed the steps behind him.

The smell was unbearable: sweetness, vomit, shit, bad meat and rotten flowers. At the top he stepped aside to let me pass. I hesitated on the threshold and Townes pushed me from behind. I held my breath and stumbled into hell.

It was the same room as before—the posters, the bed, the kitchenette, the mirror with the serial killer fan photos—except it had all been repainted in blood. As my eyes focused in the dim light, my mind fought to grasp the images that swam before it: The mattress like a black sponge buzzing with flies. The oozing carpet. The slithering walls. The headboard strewn with intestines like skinless snakes. In the middle of the bed, someone had made a kind of mandala: shoulder blades, flared on either side of a pelvis, bordered by two legs and two arms. In the center lay a heart.

I gasped, inhaling deeply, and instantly realized my mistake. The poisoned air rushed into me, filling my head with black vileness, and the walls began spinning in a bloody whirl. As my vision went dark, I flailed for the door in terror, as if losing consciousness inside that room, even for a second, meant I would never escape. Townes caught me as I fell into a faint.

42

The police kept me for the next eight hours. Since the killings had now crossed state lines, Agent Townes was officially in charge, although all the various local cops were allowed a crack at me too: Detective Bronchovich from Brooklyn, the Manhattan duo, even a skinny Asian-American guy from New Jersey. They didn't touch me, it wasn't like that, although a simple beating might have been quicker. As it was, I told them everything I knew in five minutes, then sat there all day and night while they convinced themselves. The method was tag team. Each cop would make me tell the whole story, then leave me sitting there staring at the one-way glass for a while. Then the next one would come and ask the same questions with a slightly different approach—angry, nice, sincere, suspicious—like a series of bad actors all auditioning for the same lame part.

And I, of course, had written the bad dialogue for this scene, more times than I care to tally: Mordechai Tasered by racist cops or dunked into a vat of moonshine by hillbilly gangsters, Sasha tied to a stake and slow-roasted by vampire hunters. In my books, my people always kept up a brave front, cracking wise while their hearts trembled around their secret knowledge. They never told. I was just the opposite. I was traumatized and eager to spill my guts—just that phrase made me want to swoon again—but I had nothing useful to say.

It was the female Manhattan detective, Hauser I think was her name, who finally broke me. My patience, that is. I felt bad for her at first. No doubt being a woman on the force, she felt a special need to act like a dick.

"So why'd you do it, Harry? Did you want them but they said no? Or maybe they said yes but you couldn't get it up? Or maybe you just wanted to be like your hero?"

"What hero?"

"Darian Clay."

"What? What're you talking about? Why did I do what? Agree to write the book?"

"Why did you kill the girls, Harry?"

"Are you crazy?" The images of Sandra, Morgan, Marie cracked opened in my head. I was helpless to stop them. I tasted bile. At least I didn't have to worry about getting sick anymore. I was empty. "Look, I understand you guys need to question me. Even be suspicious. But this is offensive and I'm done. I want my lawyer."

She frowned and glanced at whoever was behind the glass, her boss. She leaned in. "Sure, if you want. But that just makes you look guilty."

"You already think that."

"Not necessarily."

"You just said so. I want my lawyer."

"Let's relax a minute."

"Let me go or get my lawyer. Now." I sat back with my arms crossed. Hauser looked worried, like she'd blown the play and was going to get towel-snapped later in the locker room. The truth was I didn't even have a lawyer. I was going to call Claire.

Hauser stood, hitching her suit pants. "Look, Harry. We're almost done here. If we bring lawyers into it, we're back at square one."

I silently mouthed the word *lawyer* one more time. She cursed and walked out. I waved at the glass and then sat back, hands folded on my crossed knees. Townes came in, so quick he had to be watching.

"OK, you can go," he said. "But I want to be clear. Right now you are our top suspect. Actually our only suspect. You were there when Sandra Dawson was killed."

"I wasn't there. I discovered her. The killer knocked me out. I could have died too."

"So you say."

"Feel the lump on my head."

"I'm sure we're going to find your DNA all over those other crime scenes too."

"You know I was there. I was there again just now with you."

"What else will we find? Semen?"

"Fuck you. Is that why you made me go back in? To try to frame me?"

"Fuck you. I don't have to frame you. It's already done."

"Whatever. I'm going." I stood up.

"There's something else. Something you can't explain away. The only person who could have done this is Clay, who's got a pretty good alibi, or someone he told about his girlfriends. Like you. No one else could have known."

"Except the cops," I said, and regretted it immediately, even before he hit me. I flew back onto the table.

"You can file a complaint if you want," he said, walking out.

"No fanks," I said. Or tried to. My bottom lip was numb.

PART THREE
May 5—17, 2009

43

I got home around four in the morning, and despite my exhaustion and the various scuff marks on my head, I didn't think I'd ever sleep again. Every time I shut my eyes I saw them, the girls, or what used to be girls. I finally drifted off around dawn and slept sporadically through most of the following day. I'd wake up from nightmares, then roll over and pass back out. Claire called at noon. I told her I was sleeping and hung up. She called again at six. The killings were on the news by then, so I told her a brief version of events, minus the horror show details. She wanted to come over but I said, no, tomorrow, I just needed to rest. I ate a peanut butter and jelly sandwich standing at the counter and went back to sleep. Claire called again at ten.

"Jesus Christ, Claire, will you please leave me alone?"

"Put on the news. Channel nine."

"I don't want to. That shit's already playing in my head around the clock."

"Just do it."

Sighing, I sat on the couch and picked up the remote. I hit the local news. Carol Flosky was talking into a forest of microphones.

"All I said was that it raised important questions. I will be meeting with authorities tomorrow to extend every assistance we can. I spoke to my client today and he expressed his deep sympathy for the families of the victims and his sincere hope that the killer is apprehended quickly and that justice is done, in this case as well as his own."

"You know . . ." Claire was still on the phone, watching with me. "If he doesn't get fried, you don't get a dime."

"You're too young to be that cynical." Then I thought, maybe it's because she is young, each generation a bit harder, designed for survival in a world with Darian Clays.

"Sorry," she said.

"And they don't fry them anyway, it's lethal injection."

"Right, the spike."

"And meanwhile, the cops think I did it."

"That's ridiculous."

"Tell them."

"Sure you don't want me to come over? I'll just get in a cab."

"No thanks, it's fine."

"OK, but one more thing. If the cops ask, don't tell them you dress like your mother."

She hung up and now I didn't go back to sleep. I watched the news as it repeated the whole thing from the beginning. It felt uncanny to see places and people I had just visited and then had bad dreams about suddenly appearing on TV: Sandra's building and a picture of her, Morgan's street and her photo, Marie's house and her crying mother. I saw Townes talking to reporters with the other detectives shuffling behind him. When they returned to Flosky for the third time, I shut it off and ran a shower. I was just getting in when the phone rang. It was Dani. She'd seen the news. I told her about my day, and my night, again leaving out the gory details, but there was enough on the news by then so that she could imagine the worst, almost.

"That would give me nightmares," she said.

"It is. I keep waking up. And falling asleep. I can't do either one."

"I know the feeling. I used to dream about my sister all the time. About her asking me to help her find her head."

"Jesus, that's horrible."

"Do you want me to come over?" she suddenly blurted.

"What?" I heard a jet engine screech by over the phone.

"I mean, not if you don't want me to. I'm at work but I'm leaving anyway. It's on the TV in there. I left to call you, but I'm not going back. I'm sitting in my car in the parking lot. So can I? Do you mind?"

"Mind what?"

"If I come over."

"Yes. Sure. If you want to," I said.

44

This is the part of the story where the detective sleeps with the girl. I suppose it's inevitable. It felt that way. There was no reason for us to be together except that suddenly we needed to be.

She wasn't looking her best. She was in the sweats and bulky coat she had changed into when leaving work, but with her makeup and hair still done up. Except that she'd been crying and now her foundation was streaked with mascara and her eyes were glazed. As for me, well my best and worst weren't as far apart as hers, but that night I had a swollen lip, bruises on the right cheek and the left temple, and a goose egg growing on the back of my head, plus the effects of whatever the mixture of no sleep and too much sleep and nightmares does to a person. Plus that smell I kept smelling. But I guess I was lucky. Dani liked the pathetic type.

"My God," she said, when I let her in. I flinched as she hugged me and her hand brushed the lump on my head. "You should have ice on that."

"I should just soak my whole head in a bucket."

"It's true." She laughed. "You look awful."

"Well, thanks for coming over to cheer me up."

"Sorry." She laughed harder. "I can't help it. Your lip is huge."

"Look who's talking. You look like the sad clown."

She wiped her eyes and peeked into the bathroom mirror. "Eek!" she said. "I look like a witch. A blond witch."

"A bitch!" I said, and she giggled. She considered us both in the mirror.

"Two losers," she said, sniffling. "I guess we belong together." She smiled at me and I kissed her.

I wasn't like that, normally. Actually that's a huge understatement. I hadn't kissed anyone since Jane, and she was the one who made the first move on me. But I guess something about the last day, awful as it sounds, made me brave for once, or reckless, or just desperate. Anyway I kissed her and she kissed me back, harder. She pushed against my body, grasping with all her strength, and crushed her mouth into mine.

"Ow, shit, my lip, my face."

"Oh sorry, I'm sorry," she said, pulling back. Then she burst into laughter again. "You're really the sensitive type, aren't you?"

I laughed too. "I know. I'm blowing the chance of a lifetime."

"Totally. You're so lame. And what about me? Throwing myself at a guy and getting rejected."

"For excessive roughness," I said and kissed her again, softly. She kissed me softly back. Then I pulled her to me and kissed her hard. It hurt. I tasted blood. But I didn't care. We stumbled into the bedroom together and fell onto the bed. My head banged loudly against the headboard. She froze and waited.

"Ow," I said quietly.

She broke out into wild laughter again and then I realized she wasn't laughing anymore. She was crying.

"I know," I said, rubbing her back, though I wasn't sure I did. I let her sob into my chest while I stared at the ceiling in silence. Tears slowly filled my own eyes and ran down into my ears. I fell asleep and woke up in the darkness to feel her squirming out of her clothes. I did the same and she crawled into my arms, pressing her skin to mine. It wasn't like any other sex I'd ever had. It wasn't like two people in love and happy. It wasn't like two people drunk and lustful either. It was rageful, tender, blind. It was sad sex. It was angry sex. And it was sweet.

45

From *Double Down on the Deuce*, chapter 2:

Cherry Blaze and I drove out to Queens, where old Manhattanites bury their dead. Maybe you've seen it from the highway, on your way to the airport—acres of tombstones mocking the skyline behind them, the real eternal city, the necropolis. At least that's how it looked to me just then, with that knot in my gut telling me something was wrong. Or maybe it was just my old Impala SS knocking, like it always did, and flicking its low oil light in warning. Either way, I should have listened.

We parked, and I got a shovel from the trunk, wrapping it in a blanket. I also grabbed a pint of rye and a flashlight from the glove box. In the cemetery, she pointed out her dad's stone. Then we wandered off, found a tree to spread the blanket under, and settled in for a macabre little picnic while we waited for the graveyard to close.

Night came slow that day, and while the sun slipped into

the river behind the city, we had plenty of time to talk and drink. Then we fell silent and just lay there, watching the sky change. When darkness finally fell, and the last light in the guardhouse blinked out, and the night-lights, man-made and otherwise, came on, I flicked my orange butt into the shadows and turned to Cherry.

"OK, let's go."

"Wait," she said in a small voice, and her small hand gripped my wrist. "Please."

"What's wrong?" I lit a match to see her, but she blew it out.

"No, please." She gripped me harder. "Now that we're here, I'm scared to see him." I felt a tremor run through her bones. Her teeth knocked. "Mordechai?" she whispered.

"Yeah?" I whispered back.

"Hold me, please. I'm cold."

Well, what can I say? I'm half-Jew, half-Indian, and neither tribe has the best history with white girls, but I guess the combination of too much booze, too much talk, and then too much silence and too many stars went to my head. I pulled her close. Her lips found mine in the dark. Next thing I knew that dress was peeling away and we were down on the ground, doing dirty. She moaned like a ghost when I entered her, and her skin was ghost white in the moon glow, but when I shut my eyes, she was hot and alive like an animal beneath me.

"Smack me, smack me," she pleaded, and I brought my hand down hard on her high firm haunches, pulling her hair back, like I was bucking a wild thing. She gave as good as she got, too, scratching and biting like an alley cat. Finally, we lay back, exhausted. She lit a smoke. I checked my watch. It was midnight. Time to work.

We found her dad's grave and I dug. Now it was as if both the fear and the fight had gone out of her and we were silent. There was nothing left to say. The moon came out from the clouds and filled the grave with light. About an hour later, the tip of my spade hit wood.

"OK," I said, catching my breath. "This is it. You ready?"

"Yes," she said, in a quiet, calm voice. She trained the flashlight's beam on the box. "Go ahead."

The coffin was old and rotten and it was easy to wedge the shovel in the lid. I leaned hard and popped it open. And there, lying in the open grave, resting very peacefully and even shining in the moonbeam, was a trumpet.

Cherry gasped. The flashlight went out. And then I heard a man laughing. A laugh I'd heard somewhere before. I scrambled to climb out, but a foot kicked me back and I fell into the grave, beside the trumpet. The flashlight came back on, shining on me, though even in the moonlight I could see who it was.

"Hey, Fats," I said. "What're you doing in the neighborhood? Dropping off a date?"

The throaty laugh boomed again. It was Fat Daddy Slims, trader in flesh, dope, corruption and most recently, condos. I'd put him in prison once and shot him twice, but at three hundred pounds I guess he was hard to sink.

"Hey, Rabbi Jones," he said. "I could ask you the same thing. Jewish cemetery's next door. Now get up slow and hand me the trumpet."

I grabbed the horn and stood, handing it up to Fats. He was dressed flash as always, in a three-piece, hat and a long fur, hands and teeth glittering. But the most impressive part of his ensemble to me was the .357 Magnum pointing at my brain.

"OK, Fats," I said. "Whatever business you got with me, leave Cherry out of it."

"Cherry? Who dat? Oh . . . you mean this fine bitch here?" He grabbed her. "She belongs to me. But she ain't been cherry for a long time, have you, baby?"

He squeezed her and she squealed gleefully. "That's right, Daddy."

"But don't worry, Rabbi," he went on. "Cherry's safe and sound. Show him, baby."

She waved the flashlight, and there beside the stone marked Juniper "Honky" Blaze, was another just like it. It read Cherry Blaze, Beloved Daughter, 1980–2008. Then the light went out again and the shovel hit my head.

A second later I came to, flat on my back in the grave. What a way to end up, I told myself. Tits up in the dirt, like a five-dollar ho. But isn't that where we all end up? The wise guys, the tough guys, the big shots and the ladykillers: they were all here, lying right beside me. Sooner or later, every player gets played. And then I started to laugh, like a madman, as the first shovel of earth filled my mouth.

46

At eight the next morning, I was woken from a deep and mercifully dreamless sleep by Special Agent Townes and Co. relentlessly buzzing at my door. I pulled on my robe, checked to make sure Dani was really there curled beneath my sheet, and staggered out to squint through the peephole.

"What is it? I'm sleeping."

"FBI. Police. Open up." A cop in a blue cap held ID up to the fish-eye lens.

"I'm not dressed. Let me come down to the station."

"Open up, sir. We have a warrant. We can break it in."

"Hold on." I unlocked the door. The cop handed me some paper and a whole crew swept in. Townes was last.

"Good morning," he said.

"Is this really necessary? Why don't you just tell me what you're looking for?"

"It says on the warrant."

"It's too early to read."

"All materials relevant to Darian Clay, including but not limited to notes, transcripts, tapes, photos, notebooks . . ."

Dani came out of the bedroom. Her hair was a mess and she wore my old Ramones T-shirt with her sweatpants. She looked stunning.

"Ms. Giancarlo." Townes grinned at her. She gave him a look of utter disdain.

"Come on," she said to me. "Let's make coffee and wait for Agent Asshole and his friends to finish."

Townes chuckled. "That's Special Agent Asshole to you."

Then the door buzzed again, frantically, but before anyone could reach it, the lock turned and it opened. Claire stormed in, trailed by a gray-haired man in a dark blue pinstriped suit. She was wearing her uniform, complete with blazer and kneesocks, and her hair was up in pigtails. Livid, she took in the scene, hands in fists on her hips.

"What the fuck is going on here?" she demanded. She seemed to be equally accusing of Townes, Dani and me.

"Is this your daughter?" Dani asked.

"Ha," Claire barked. "As if."

"The feds and cops are searching the place," I said. "They're confiscating all my stuff from the book."

"The fuck they are. Who's in charge?"

I pointed at Townes. He frowned at the angry teenager and turned back to me.

"Who the hell is this?"

"My business partner," I said.

"That's right," Claire said, stepping up to him. "And this is our lawyer."

"Good morning, gentlemen," the lawyer said, stepping forward with the confidence of the man with the most expensive suit in the room. He took out a card. "My name is—"

"I know who you are," Townes said, ignoring the proffered card.

"I don't," I said.

The lawyer smiled and handed the card to me. "Don't worry. It's pro bono. I'm a family friend. Can I see the warrant?" I handed him the paper I was holding and he glanced at it. "Ah, Judge Franklin. We're having lunch tomorrow anyway."

I glanced at the card. Turner C. Robertson, Esq., of Mosk, Porter, Robertson and Leen. The card was a rich cream with raised ink and it felt like it would crack if you bent it. I dropped it in my robe pocket. He and Townes put their heads together and mumbled. Meanwhile Claire had sidled up to me.

"Who's that?" she said under her breath, and cut her eyes toward Dani.

I told her and she sighed. "Figures. The stripper." Then she turned, smiling sweetly. "That T-shirt looks good on you."

"Thanks," Dani said evenly.

"It's comfy to sleep in, isn't it? I love it."

Dani didn't react but her eyes scanned Claire's nubile form and then slid to me.

"Claire helps handle my affairs," I explained.

"Is that what you call it?" Dani asked. Claire narrowed her eyes and I could see her back go up.

"What do you call your job? Dancing?"

I gulped. "OK. Let's focus on keeping me out of prison here."

Then one of the junior agents, the one who'd cried yesterday, came out of my office looking upset again.

"There's nothing here," he announced.

Townes looked over. "What do you mean?"

"Yeah, what do you mean?" I chimed in.

"There's nothing here about Clay. No notes, interviews, nothing. Just a lot of crap about these other books. Vampires and planets and shit like that. And a bunch of old porn."

"Well?" Townes turned to me. I was in a panic myself.

"What are you pulling?" I asked him. "Where's my stuff?"

"You tell me. You understand it's contempt if you don't turn everything over."

"I don't know where it is," I insisted. "You guys must be hiding it. Search everyone," I ordered, inanely, as if I were the head detective.

"Don't worry," Claire said, proudly stepping forward. "I have everything. As soon as I heard you got arrested, I came right over and moved it all to a safe place."

Townes sighed. "Look, little girl, I don't care who your friends are. It's illegal to withhold or conceal evidence in a murder."

"Excuse me, Special Agent." Robertson now stepped in. "But this warrant gives you permission to search these premises only and compels Mr. Bloch alone to turn this purported evidence over. Ms. Nash is under no such compulsion, and I will ask you to refrain from threatening and coercing a minor."

Townes shrugged. "Counselor, you know full well all you're doing is wasting time. I'll get a new warrant."

"Yes, and this time I'll be there to argue it. This is a First Amendment issue regarding the freedom of the press and my clients are prepared to defend it."

"Are they prepared to go to jail?" Townes asked.

"Yes," Claire announced, stepping forward and tossing her pigtails. "We are."

"I'm not," I said.

"Quiet," Claire said. "We won't go anywhere. My lawyer will handle it."

"Yeah, be quiet, Harry," Dani agreed.

I retied my robe and sat down on the couch. Dani and Claire sat beside me. Robertson and Townes went into another huddle and quickly came to an agreement: all the materials, including the stuff they had already confiscated from me yesterday, would be copied, with me retaining sole rights to publication and distribution at the end of the investigation.

"That sounds fine," Claire said, when the two men came over and explained the deal.

"Yeah, that's good," Dani concurred.

I lifted my empty hands. "I guess it's fine then."

"This is conditional," Townes pointed out, "on Harry not being arrested or charged with the murders. Then he forfeits all rights, of course."

"Of course," Claire said.

"That's fair," Dani said.

"What?" I spoke up. "Who said it's fair?"

"God, don't worry," Claire said. "Lighten up. You didn't kill anyone." She chuckled at the thought.

"You should see the lump on his head," Dani said.

Claire stood. "OK. I'm going to leave you to finish up," she said. She shook hands with Townes, gave Robertson a kiss on the cheek, and jingled her keys at me. "I'll check the mail and then I've got to run. I've got school."

"She has keys?" Dani asked as the door shut.

"And where does she go to school?" Townes put in. "It's after ten o'clock."

"Don't worry about it," Robertson said. "She's getting straight A's. Right?" He asked me. I nodded and he explained to the others, "He's her tutor."

Dani frowned. "We'll discuss this later," she told me, as Townes and Robertson went off to supervise the wrap-up.

"There's not much to discuss," I said, trying to assert myself a bit. "It's a business relationship."

"That's even weirder. If you were just a normal pervert, I could understand. But this is, I don't know what."

"We're partners," I offered.

Dani wrinkled her nose. "Pick another word."

"Colleagues?"

The door opened and Claire burst back in. Clutching the mail, she ran to my bedroom and shut the door.

"What's going on?" Dani asked.

"I don't know," I told her. "Wait here."

I knocked on the door. There was no answer. I opened it slowly and stepped in, shutting it behind me. Claire had flung herself face down across the unmade bed, the mail sprawled out on the floor beside her.

"Hey," I said in a low voice. "What's going on?"

She shrugged but didn't move, her face sunk in a pillow that I knew smelled like Dani. The whole room smelled like sex. "Come on, you can tell me," I said, and sat down on the edge of the bed, preparing to pat her back and tell her not to mind Dani, or to thank her for standing up for me and handling everything brilliantly as usual, but then I saw the photos.

They were spilling out of a plain manila envelope that had my name typed on it, but no stamp or return address. Claire had torn down the edge. They were eight-by-ten color prints with a white border. The one on top was Sandra Dawson. I knew because I recognized the room in the background, her bed and white dresser and on the wall the photo of a woman in a slip and lace veil. Also I could tell because she was hanging upside down with her head cut off and her entrails dangling, like the pink and white vines of a hanging plant in bloom, ending in the bright red puddle of blood that spread like a blossom on the floor.

I reached for it, but then thought of fingerprints. "These were in the mail?" I asked. Claire nodded. I got the lawyer's card from my pocket and used the stiff edge to push the photos apart. There were three altogether, one for each of the victims, full color head-on shots of the crime scenes I'd just witnessed, carefully composed and framed. Again, like at Sandra's, I felt someone there, just behind me. Wherever I'd been, he had been, and whomever I saw, he visited next. Now, he was letting me know, he'd been here.

I patted Claire on the shoulder. "I'll be right back, OK?" She nodded into the pillow. I used the card to push the pictures back into the envelope and then used the sleeve of my robe to pick it up. I went into the living room and then the kitchen, where Dani, Townes and Robertson were sitting in the breakfast nook and drinking coffee from my mom's mugs, brown with yellow flowers. I put the envelope in front of Townes.

"This was in the mail." I squeezed Dani's shoulder. "You might not want to look." Then I went back into the bedroom, where Claire still lay facedown.

"Can I hug you?" I asked, kneeling beside her, and she nodded, so I did.

47

Who? This was the word that I repeated to myself, ceaselessly, as I ate, showered, dressed, walked around and held full conversations on completely different topics. Who? Whatever the reason for killing off Clay's girlfriends, only someone in contact with him, or with access to his mail or prison cell, could know who the women were or the specifics of their fantasy lives with Clay. Who, then, could this be? A collaborator of course. Or else a copycat: a cop, a prison guard, a nut who somehow had access to these documents, a demented clerk in the system somewhere. Or else some kind of stalker: another jealous lover perhaps, or someone envious of Clay's fame and female fan club. Which in turn would mean that person had been following me, stepping into my footsteps and killing each girl after I left. Each time my thoughts revolved back to this starting point, a new shot of fear burned my stomach and closed my throat and I saw Sandra's body turning, inverted, then felt the blow to my head, and I asked myself, Who?

And what did Whoever want from me? Was I a victim being toyed with by a sociopath, like in a Jim Thompson dime novel? A patsy being framed, like in all those Hitchcock movies? Or, like in every other thriller, including my own, was I just a clueless witness about to be eliminated, too dim to realize the truth, until I washed up dead in the next chapter? And then there was the thought I could barely let myself think, much less say aloud, the idea that would have been ridiculous just the day before: was Clay somehow innocent after all? And was the real killer back in town?

One thing was certain—I couldn't count on Townes for protection. He had done everything but spit on my shoes before he left, and even Robertson, my own lawyer, had made it plain when we shook hands good-bye: "You might want to tie up some loose ends now. An arrest could come anytime."

"Don't worry," Claire had added. "I'll bail you out. This arrest thing is just a formality, right?" Robertson shrugged.

Claire, meanwhile, was fine. Once her tears dried, she shook the horror off like a bad dream after a movie, and bounced back with the resiliency of the young, desensitized by all the media nastiness provided by people like me. She was right back at work the next day, sprawled on my couch, chewing a Twizzler. Straight from field hockey practice, she wore space-blue fractal sneakers, red kneesocks, a pleated skirt and a hoodie. Stick at her feet, and with her blond hair pulled tight to the skull and bound in a high ponytail, she looked like a cartoon warrior girl in a golden helmet.

"I know it's a total tragedy," she said, gnawing her licorice, showing her red tongue, "but the value of this book in the marketplace just like tripled. I mean it already had historical interest, but let's face it: there's nothing like fresh bodies to give it that torn-from-the-headlines feeling."

"Yeah, I know that feeling," I said. "I've been eating Tums for two days to get rid of it. I'm changing my name and moving to Kansas. You can have my couch."

"Don't be so dramatic. You already have like six names. What would those Watergate guys do, Woodsteen and Burns? Did they run away the first time Nixon tried to kill them?"

"Nixon didn't chop their heads off with a cleaver. Rent the movie."

"You're a writer, damn it." She poked her Twizzler at me, like some muckraking old editor with a stogie. "At a time like this you should be working. Tracking down leads and stuff. Doing what you do best."

"Spare me."

She shrugged. "At least show up for your Clay interview tomorrow. That's inside a prison. You'll be nice and safe."

She had a point there. I did have an appointment to see Clay the next day. As was our routine, I was supposed to interview Sandra, then go up to deliver his story and collect my interview. I had written nothing, of course, reality having intervened. Even the most extreme and disturbing fantasy was a fairy tale compared to the newspaper. And what about the book, Clay's book? Was that still a reality? For now, let's just say I was blocked: all I could think about was not becoming a character in it. But my appointment was still on the calendar, no one had canceled, and I supposed it wasn't a bad day to be behind bars and under armed guard, talking to the one person who I knew for sure had not attacked me, and who might even know who did. So I packed my bag and rode the night train and checked back into the sad motel. I tried Dani but got no answer. Perhaps she was at work, hanging naked from a pole.

Prison, however, was not as warm and cozy as I'd hoped. Although passing through the gates was a lot less scary than walking down my block to the deli, I still felt exposed. It seemed like everyone knew who I was. I was "that guy," and I felt both select and ashamed as people stared, muttered and then quickly looked away. I was tainted with Clay's Disease, and as I went through security, the friskers seemed reluctant to touch me. But like some scandalous VIP at a nightclub, I was swept right through to the visitor's waiting room, where I found Theresa Trio, tapping her toes beside the battered soda machine. She stood when she saw me.

"Good. You're here. They're waiting for you."

"They?"

"Carol wants to see you too. Ms. Flosky." She was worked up about something and it made her skittish, girlish. Her eyes sparkled. "We, I mean she, has meetings with the judge and the governor's head legal counsel later. Actually things are looking up."

"I'm glad the evisceration of three women has an upside for you."

Stung, she looked away, picking at a chip in the table. "That's not what I meant. I'm sorry about those women. But maybe now the police will catch the real killers."

"The police? Please. You know who their main suspect is? Me."

Theresa raised her eyebrows and I laughed.

"And what's even scarier is that the real killer knew all about those girls, when I saw them, their addresses, everything." I leaned in to make eye contact with her. "Who knew all that? Clay. Your poor innocent victim."

Theresa eyed me evenly. "Lots of people could have known. Even me."

Even you. I remembered the tattoos I'd seen peeking from under her clothes, the online correspondence of vampT3, the streak of perversity I'd found so intriguing, the hidden inner life. My fan. The vampire-loving freak. I asked myself, Did she know who I was after all? I answered myself, So what? I was getting dizzy. Once again, that bitter, bilious taste, the terrible taste of terror touched my tongue: a mixture of nausea, adrenaline, and Amtrak hot dog. Then the guard appeared in the door and called my name.

"See you later," I said. I thought she smiled weirdly at me before reaching into her bag and pulling out my book.

48

"Harry," Clay said, smiling and shaking his head. Flosky sat across the table. Another plastic chair waited for me. "Wow. You look like shit. But I guess it's all relative. Considering what you've been through."

Flosky puffed on her cigarette and peered at me through the cloud, as if reading my fortune or my character. As I took my chair, the smoke brushed over my face. I wanted to sneeze.

"Yeah," I said. "It's been a rough few days."

"No doubt," Clay went on. "We've been following it in the news. Now you know how I feel." His smile widened. Flosky watched me impassively. I looked from one to the other.

"I'm not sure I know what you mean."

Flosky dropped her cigarette and ground it into the scarred linoleum. "He means you know what it feels like to be hounded by the press, brutalized by the police and suspected of a horrific crime of which you are innocent."

"I hope you've got a good lawyer," Clay said, chuckling, but cut it short at a glance from Flosky. "Sorry." He put his fingers to his mouth and chewed. His big white teeth seemed to cut into the gums when he smiled. "Nervous laughter," he said. "Gallows humor, right? I don't know what to say. I never met the girls, of course, but I feel like I did from their letters and pictures. It was very intimate in its own way, you know. Their parents, friends, families are all mourning them now. But I knew a side they never saw, a part that they only trusted me with. People don't realize how deep that connection can be. But you do of course. You knew them all." He sat forward. I could see the place where he'd nicked himself shaving, near the base of his throat. I could see food in his fake teeth. "You don't happen to have that story with you, do you? The one about Sandra?"

I jerked back, as if he'd tried to kiss me. "I didn't fucking write it."

"OK, OK," Flosky spoke up. "That's enough. I don't have time for this bullshit. Of course you didn't write it. And you," she told Clay, "shut up and let me talk."

"Sorry, Carol," Clay said, and to me, "Don't worry, bro. I won't hold you to our deal on that one."

"Darian," Flosky repeated, through a clenched jaw.

"Sorry. Go ahead."

She took a breath, the kind you take while silently counting to ten, and turned to me. "You know I've been against this book from the beginning. Now it looks like maybe it's turned into a whole different kind of mess. On the other hand, I admit I might have misjudged you. Anyway, we have no choice now, we're going to have to trust each other. Three more girls have died. And your own safety is at stake."

"Trust me how? What are you talking about?"

"What I'm about to tell you is privileged. The kind of thing an attorney only discusses with their client. But you're involved, so . . . Do you know what disclosure is? In the legal sense?"

"Sort of."

"The defense has the right to see all the evidence, everything the prosecution has in their files. We were privy to information that was never released to the public. Things only the cops knew. And the killer."

"Yeah, so?"

"So I saw the photos of those murders ten years ago and read the reports. And yesterday the judge made Townes show me the reports on the new killings. They fit the profile exactly."

"How exactly?"

"Like handwriting. Why do you think Townes is shitting a brick? This case made him. Now I intend to argue that the signature on these crimes is so close that the same killer must have done them all, or in any event they certainly raise enough doubt to warrant a new trial."

I frowned. "That's one view, I guess." I was unwilling to admit that the possibility had already crossed my mind. What if the creepy killer across the table from me was just a regular old creep?

Flosky put another cigarette in her mouth and lit it, waving the match out furiously as if it were a gnat. "Whatever. I'm not going to argue my case here. What I need to tell you is this: I do believe that the Photo Killer is back. The real one. I think he's back because of the publicity surrounding the execution, and even more so, I think he surfaced because of your book."

"What?"

"These people, these psychos, whatever, they have huge egos. Does he want to get caught? No. He's not stupid. When Darian got arrested, he was happy to go underground, to stop killing, or at least change his signature, move away, who knows, and let someone else take the blame. But the idea that someone else will get the credit, the idea that someone else will go down in history, in a book, as having done what he did? That got to him. It ate at him until he started killing again, to show the world who he really was and what he could do. Like I said, he's not stupid, but he is crazy, and I think it's my duty to warn you. There's a good chance he could come after you."

"Me?" I sat back to consider this, and they both considered me,

Flosky glumly smoking and Clay with a sadly mocking or mockingly sad little smile. Again I wondered at how seminormal he seemed, how nonlethal. Teeth and nails, was that enough? Were they the mark of the beast? Was that what I needed to watch for, walking home tonight? "What did I do?" I asked them, as if they knew or cared. "I'm just the writer."

49

"So the answer lies in the past," Claire mused, after I filled her in on my meeting with Clay and Flosky. She sucked Diet Coke thoughtfully through a bent straw, spindly ankles crossed on the coffee table. "Sounds to me like you need to do some legwork and find that connection. Dig up the backstory on this."

"Only if I can solve it safely from here, while I water my orchids, like Nero Wolfe." I leaned back in the armchair, wriggling off my boots, and put my feet up across from hers.

"Who's he?"

"This detective. A fat genius."

"Well, you're not there just yet," she observed. "But with all the books you wrote, you should be a pretty good sleuth by now. You could go out there and find some clues. Just do what Mordechai would do."

"You're right. I am pretty good at finding those clues. Want to know why?" I poked her little feet with mine. "'Cause I'm the one who put them there. That's the difference between playing detective in a book and real life. I make up the crime and then I solve it. And even then it gives me a headache."

She kicked me back, heel to heel. "All I'm saying is it would make a great book if you cracked it yourself."

I snorted. "Did I forget to mention the part about my life being in danger?"

"Well, isn't catching the killer the best way to save it?" She sat up and earnestly squeezed my feet in her two hands. "What if they're right? What if Clay is innocent?"

"Stop." I shook her off. "That tickles."

"Seriously, Harry."

I shrugged and faced her bright eyes. "If Clay's innocent, then there's a serial killer loose and after me."

"And who's going to catch him? The cops?"

Before I could think of an answer to that one, the intercom buzzed, and Claire leapt up to press it.

"Who's that?" I asked, suddenly worried.

"That is a very important magazine person who asked to see you. Your cell was off in the prison, so I told them to just come over. But I have debate team at school, so I'm going to have to leave." She pulled her backpack on and headed for the door.

"What's debate on?" I shouted.

"Illegal immigration," she yelled back. "I'm pro!"

The door slammed. Magazine person? I took a quick look at myself in the mirror. I was demon-eyed and unshaven, my dirty hair flattened by train sleep. I even found a tiny puff of white pollen hiding in it, like a spring motif. The doorbell rang.

"Coming," I yelled. "One second." I hurried to the door, retucking my shirt, and noticed the large hole in my sock. It had started small that morning, but now my big toe poked through, like a pink turtle testing the air. I looked back longingly at my boots, but the door buzzed again, so I put my toe behind the door and opened it with the traditional greeting, "Sorry!"

It was Jane.

"Sorry," she answered, as if we both hailed from the same Sorry-land. She could see the shock on my face. "Is it bad that I'm here?"

"No. I. No. I. Just wasn't expecting . . ."

"Sorry. I spoke to I think it's your manager? Claire? She set it up."

"My manager? Right."

"Then this girl in the hallway told me which was your door."

"Yes, that's her."

"Who?"

"What?" I flashed on Dani's reaction to Claire the day before. "No one. What did I say? Forget it."

"Sorry about this," she said. "I can go."

"No, please. I'm sorry. Come in. Sorry about my sock."

A few more apologies got us through the door and her out of her coat. Like compulsive samurai trading gifts we moved crabwise, smiling and sorry, into the kitchen, where I set about making coffee, more or less. Anyway, sprinkling coffee and water around the counter.

"So I'm here on business," Jane said. "In a professional capacity."

"Selling magazine subscriptions door-to-door?" I got the coffee grounds in the filter finally and pressed the red button. The machine began to hiss and gurgle.

"No." She laughed and blushed, and her discomfort calmed me down. I wiped the counter with a sponge and put an Entenmann's coffee cake on the table. "Though I have noticed your name absent from our subscribers list."

"Well, you know I only read porn and comics," I said, fetching the daisy mugs. "Plus, come on, four issues a year? What kind of magazine do you call that?"

"We call it a quarterly."

"Now, I thought that meant it cost a quarter, like the *Post* used to. Yours is more like a ten-dollarly."

Another, bigger laugh. "I forgot how much fun you used to be."

"Gee, thanks."

"You know what I mean. This is nice."

I poured coffee and sat across from her, with a quart of milk between us. "It is nice," I said.

"To be honest, I'm surprised. With everything that's going on, I thought you'd be more distraught than you seem."

"I am more distraught than I seem," I said, suddenly feeling distraught, mainly in the stomach and across my forehead. I ran my hands through my hair. "But I'm also sort of OK," I added, and I was.

"Well, I think you're being terribly brave. We all do." I wondered who they all were, but I didn't want to interrupt her flow of praise. "That's why I'm here. To offer whatever help I can. Not that we can do much about the physical danger you're in, though I suppose we might organize a brigade of writers. Like during the Spanish Civil War."

I had an image of Dave Eggers and Jonathan Lethem, dressed in matching windbreakers and parked outside my building with flashlights, waiting for Squad Captain DeLillo to call in on the walkietalkie.

"Right," I said. "A gang of armed neurotics. We'd all shoot ourselves or each other."

"Exactly. Our powers are useless against reality. But we can fight your abstract literary battles for you. This police harassment you're receiving. The FBI subpoenaing your files. I already have enough names for a petition, believe me. People are emailing and asking what they can do."

"What people?"

"You know. Book people. Some of the writers you met the other night, for instance. I'm thinking an open letter in the *Times* to start. I spoke to Ryan and he'd be happy to cohost a benefit reading to help with legal bills. And I put in a call to PEN."

I laughed. "I'll manage. But thanks."

"You're sure?"

"Yeah. Very."

"I knew you'd say no. But don't let them bully you. You have to write this book. Promise me."

"I promise."

"And you'll think about it? What I said. And let me know if I can help?"

"Yes."

She stood and I did too. Then she reached across and touched my face. I stayed very still, as though a butterfly had landed on my hand.

"You know," she said. "Speaking objectively of course, you're looking very attractive right now. This whole thing has done wonders."

"Want to feel the sexy lump on my head?"

"I do. Sort of." She kissed my cheek. "But I won't."

After Jane left I thought about it, and I realized what it was, the change she had noticed that I hadn't seen in myself. True, I was exhausted and stressed and confused. I was broke and desperate and, most of all, very, very afraid. But for the first time in a long time, I was no longer depressed. Here's a self-help tip: nothing brings us back to life like fear.

50

I decided to begin my investigation at the beginning, with Clay's house, where he lived and committed his crimes, and where he took the photos of his victims. Dani insisted on driving me. I resisted at first—I couldn't imagine it being anything but traumatic for her—but she was adamant and I was secretly glad, as much for the company as the convenience of a car. Then Claire announced that she was coming too. She was appalled beyond words when she heard that I'd passed on Jane's proposal, and seemed to feel that I could no longer be trusted to wander the streets unmanaged. Plus she had a better car.

Thus, I ended up sitting behind the wheel of Claire's dad's black BMW 750i, with Claire beside me, waiting for Dani to emerge from her building in Jackson Heights. Claire sucked the last of her Diet Coke through a straw with a strangling sound and then dropped the can on the floor of the car. She was still holding a grudge.

"PEN," she said. "PEN!"

"You didn't even know what it was till you Googled it."

"Well, I know what a benefit concert is. It could be huge."

"Benefit reading. Very different and not at all huge. No Bono. Besides, I couldn't accept, because of our prior relationship."

"No, duh. That's why you have to work it."

"No way, too weird. Plus this way I look heroic in her eyes, not helpless. She said I was attractive!"

"Big whoop. She's just having buyer's remorse. Don't fall for it. Besides, I think you've got more than you can handle with the stripper."

"I'm not sure. It was only that one night," I said as Dani came out of the building and waved. We both waved back.

"Just be careful," she said and turned around in her seat, bouncing onto her knees as Dani got in the back.

"Hi, Dani," she chirped.

Dani smiled angelically. "Hi, sweetie."

I gripped the wheel and drove.

Clay's old place was in Ozone Park, near the Brooklyn border. It was a normal residential block of saggy homes and older cars in the drives. Others were fixed up, like Clay's probably, by younger arrivals, many of them immigrants. Ten years ago, this street would have been dimmer, dingier, aging and abandoned. I had a newspaper photo that I'd printed off the Web, and at first it seemed as if the "Hell House," as it was called in the caption, had been demolished and replaced. Repainted, with an addition on the side, a new deck in back, and a replanted front garden of high shrubs and young trees, it had, maybe purposely, been made almost unrecognizable, but it was there.

"So this is it?" Claire asked, sounding disappointed, as I parked across the street. "Not very spooky." Nevertheless she pulled out her camera and started to snap pictures that she hoped would go in the book. I stared at the twin front windows, the shingled roof with the deep eaves, the small porch. Coming here had seemed like a logical first step, but now I didn't know what to do. Dani didn't hesitate.

"Wait here," she said, and strode across the street, while I stood by the car and watched. In old jeans and a turtleneck, she was a knockout, but I felt more like a smitten pal than her lover. I had not seen her since the other night, and this morning there had been no kissing, hugging, or anything else that normally came under the heading of romance. Nor had there been any mention of what had happened or not happened between us. I could only assume that she regretted it and wanted to pretend it never happened, a grief-drunk mistake best forgotten. Dani marched onto the front porch and rang the bell. She knocked, then knocked again. Then she waved me over. I crossed the lawn to meet her, Claire trailing along, observing the scene through the digital square of her camera.

"No one's home," Dani said. "Let's take a snoop around."

"What would you have done if they answered?"

She shrugged. "I don't know. I'd have come up with something."

She was probably right. Girls like her and Claire lived in a different universe than I, one where people tripped over themselves to be helpful. I lived in a world where no one had change for a dollar and every store's bathroom was permanently out of order. Why these women, with their magical powers, took pity on me I don't know, but I am eternally grateful.

We peeked into the front windows, which were curtained with sheer white fabric. I saw a soft white leather couch, big and loose like an Oldenburg sculpture, and a huge-screen TV on the wall, as well as several crosses and Jesus-related items. I could see from the photos on the shelving unit and some writing on the books that the family was Korean. Most likely recent arrivals, who had no idea about their home's unholy past. When we turned from the window, I saw that Dani had a black smudge on the tip of her nose from pressing it against the screen.

"Hold on," I said and licked my finger. She waited patiently, watching my eyes, while I wiped it off.

"OK?" she asked.

"All better."

Claire took a picture. "How cute," she said.

Without discussing our next move, we all three left the porch and walked together around the side of the house, trying not to trample the flowers that bloomed limply in the newly turned soil. Out back, in the small yard, were a white wrought iron table and chairs and a white stone birdbath along with a few roses and a square of lawn. We crouched down, side by side, and peered into the basement.

This was it. Once both of these low windows had been sealed, one for the darkroom Darian kept and one for the "studio" where he constructed and dismantled his scenes. Then there had been chains and whips and knives and saws, hooks bolted into the wall and low ceiling, a drain in the concrete floor and a hose for washing down the blood. There had also been props, costumes, wigs, makeup and lights, all the accoutrements of a cheesy photo studio. Now of course all that had vanished.

I realized that Dani, squatting beside me with her hands shielding her eyes, was staring at the same scene, thinking the same thoughts, and probably imagining her sister's end. I could hear her breathing, so close that her hair tickled my cheek. When I breathed, I smelled her shampoo.

"Is this . . . ," Claire began, but I pressed her leg and she took the hint. She quietly raised her camera and took a few shots, then put it away and went back to silent staring. There was nothing to see. The walls and floor were freshly painted and extremely clean for a basement. One end contained a Ping-Pong table, a fridge, posters of anime heroes and an old stereo. On the other side there were cartons, a slop sink that had once probably been part of the darkroom, a washing machine and a dryer. There was a freezer but I doubted it held any missing heads. The only ominous reminder of what had once been was an old-looking workbench, its rough wood scarred and splattered with paint, from which a couple of big vices hung like rusty steel jaws.

51

From *Whither Thou Goest, O Slutship Commander* by T. R. L. Pangstrom, chapter 2:

Time travel is a lot slower than you'd think. Since one is
using the folds and tears in timespace to galaxy-hop, there
is no sense of movement, of progression from one point to
another. A light-year passes while we seem to stand still, at
rest in our ship, floating in icy darkness. Yet the body knows
the truth, and the brain struggles to catch up, adjusting forward or back, trying to account for the lost time. It's like that
simple relativity problem that Zorgon kids learn in preschool
physics class (Einsteinoid, Post-Quantum, Proustian and
Dwarf-Magical Theory). If your particle-train leaves Greater
Mylar at ghostdawn, flying at 500 km/persec, why, when it
gets stuck in the Blabdok station for five minutes, does it feel
like five hours? With timespace travel the concept is the same.
Decades pass in minutes but those minutes are excruciatingly

slow. They seem to take forever. You grow restless, paranoid or enraged. Your stomach hurts or else you are hungry but nothing on the menu looks good. You feel like your whole life will pass just getting through these few million year-miles.

As a result of these stressors, travelers have been known to suffer from space sickness, black-hole depression and swollen ankles. More seriously, cases of psychotic meltdown have been seen, with crewmembers and passengers alike becoming violent, most notoriously in the Sirus Six Massacre of 5321 (although, due to time differences, the bodies were discovered in 4440). To avoid such tragedies, as well as lesser inconveniences, like cosmic acid trip reflux, which I suffer from myself, all Zorgon ships traveling at Timespace Level 5 or above (or at Spacetime Level 6 or below) must institute Deepsleep Shift procedures. A combination of superdrugs and suspended animation technology is used to put several of the crew into hibernation for up to a century at a time. Meanwhile waking members try to "live" in realtime, carrying out a "day's work," eating "three meals," and finally going to "sleep." This way, when the next shift wakes, the mindbody is tricked into thinking it has only been gone since yesterday, though "yesterday" might be a thousand years ago, and "today" might last for only an hour.

This all sounds simple enough, and in theory it is, but as Master and Commander of *Phallus Twelve*, a standard love-slave ship carrying, besides myself, an all-female crew of six high-performance wenches, I found life anything but simple, especially when intergalactic clan war erupted, destroying our Homebase and leaving us adrift in Deep Space, searching for a time of refuge. Realizing that we might be in transit for ages, I decided to implement Deepsleep. Each crewperson would work a hundred-year shift, waking in rotation every

500 years, while I lived on Half-Life, waking each century to oversee ship functions.

At first things seemed to proceed smoothly enough. I aimed the trusty old *Phallus* straight into the Far Past, drank my sweet blue medicine, and went to sleep in my ipod. One hundred years later I awoke to the smell of frying bacon.

Polyphony was in the galley making pancakes, bacon and eggs. She was a Type A Pleasure Slut, fully equipped, and had woken up with a huge appetite. Nude in the warm spaceship, she hummed happily as she cooked. She was young, and time travel barely affected her. Fresh from the airbath, her blond hair hung straight to her waist. She wore only her mandatory collar and, as per regulation, her body was hairless. Her pert, upturned breasts were scented with oil from the spice planets, and her lips as well as her labia were tastefully dusted with glistening starpowder, the granulated dust of extinct suns. In addition to her expertise in cooking and Erotic Arts, she was also the *Phallus*'s Systems Expert (SX), responsible for maintaining the ship's onboard computer.

"Good morning, Poly," I said as I entered, and gave her ample but firm buttocks a playful flick of my whip. I'm a by-the-book commander, and although we were alone, I wore my standard uniform of utility belt, boots, gloves, cape and ceremonial headband. "Something smells good."

"Good morning, Commander," she said. "Breakfast is ready."

While we ate I heard her report. All ship functions were normal, but no safe harbor was in sight. Still we decided to make the best of it and enjoy the next hundred years. We started with a bath. Poly scrubbed me head to toe and then playfully rinsed me with warm synth-water, recycled from our used hydrogen fuel cells and the urine of the sleeping crew. Then, following the Health & Wellness Code, we made Vigorous Love, first in the Cloud Chamber, laughing and floating, and then in the more demanding Sexagon, setting it first on Pulse, then Full Thrust, then Combo, which was Poly's favorite. Then we checked the engine and had a light lunch. In the afternoon we played four-dimensional Scrabble and walked through the hydroponic forest, gathering truffles for dinner. We laughed and held hands and even had Analog Sex right there on the pseudo-grass. But at dinner, Polyphony hardly touched her food.

"What's wrong?" I asked. "You barely consumed your recommended calorie quotient."

"Nothing," she sighed. "I was just thinking." But I knew she was lying. It was not Nothing. It was Something. As we lay down to sleep, I saw tears in her eyes.

"Please, Poly, what is it? Tell me?"

"It's just that I will miss you when you're gone, Commander. After you put me to sleep. For all those five hundred years."

I smiled and wiped her tears. "But it will only feel like one night. And besides, we still have a whole century together until then!"

"I know," she said. "It's silly, but I can't help it. I can't stop thinking about how each day together, however wonderful, is one day less, and how long we will be apart once they're gone."

At last I convinced her not to think of it, and she curled up to sleep in my arms. But now I was troubled. Although Sexbots like her were designed with genius IQs, this was far outside her emotional range. She was meant to be a Pleasure Unit, happy and carefree. But here she was, not missing the past even (since she had none) nor fearing the future, exactly, but mourning, in the present, a loss that was yet to come, the loss of the very moment she was in. While she slept I got my toolkit and silently checked her vitals. Sure enough, something, a suspension problem in her u-pod, bad medicine, or an inherent design flaw, had damaged her brain. Her sense of time was painfully acute. When you and I speak of the present, we really mean an approximation, or even a memory, since the actual persistence of a moment is so brief as to be beyond our senses, just like the turning of a planet seems still and the growth of a plant invisible. Not for Polyphony. For her, each moment in the river of time came and went separately, drop by exquisite drop, so that the moment and its loss were simultaneous and inseparable. Joy and sadness were one.

I know what you're thinking. My duty as Commander was clear: turn her brain off and dispose of the body. But I hesitated. Why? I told myself it was because we were on a long mission to unknown destinations, that I needed her skills and was dangerously low on spare body parts. But maybe it was the way she bathed me, or the look on her face when I turned the Sexagon up to full volume. Or maybe it was just the way her breath sounded, sleeping there in my ipod. I didn't have the heart to press the reset button. And that was how my troubles began. I, Commander Julius Dogstar, Master Twelfth Degree, should have checked my own vitals. I should have taken my pulse and felt the microscopic black sun in my blood as it sped invisibly toward my heart.

52

When we got home, we ordered pizza. It was my idea. After our fruitless visit to Clay's, the mood of my little investigative team was somber and I thought it might cheer us up. We got a large (half plain, half pepperoni), something we were only able to order thanks to Dani. For Claire and me, a whole pie was usually too much. I can eat four slices at my best, and Claire gives out after one or two. When snake-hipped Dani announced she was up for three, Claire regarded her with a new-found respect.

"Really? Three? But you're so skinny."

She shrugged. "It's all the dancing. You burn it up. Also I do yoga and Pilates."

"I do yoga, but I want to try Pilates. They say it's really good for your core."

"Totally."

I nodded enthusiastically. I wasn't sure what a core was, or if men had them too, but I was extremely pleased that my two lady friends had something in common.

"I went to yoga once," I offered.

"You?" Dani scoffed.

"It's true," Claire said. "He was the worst in the class. He doesn't even know right from left."

"I got flustered," I said. "I admit my balance isn't that great."

"No shit," Claire said. "He almost knocked over a pregnant woman."

"And you're stiff as a board," Dani added. "When you stretch it sounds like Velcro."

"That's true," Claire said. "The instructor wouldn't even let him try the headstand. She was afraid of a lawsuit."

They laughed gleefully as I tried to rally a defense: "She complimented my child's pose."

"Yeah. That and coffin," Dani said, and this was apparently so witty that Claire laughed into her straw and squirted soda. At last they'd found something they could enjoy together—criticizing me. Then, stuffed with cheese and coated in grease, we sat back, cracked a second round of sodas, and I tried, as team leader, to reflect on the day's lessons.

"Well, I guess I'm not much of a detective, am I? I don't know what I thought I'd find there today. Bloody footprints, maybe."

"Isn't this what detectives do, though?" Dani asked.

I shrugged. "How would I know?"

"They revisit the scene, look around, find clues," she said. "How do you know what you're looking for till you find it?"

"Columbo seems to know," I said.

"I love Columbo," she said, picking dried cheese off the cardboard with her nail and eating it.

"Gross," I said.

"Who's Columbo?" Claire piped up.

"An old TV show from before your time," Dani told her. "Before mine too." She grinned at me.

"He'd always notice these little things no one noticed," I said. "Like where were the victim's car keys or why would a girl fold her clothes before jumping out a window?"

"Why would she?" Claire asked.

"She was hypnotized into jumping."

"Monk notices those things too," Dani said. "I like him."

"Well, so did Sherlock Holmes," I said. "He wrote a whole monograph on cigar ash."

"That's what we need," Claire said. "Some CSI-type evidence. Like a body hair in a drain. Or a tooth."

"Come on," I said. "What should I do? Get out my old microscope? I think the FBI has that covered."

"I like those English detectives on PBS," Dani said. "Inspector Morse. Inspector Lynley. They're dashing."

"I like Inspector Frost," I said.

"Me too, but he's not so dashing. Just good old-fashioned police work. Experience and instinct, right, gov?"

"Well, that's not going to be me either, is it?" I said. "Like Ed McBain says in his books, based on established police routine."

"Then there's *Prime Suspect*," Dani continued. "What's her name?"

"Helen Mirren."

"She's pretty hot in that."

"She is," Claire agreed. "The one where she makes it with the younger black dude?"

"Then you have your psychological-type detectives," I said.

"Profilers," Dani said. "Like *Wire in the Blood* and the Hannibal Lecter guy."

"I was thinking more of Inspector Maigret," I said. "Or Poirot even. Detectives who kind of soak up the atmosphere and empathize with the characters. In a way they're like writers, creating plausible narratives."

"There you go," Claire said. "You can do that. Like you're writing one of your books. Except plausible."

"I just hope I'm not the Lew Archer, Philip Marlowe type."

"How's that?" Dani asked.

"They just stumble around until someone kidnaps them or beats them up," I said. "Hammett's heroes too, like Sam Spade, getting hit on the head all the time. Marlowe gets drugged on almost every case, still he can't resist. When the bad guy offers a cigarette, he lights right up."

"'Cause he's drunk," Dani said.

"And did you notice," I went on, "how they never bathe or sleep but they shave constantly? They're like, 'I stopped off at home to shave and change my shirt.'"

"But they look good, in those suits and hats," Dani offered. "Even the bad girls like them."

"And they get to make a lot of smartass comments along the way, like Humphrey Bogart," Claire said. "And not take shit from nobody."

"And they smoke unfiltered cigarettes and keep whiskey in their desk," Dani said.

"And then the girl leaves them flat broke in the end," Claire said, and as if we had emptied the bookshelf, a silence fell over the room. Claire pushed her chair back and, burping softly, went to lie on the couch. Dani got up and started clearing the table. I gathered the empty cans and followed.

"I remember," I said, "when I was a kid, I'm not sure how old, in grade school, a rapist was loose in the neighborhood and I saw this sketch and description of the suspect that the cops taped to a lamppost. I can still remember, he had glasses, a mustache, parted hair. Anyway, it said to watch out for this guy and report any information or clues. And I took it literally. Like I just started walking around, on my way home from school or whatever, looking for this guy or, even weirder, looking for clues. I even had a magnifying glass."

Dani laughed mildly, rinsing the dishes. Claire was now sprawled on her back, snoozing. I went on.

"I remember I collected these random things that for whatever reason I thought of as clues. A little medallion I thought was gold but I'm sure was tarnished brass at best. An electrical cap—you know, the plastic thing with a cut bit of wire hanging out. The tube from a cigar that still smelled. It was purple with gold printing, which seemed fancy to me. I kept these things in a shoebox and I'd sniff the cigar tube and pretend to be smoking it while I went over the items, waiting for them to add up to something. Then one day I was walking past this alley and I heard a scream. Of course I was terrified. I was certain the rapist was attacking someone right there. I wanted to run away but I forced myself to walk down the alley to the end, where it wrapped around the back of a building. I remember creeping along, my heart pounding, with my back to the wall. And then, summoning all my courage, I peeked around the corner."

I paused and Dani glanced over. "So? What was there? The rapist?"

"Of course not. There was nothing. A stairway down to the basement. Who knows where the scream came from? Someone arguing or a TV. Maybe it wasn't a scream even. Maybe it was a kid laughing. But when I looked around the corner, completely terrified and like rigid with anxiety, my eyes fell on one thing: a cigar, half smoked, sitting right on the ground, directly in front of me. And its band was the same purple and gold as my tube."

"Wow. So then what?"

"Nothing. I grabbed the cigar butt, which I thought of as evidence, and got the hell out of there. I ran home. I put the butt in my tube, and then my mom smelled the stink of it and took the whole thing away. She promised me she was turning it over to the cops, but for some reason they never followed up with me."

Dani laughed.

"But the point of the story—"

"Yeah, I was wondering," she said.

"Well, obviously none of this had anything to do with the rapist."

"Obviously."

"It was only in the mind of a kid. And even the cigar matching. What was that? Just a random connection."

"A weird coincidence."

"But not even that weird when you think about it. A cigar and a cigar tube? It was probably a cheap brand, sold everywhere. There were probably dozens around. I just noticed it because I was looking.

Something takes on meaning to us and we start seeing it. Like Diet Coke cans, or broken shoelaces, or redheaded men with blue socks. Who knows what else was in that same alley, invisible to me, that I suddenly would have noticed if I'd been tuned in to seeing, say, packs of Newports or torn lottery tickets with the number six in them? Instead of the clues leading us to a mystery, I sometimes think it's the mystery that suddenly turns everything into a clue."

"I know what you mean," she said, turning off the faucet and drying her hands. "It's like after my sister died. I hadn't seen her in years. But suddenly, everything reminded me of her. A commercial about paper towels, an old song. I kept seeing her everywhere. Like really thinking for a split second that it was her, turning a corner or going by in a car. When she was alive, she didn't exist for me. But once she was gone, she was everywhere."

I reached out and touched Dani's hand. She squeezed my wrist, hard, but then let go and went to her purse for a smoke. I looked over at the couch and realized Claire was awake after all, lying on her back, eyes open, listening.

"I've got to get back and change for work soon," Dani said, smoking by my open window. The curtain ruffled as if someone was back there, about to appear.

I grabbed Claire's keys and we went. Now that we were alone together, in the elevator and walking to the car, the awkwardness returned and I struggled for something to say. Again Claire's question from the day before asked itself in my head: What if Clay was innocent? It was easy to dismiss Flosky and Trio's doubts as opportunistic. But what about the certainty of others? Was it any less self-serving? To prove Clay innocent would be a disaster for Townes, the cops and the courts. To even suggest his innocence would enrage Toner and the other victims' families. And I felt horrible just thinking about the possibility near Dani. I unlocked the passenger door for her and then went around and got in.

"Dani," I said, as I shut the door.

"Don't say anything." She cut me off. "Just let's do it."

I nodded and started the engine, then drove a couple of blocks before turning down a quiet street. As I pulled into a secluded spot behind a truck and under a tree, I happened to look in my side mirror and see, I thought, a late-model black Impala parking discreetly up the block. We were being followed. Or at least it seemed like that to me. Dani grabbed my arm and I climbed after her into the back seat. As she pulled off her sweater and unbuttoned her jeans, I glanced through the back window. I didn't see the Impala. Then she pressed against me and I shut my eyes.

53

For the next few days we followed Darian Clay, even if at a distance of years, and despite the grim sites we were seeking, Claire, Dani, and I settled into the rut of any unhappy family on vacation: I drove, Dani misread the map, and Claire lounged in the back, making sarcastic cracks, complaining of nausea, hunger and then, after lunch, nausea again. She and Dani didn't seem to hate each other any more than most relatives, and the feeling of normalcy, however false, gave me a sense of safety. What could happen to a carful of regular folks cruising around and bitching at each other in broad daylight? Evenings, we ordered in, Chinese, Japanese, Malaysian, and watched *Law and Order* reruns in the thin hope of picking up a useful pointer. But all I learned was that, if you want to know whom a suspect called from his phone, you checked his LUDs (local usage details), which won me a dollar from Claire. ("Why would they check his lungs?") Dani helped Claire with yoga and Pilates and then, to my great consternation, showed her some basic "dance" moves, which led Claire to modify her antistripper stance.

"I mean it's not my chosen career path," she told me over morning cornflakes.

"Good." I waved my spoon for emphasis. "That's why you've got to do your homework. I mean do it yourself."

"But at least Dani's fun and she has interesting stories. For instance, did you know Preparation H, the butt cream, can get rid of those bags under your eyes?"

"I'll have to try it."

"I'd rather my dad date strippers than those phony junior miss executive types in their miniskirt suits who always try to hug me. Blecch."

The three of us drove out to Astoria to find the Jarrels' home, where their daughter Nancy had been living with them when she was killed. The whole way there I looked for the black Impala, but it was nowhere in sight and I decided I had just been paranoid.

We found the block, but the address no longer existed. After several trips up and down the street, we concluded that their old house, as well as most of the one- and two-family homes on the block, had been leveled and a ten-story glass and steel structure stood in their place. We parked and walked by the entrance to the new office building. People dressed in business clothes stood smoking with IDs hanging around their necks. I wondered what the Jarrels thought. After the murder and the circus of the trial, they sold out and moved upstate. Perhaps they were glad to find a buyer who would wipe away what for them was only a sign of their pain: a home that had become a memorial. Still, it made me sad. Clay stole the girl's future. Now her past had also been erased and replaced by a blank box, in which, standing before it, we saw only our own reflections.

The Hickses had been country people, at least by my standards, and had lived someplace in Pennsylvania, but their daughter had been living up in Washington Heights while she studied acting and waitressed at a restaurant downtown. We ate at the restaurant, for no particular reason except that it was lunchtime, sitting outside despite the chill. It was the kind of place that called fries "curlies" on the menu

and the bacon cheeseburger Dani ordered was called an "Oinker." I
felt sorry for our waitress, smiling desperately in her striped polyes-
ter outfit and giggling about the "humongously awesome pepper jack
nachos."

Claire gave her a very Claire look from over her shades. "I doubt
they're really that awesome. I'll just have the cheesy weezy quesadilla.
Isn't that a redundancy?"

"Totally," the poor girl squeaked, giggling in fear. I could see
Janet Hicks in her. Needy, hungry, frantic, so terrified of not being
a star that she forgot to be scared of Darian Clay and rushed eagerly
to her doom. We drove past the acting school, which was still there,
upstairs in a midtown office building, where Darian had posted his
notice looking for models, then continued up to Washington Heights.
I thought I spotted the black Chevy behind us again on Broadway,
running a light.

Janet Hicks had lived, with two roommates, on the tenth floor of
a building close to Riverside Drive. She went running by the water in
the mornings, got a juice in the Dominican bakery, went down to her
improv class in the afternoon and served bad, overpriced burgers all
night.

We walked along her street and took a turn in the park. Although
you could feel the encroachment of Columbia University and the
condo developers pushing people out, the Heights had changed less
than most parts of the city and for now it was clinging on. People
spoke Spanish in the stores. Old ladies hung out the windows and
mothers sat on the stoops while their kids played in the street. The sun
was setting, and all along the block, the grand old buildings loomed
like ships easing down to the river. Soon night would fall and someone would blast salsa music from a window or car, so loud the whole
street could hear. Soon summer would come and someone would
open the hydrant for the kids.

And at night, after visiting those monuments that only we could
recognize, Dani and I hid in lots and alleys and performed our own
strange ritual, grasping and struggling wordlessly in the backseat.

54

Although it had been sold and resold several times, the Toners' old home in Great Neck still looked like the photo I had of white columns and a long lawn behind a high gate. Toner himself now lived with his new wife in an even bigger house in an even richer neighborhood nearby. More significant to us, however, was the factory, which Toner had inherited from his murdered wife's father and still owned, and where Clay had been briefly employed. It was a long, windowless building, fenced in and topped with barbed wire. I knew from Townes that they made plastic bags, but really almost anything could have been going on in there. We drove around the perimeter a couple of times and then parked out front and watched some trucks come and go. It was getting toward the end of the day and we were tired. We were all on our phones when someone knocked on Dani's window. She jumped.

"Fuck."

It was the security guard from Toner's factory. Dani rolled her window down.

"Yes?"

"Excuse me, but you folks looking for someone?"

"No. We were just sitting here," she said. "That all right?"

"Well, you were seen driving by before, so that's all."

"Seen?"

"On the security cameras." He pointed and we all peered at the cameras mounted on the posts of the fence.

Claire said, "Hold on," into her phone, and leaned into the front to face the guard. "Well, that sign says no parking on Thursday and this is Friday, so that's OK, right?"

"No problem, miss." He smiled stiffly and touched his cap in a sort of ironic salute. "Just checking. Have a nice night."

We watched him walk back across the street and through the gate, which shut behind him.

"That was weird," she said.

"Let's go," Dani said. "That guy gave me the creeps."

"And you know what else is strange?" I started the car. "Don't freak out, but I keep seeing this black car following us. I think it's the cops. Or the feds."

"I know," Dani said. "I keep seeing it too."

"Me too," Claire added from the back.

There was one more thing on my mind that I did not mention: Dora Giancarlo was next on our list for tomorrow. I'd been thinking about this eventuality since our morbid tour of Darian's high spots began, and I knew that this had to play into Dani's insistence on accompanying me. Nevertheless, we had avoided all discussion of the topic. Nor did we say anything about it that night, on the ride from the factory to her place, where she declined my invitation to join us for a bite. When I tried to kiss her good-bye, she gave me her cheek.

"Cold-shouldered you again, huh?" Claire asked. She hopped up front and I watched her buckle her belt before pulling out.

"You noticed."

"Yeah. I also noticed one of her socks jammed between the back seats."

I winced. "Sorry."

"So I take it she wasn't so cold last night. Not too cold to take her clothes off."

"Well, they weren't exactly off. Maybe she is shy around you."

"Shy? She's a polecat. That's not her problem."

I headed toward White Castle, which Claire had requested for dinner, another reason Dani might have declined. The silence ticked by. I could feel Claire looking at me.

"OK, what?" I asked.

"Not to be blunt, but you're kind of dense so . . ."

"Yeah?"

"Look, Dani's an OK person, but she's got some kind of weird fixation on the murders and her sister and all. It's not you that she's turned on by. It's him."

55

Dani's sister had been living on the Lower East Side. She had a scholarship to study acting and singing and she modeled for extra cash. We drove past her old building on Clinton Street and then up through the sprawl of NYU, which seemed to spread like an anthill, colonizing the once wild territory of downtown New York and filling it with drones. Even twelve years before, when Dora lived here, the neighborhood had lost much of its menace. In the 1990s, gentrification swept out the drug dealers and thieves along with the poor people, artists and minorities, and Dora should have been safer than at any previous time in New York history. Perhaps she was just unlucky, or perhaps prosperity and an influx of fresh, eager youngsters drew its own more insidious brand of predator.

It was in one of the student lounges that they thought Dani's sister might have seen the poster offering generous pay for models plus free prints for their portfolios. She called him from her apartment and then, on February 9, 1997, she headed out to Queens to meet Darian Clay.

"At least that's what they think," Dani said, sitting beside me in traffic while Claire, I now realized, only pretended to ignore us from the back. "That's all based on what she told my parents. She didn't say a name or anything. Just that she was going to pose for some photographer the next day and that it was no big deal moneywise but she was hoping to get some good shots for her book. Or else they think maybe he approached her in a coffee shop or even on campus. People approached her all the time, you know, because of her looks." Here she frowned in embarrassment, realizing she was describing herself as well. "She was a lot more outgoing than me, very charismatic. That's why she was the star." She laughed. "Well, that and talent. Anyway, he got her out there somehow to pose for those pictures."

"You saw them?" Claire asked. Dani looked back and gave her a small smile.

"Not any bloody ones, no. But I saw the regular ones, the ones they found in Clay's studio and that he claimed they did willingly. The cops showed them to us to ID her. They were just regular pictures. But somehow I felt there was something about them, about her. They made me sad. But then of course they did, right? After the fact. The truth is, I hadn't seen her in a few years or my parents. I was living out in San Francisco and only came back when I heard she was gone. When I saw those pictures, I felt bad for her suddenly. I remembered all the pictures and videos of her everywhere in our house growing up, the singing and dancing lessons, the lines we'd have to hear her recite for practice at dinner, the photos she did for her first head shots, with makeup and hair and all, her first jobs, seeing her smiling in some pajamas in a catalog, all of which my mother cut out and kept and who knows what my dad did with it later, and instead of feeling jealous or resentful or condescending like before, I just felt sad for her, that she had to go through what she did. All of it. Not just the end. And I'm sure it's like you said, it's what happens later that makes the past seem sad, seem destined, like the sadness of what is going to happen is there already, when it's us who put it in, we who are alive to know what happened, but still when I look at those pictures of her young and staring into the camera like that, I think poor girl, you poor poor girl."

56

From *Whither Thou Goest, O Slutship Commander* chapter 7:

"Bedtime" in zero-gravity. The Timespace Wellness Guide recommends rotating the viewscreen away from the nearest sun and toward those farther out, the tiny cracks and pinholes in the worn black dome of the universe. It also prescribes Storytime as a before-sleep ritual. Not only does this help regulate the bio-clock, it also provides material for dreams during the prolonged centuries of REM, reducing the incidence of space-mares, epic bad dreams in suspended animation that leave the sleeper confused, exhausted and occasionally mad. While true psycho-breaks were relatively rare, many awoke in their ipods to find their pillows drenched in tears or their skin scratched raw. Hours or even days were spent reconstructing what was real, after a decades-long dream involving dead relatives and monsters.

Commercial travelers even prerecorded video-chips to remind themselves who they were.

Tonight I rest my head in Polyphony's lap while she combs out my ponytail, trims my beard and ear hair and, as we journey across time toward the far star our charts call Sol, soothes me with an old, familiar tale:

"There once was a Zorgon Artisan (Ninth Degree) named Rufus Camilius, who had a small workshop in downtown Mylar, in the old Pleasure Center, where he built sex-droids and lived in the back with his beautiful daughter, Clio. His skills were unsurpassed, his flesh work especially was amazing, and it was said that the Duke of Drago himself carried a piece of Rufus's butt skin in his pocket, as a kind of charm, and that during the long cold march to Swampland and all through the great battle of Dork, he would reach down and stroke it for comfort. Nevertheless, fashion changes, and Rufus found that the vogue was no longer for finely made androids. Genetic engineering was all the rage and everyone wanted mass-produced clones. Science was the future, and no one appreciated high art or old-fashioned craftsmanship. Poor little Clio lived on a bowl of gruel a day, while Rufus was reduced to chewing scraps of his own once-vaunted skin to ward off hunger pangs. Though he had many offers to sell comely young Clio, he had always refused for sentimental reasons, but now it seemed inevitable. Then he had an idea: combine the ancient art of android design with the new science of genetic cloning. It was his last, daring hope. He melted down all the flesh in his workshop, stripped the circuits from his own prosthetic foot, and while she slept, plucked a golden hair from the head of his daughter. Then he labored, without sleep or food, day and night until he produced his first model, the Clio II.

"It was a hit. He sold many Clios and soon rolled out the second part of his plan. He approached celebrities, top performers from the Satellite Casinos or the Holo-Tube and licensed their genetic material. Now anyone with enough money could keep his or her favorite actor, singer or politician as a sex slave. Rufus prospered greatly. He built a fine house and dressed his daughter in beautiful gowns. They feasted on mutton and fresh space-mold every night.

"Then, late one evening, an unmarked hydro-carriage arrived at the door, and Rufus received a visit from none other than High Lord Malodour, disguised in a black hood and cape. He was deep in mourning. His beloved wife, Lady Plumm, had died and he was going mad with grief. He offered any price, as well as all his influence and protection, if Rufus would do him one service. He opened a velvet case and removed one of Lady Plumm's hairs.

"Well, what could Rufus do? To disobey Malodour was certain death. So he returned to his workshop and produced an exact replica of the High Lord's lady, asking only that he promise to keep her locked in his dungeon at all times. The High Lord's gratitude was immense. He showered Rufus with riches and favor. But all for naught. The die was cast, and from then on, Rufus's life was a torment, for just a few days later, there came another knock on the door. This time a Prince of the Blood, whose fair maiden had perished in a dragon accident, was there on his steps, holding all that was left of her, a dainty right hand on a satin pillow. What could Rufus do but obey the Prince? Then a spice merchant from the outer Pleiades came begging. His beloved boy slave Bono was gone, having fallen in love with a passing star minstrel and fled. He threatened to expose Rufus if he did not grant his request. Rufus reluctantly agreed. One after another they came, an endless stream of the heartbroken and bereft, those whose beloveds had left them, or betrayed them, or simply turned them down. Then at last, one dawn, Count Stark, a famous knight and lute composer, arrived with a chest full of jewels.

" 'What is it?' asked the weary Rufus. 'Has she died? Left you?'

" 'No,' said the sorrowful knight. 'She is there, right now, in my bed at home. But she is different than when I met her. She has changed . . .' "

57

The next day, Dani, Claire and I initiated Phase Two of my plan (Phase One of which had so far yielded nothing whatsoever): revisit the homes of the more recent victims, those whom I'd already seen, and discover some pattern or link that would connect them to the past murders. The one minor hitch was that, since the dead girls' apartments were still considered crime scenes, and since I was a suspect in those same crimes, our police escort might not be as discreet and accommodating as before.

And so, on a bright, clear, cold spring morning, Madam Sibylline Lorindo-Gold emerged from her chamber once more. I was in full Mom drag this time—black dress, stockings, everything except the shoes. Claire had pushed for the heels but there was no way I could even get my mom's orthopedics on, so I was wearing the only high black shoes I owned, combat boots. My face was hidden behind foundation thick as spackle, cherry red lipstick, eyeliner and blush. My eyelids were midnight blue.

Dani and I gathered our belongings, including a small overnight bag with my normal clothes. Claire kept watch by the window.

"There he is," she called out, her head in the curtains. "Black sedan at ten o'clock."

"Where's ten o'clock?"

"That hydrant across the street."

"Perfect," I said.

Dani made a call on her cell. "OK, it's a go," she said into the phone. "Black cop car in front of the hydrant on your left." She shut the phone. "Let's do it."

"Good luck," Claire called from under the drapes. Her sneakered feet twitched excitedly.

"Right." I put my black straw hat on, the one with the little roses, and we went.

Down in the lobby, I gave Dani the suitcase I'd been carrying and took the rubber-tipped cane, but we didn't go out yet. We waited at the door. Then from up the block we heard it. Like sonic depth charges were going off in the sewer beneath us. Like Godzilla was stomping over after eating Brooklyn.

"There he is," Dani said, and there he was, in a gold Caddy Coupe with wire rims, that huge bass thumping out the ass. RX738 to the rescue. He rolled up and stopped, double-parking right in front of the cop. Then we stepped outside, Dani holding the door and then taking my arm while I leaned on the cane and pretended to be an old arthritic woman. Together we strolled to her rusty Datsun parked down the street. She unlocked her passenger door and helped me in. As she went around her side, I looked in the rearview and saw our shadow, the cop or agent, yet another white man in black sunglasses, arguing with RX.

"Here we go," I said to Dani as she got in. She peeked into her side view.

Meanwhile, RX got out, even bigger than I remembered, six feet three with a 'fro like a hedgerow planted on his head, and invited the skinny young cop out for a talk. As Dani started the engine, I saw the chat grow heated. The white boy waved his arms and RX closed in on him. The white boy waved his badge and RX laughed. Then the white boy waved a gun.

"Fuck," I said. "This is bad. I think we should abort."

"Don't worry," she said, putting the car into gear. "Rex has it covered."

Still without any visible hurry or worry, RX stepped back, raised his open hands, and turned to place them on the roof of the car. As Dani pulled into the street, I watched a passenger I hadn't noticed get out of the Caddy, a heavyset white man in a dark blue pinstriped suit. He also had his arms raised in surrender, but one of them was holding a business card.

"Who's that?" I asked.

"His lawyer," Dani said, as we drove away.

"God bless lawyers," I said. "If I ever get rich, I'm buying one."

She kept it slow to the corner, as the little scene behind us shrank in the mirror, then stepped on the gas as we pulled onto Northern Boulevard. I changed into my male clothes and scrubbed my face with a Handi Wipe while we headed into the city, to Horatio Street and the home of Morgan Chase.

We cruised down her block and then around again, looking for parking and lurking cops. But no one was watching. It was like nothing had ever happened. A UPS truck puttered down the street and a cabbie leaned on his horn. Young mothers pushed militaristic strollers over the uneven sidewalk. Spring, it seemed, had even chosen this block to throw its welcome party. The budding trees were unfolding rice-paper hearts and butterflies, and with each breath of wind, dazzling armfuls of this confetti fell on the parade of parked cars, on the man in the suit with the cell phone, on the old lady with the two canes, rubber-tipped like mine. Morgan's building was still easy to break into, but the apartment door was locked and sealed with that police tape.

"Now what?" Dani asked, brushing a little white seedling from her hair.

"I bet the window's open, to air the place. We could try the fire escape."

So we trooped up to the roof, went to the rear of the building, and clambered back down the fire escape as quietly as possible. Luckily it was a weekday morning and the other apartments' windows were shut, blinds drawn. No one was watching. Morgan's window was open six inches or so, with only a thin curtain drifting behind it. I pushed it up and climbed through. Dani came in behind me.

The apartment had been cleaned, sort of. The blood-soaked mattress and box spring were gone, along with all the bedding. The bed's skeleton, with its steel frame and a ribbed headboard curving up, looked like an abstract sculpture, a trap or a chariot, and no longer a nest. The floor underneath it had been scoured till the finish was scratched off and was lighter than the surrounding wood. Nevertheless, all these attempts to remove the traces of the crime only made the room seem more haunted. I thought of the porn story I wrote for Clay about her, the scene that took place in this room.

Of course the police had been through the place with tweezers and a magnifying glass, but we rummaged around anyway, looking for something that would somehow connect to something else, or appear newly meaningful in the light of the nothing much we'd seen before. It didn't work. Dani became morbidly absorbed in an old family photo album while I discovered many rows of small glass jars, each filled with dried herbs and labeled in an elegant hand. Morgan was a rigorous lady, all right. The silverware drawer looked like a surgeon's tray and even the dishtowels were perfectly folded and stacked like unread newspapers. But none of this had protected her. Danger had found its way into her life through the secret crack in her heart. Desire was lawless and obeyed no one. Or perhaps it was the other way around: desire was the final law under which all others broke.

We left through the door, dipping under the police tape and letting the lock click shut behind us. Then we drove up the West Side and out to New Jersey. All along the river and the highway, I saw trees raise their colored heads like flags, into the wind, as if marking the path to the Fontaines' lawn, which was covered in the dogwood's blazing pink.

We knocked on the door, but my courage faltered when I heard the lock turning. No one home would have meant another break-in, or even a wasted trip, but I dreaded a confrontation with a victim's parent far more. Dread isn't the word. I was frightened as the door pulled back and I saw Marie Fontaine's mother, overweight, in very tight black stretch pants, a black and white striped top that didn't quite reach the pants, and white sandals. She wore black eyeliner and her dyed black hair was showing brown roots. Her toenails were pink and her rings cut into her puffy pink fingers. She was only about five feet tall. And I was afraid of her, the power of her grief. I couldn't look her in the eye. I stared down, instinctively recognizing that she had now, tragically, attained a kind of royalty in the realm of human emotions while I, with my clotted desires and petty depressions, remained a mere peasant. I was ashamed at myself for having no answer to the question that her very presence righteously asked the world: Why? Why is it like it is?

Or at least that's what she asked in my mind. What she asked in reality was "Can I help you?" But even that mild, utterly conventional greeting suddenly seemed so terrible (Help us? You?) that I was momentarily stumped. Luckily Dani spoke up.

"I'm Daniella Giancarlo. My sister was one of Darian Clay's victims."

"Oh . . ." Mrs. Fontaine's face seemed to soften. "I'm so sorry to hear that."

"Thank you. And this is Harry Bloch. We're both very sorry for your loss, as well."

"Yes," I said. "I was very sorry to hear about your daughter."

"You knew my Marie?" she asked, suddenly interested in me. I regretted speaking.

"Not well."

Dani stepped in. "Harry is writing a book about the Clay case. He spoke to your daughter because she'd been in touch with Mr. Clay."

"Yes. I had no idea. Why would she do such a thing?" She addressed me.

"I don't know, Mrs. Fontaine. Young people get confused or angry. I only met her once. I liked her though, very much. She seemed like a special person. I'm sure she would have sorted it all out."

She smiled. "Yes, she was a special girl, always. Right from childhood. Used to stand up in her crib with her hands on the bars and holler. Hated being cooped in. She was so naturally talented. Had the highest GPA in her major at college. Not in the whole class but still, in her major the highest. But always so angry. Like you said. And I never really knew what for." She trailed off, no longer looking at us but past us, to the trees.

Dani said, "Mrs. Fontaine, it would really help us a lot with our investigation if we could take a look at Marie's room."

"I can't go up there yet. I guess I'll have to eventually, but I can't. Not yet."

"No, well, of course not. But that's not necessary. We can just go up. If you don't mind, that is."

She shrugged. "I don't mind. The police said don't go up there, but I don't mind."

She gave us a key and we climbed the steps to the little studio above the garage. We unlocked the door and again ducked under some tape. Since we were here with permission, more or less, we switched on the light and opened a window. The place looked like Marie had moved out in a hurry. The bedding and mattress were gone, and across the walls, strips of tape marked where an image had hung. The police had taken all the posters and other crime- or horror-related artifacts, even the Marilyn Manson picture, a corner of which still stuck to the wood paneling. Before the mirror, where the shrine to Clay had been, there was only some dried candle wax and the shape of the beaded letter box outlined in the dust.

We sorted through her drawers together, and I looked in the medicine cabinet while Dani looked in the closet. We poked around aimlessly, flipping through folded T-shirts and stacked magazines as if expecting a clue to fall out. I remembered my first visit to this room, my one meeting with Marie.

I told Dani, "You know, I hate to say it now, but this girl was kind of awful. She freaked me out."

"How?" She unfolded an extra-large Nine Inch Nails T-shirt, held it up, and then put it back.

"I don't know. Like her mom said, she was harsh, argumentative, full of herself. Had these fantasies that she and Clay would go off and kill together. I hate that poseur bullshit."

She sat beside me on the sunken couch. "She must have been very unhappy."

"Then she started playing with herself."

Dani sat forward. "What? Really? How?"

"Yeah. She hiked up her skirt and showed me. Jesus, her poor mom. I can't believe I said I liked her."

"What did you do?"

"I got the hell out of there. Out of here. She was guffawing."

"You didn't want to just fuck her?"

"No," I said. "No way."

"Not even a little?" She smiled slyly. "Just to teach her a lesson even?"

I shook my head.

"Come on. I bet you had a hard-on walking away."

"I don't remember."

"I bet. I bet you did," Dani said, her voice thick. "What a little slut. Laughing and fingering herself in front of a random stranger." She was flushed now. She slid closer to me on the couch. "You wanted to show her what happens to sluts like that."

"No," I said. "I didn't."

She unzipped her jeans and put her hand down the front. "Show me. Show me how she did it." She moved closer and took my hand, steering it toward her open pants.

"No, come on. Let's go." I pulled my hand away.

She reached over and touched my groin through my pants. The look on her face was angry. "See, you're hard now. I knew it. Don't pretend. Show me how you'd fuck that little whore. Show me what you'd do to her if you had her here right now."

"Fuck off," I said, standing up. I turned to go. "I'll be downstairs when you're done."

"Fuck you," she yelled after me, as I opened the door. "Fuck you!"

Marie's mother was waiting on the steps.

"Mrs. Fontaine." She shifted uneasily, holding a paper grocery bag to her chest. Had she heard anything? Did I look strange? "Hi," I said.

I heard the door slam open again.

"Hey!" Dani shouted and came clattering out, stopping abruptly when she saw Mrs. Fontaine. "Oh," she said softly and backed up a step. I was afraid to look, but I prayed silently that her pants were completely zipped. I kept smiling at Mrs. Fontaine.

"We were just on our way down," I said.

"Sorry," she said, though who knows what for. "I thought of this." She handed me the bag, without meeting my eyes. "I found it before and took it. I didn't want the police to see. I know that's wrong but I didn't want them to think of her that way. But you met her and you . . ." She looked past me, up at Dani. "Well, you both might understand better."

I looked in the bag. It was the decorated box that I knew must contain her correspondence with Clay.

"We'll return this to you right away," I said.

"No," she said. "I don't want it. I just took a peek and then hid it away. I don't want to know about that part. What good would it do?" She put her hand on my arm. "I know she wasn't really a good girl, like you said. But I loved her. I did my best with her. Sorry," she said again, and this time I said, "That's OK," and squeezed her hand. I forgave her, because I was there and I could. Then Dani came down and hugged her and they forgave each other too.

58

It was quiet back in the car. We exchanged a few words about needing gas and pulled into a station. We decided to gamble on traffic and take the George Washington Bridge, then head down the East Side toward Brooklyn. Neither one of us knew quite what to say about the incident back at Marie's. The connection, in Dani, between grief and sex was typical enough—there are many stories of people spontaneously fornicating at funerals and hospitals—and frankly she had more of an excuse than I, except that I was terribly lonely and terribly horny and she was terribly beautiful, all of which adds up to its own kind of grief, I suppose. But even as I yearned and grieved, I couldn't help but wonder, was this girl nuts or what? Who knew everything I knew? Who had total access to all the information, past and present? Who could have easily followed me and tracked my comings and goings? And if she was supposedly in school, why the hell wasn't she ever there?

"Hey, how's school, by the way?" We were cruising down the ramp from the bridge toward the Harlem River Drive. On our right was a granite tower on a hill where, when I was a kid, they used to dump stolen cars after they'd been stripped. The metal carcasses would tumble down and get caught in the trees, hanging as if they'd fallen from the sky. No more. "Don't you have class?"

She gave me a curious look. "School's over. Next week is finals. I told you, remember?"

"Oh yeah."

As we rolled downtown, Queens appeared on the left, under a blue sky and across a gray river. A barge the size of a football field slid by, hauling a garbage mountain.

Heart of a failed poet, mind of an amateur detective, ass of a middle-aged hack writer—did I really suspect her of the murders? Ass of a detective, spleen of a poet, pituitary gland of a burned-out pulp novelist—what I felt was the sudden abyss that opened between us, the irreducible distance between one body and another, one mind and another. Skull of a poet, wings of a detective, claws of a two-bit sci-fi novelist—who are you when you are not with me? Sex of an angel, face of a devil, ass of a curious fourteen-year-old boy—even if we talk all night, even if we cry, even if we sleep with our arms round each other, even if I plunge my fangs as deep into your flesh as I can, that tiny crack remains, waiting to split at any time. Eyes of a mountain, clouds of a tiger, river of a soft-core poet—then anything becomes possible: you might lie to me, you might betray me, you might change, die or leave. Hands of a monster, throat of a victim, lips of a dying vampire—so then why not murder? Why not her? And in her mind, why not me?

59

We found our way into Brooklyn and arrived at Sandra Dawson's.

"There it is," I told Dani, and she pulled into a spot across the street. People were going in and out of the bodega. Dani shut off the engine and lit a cigarette. The car filled with smoke.

"You go," she said. "I'll wait here."

"We don't have to do this now if you're not up to it," I said. "I'll come back."

"No. It's fine." She dismissed me with a wave and I remembered, again, that she was not my girlfriend, not my partner. She was really no one I knew. "Go do your thing."

I got out and crossed the street to Sandra's building. The afternoon had turned clear and bright without my noticing, and now all the windows on the street flashed with the blue of the sky. Suddenly the bodega's plate glass front exploded. I heard a high shriek and a hollow, echoing crack. I paused, standing stupidly, as the people in front of the bodega scampered away and those inside it ducked. I realized something bad was happening—the thought that crossed my mind was of a building collapsing—and I started to run. I heard another crack. A chip flew off the brick wall above my head and I understood. That was a bullet. Someone was shooting at me. I hunched down, darting between parked cars. I could feel the blood in my heart. The next shot hit a tire in the car beside me and the air escaped with a soft rush. Then I heard an engine and honking. Hesitantly, I peeked up, and there was Dani, making a crazy U-turn and roaring over, putting her car between me and the gun.

"Come on," she screamed, pushing open the door, and I ran. I bolted as fast and low as I could and jumped in, rolling against the dash as she slammed on the gas. The rear window blew, hailing us with glass. We both ducked, and my door swung wide as she fishtailed out, screeching around the corner, where I managed to grab it shut. Dani turned again, sliding through a stop sign, then joined the flow of traffic. I watched out the back. There was no one behind us, except the hundreds of normal people.

"Fuck," I yelled, as numb terror and adrenaline melted like ice in my stomach. Someone had really shot at me. I shuddered uncontrollably. "Fuck, fuck, fuck."

"Are you OK?" she yelled, as she turned again. This time she pulled into an empty alley with parking spaces at the end. "Are you hit?"

"No. I'm OK. Are you OK?"

"No. I'm OK," she said. Then she hit a pole.

60

The hood and trunk of Dani's car both popped open from the impact as we bounced to and fro, then settled back into our seats.

"Fuck," I said again. "Are you OK?"

"Yeah, I think so," she said. "Are you?"

"Yeah."

We sat in silence, breathing hard. The steel pole was there to mark off the parking spots, and Dani, driving too fast and too frightened, hadn't seen it. I checked behind us again. The coast was clear. We were, I supposed, safe. My hands were still trembling though, and I tucked them under my thighs.

"I think we should just wait here for a bit," Dani said. "Just to make sure no one's out there. Just till I feel ready to drive."

"No problem. Take your time."

Dani turned to me in her seat. Her face was flushed and I could see her chest heaving.

"I just can't catch my breath," she said. "It's like an asthma attack."

"Do you have asthma?"

"No."

"It's OK. I keep shaking. It's adrenaline, nerves. Fear." I squeezed her shoulders. "It'll pass," I said. "You were great. What the fuck, you were awesome. You saved me."

"No." She shook her head. "I just wanted to get the fuck out of there." She kept gulping big mouthfuls of air between each word. I gripped her tighter. I took her face in my trembling hands.

"Careful, glass," I said, and picked a few bits from her hair.

"Thank you," she said. She brushed mine.

"No," I said, shaking my head. "Thank you." She looked me in the eyes. She leaned toward me.

This time I couldn't even say who started it. It was like something our bodies were doing separate from us, something they needed to do while we waited. Now I felt close to Dani, like she was the person I was most linked to in the world, but I was cut off from myself. We were like two couples there together in the car: she and I, us and them.

Afterwards, despite her shortness of breath, she smoked. It actually seemed to help. We slid our clothes back on. I yawned, inexplicably. All of a sudden I was tired, hungry, thirsty. I was everything.

"I wonder if my car is ruined," Dani said, finally breaking the silence. It was certainly trashed. In the backseat my wig and cane lay mixed with broken glass from the shattered rear window. I brushed the glass from my wig and stuffed it into the bag with Marie's letters, which I'd almost forgotten.

"Guess I'll check out the damage," I said, thinking it was the polite, manly thing to do, although I know nothing about cars. I got out and looked at the front. The bumper was crumpled and the hood was creased. I lifted it up. Nothing was cracked or smoking.

"Looks OK," I shouted.

"Anything leaking?" she asked.

"Good point." I got on my knees and peered under the car. "Nope. Looks good."

She started the engine and it took. Smiling, she gave me a thumbs-up.

"Let me get the trunk," I said. While fumes rose from the tailpipe, I hustled around back. The latch had popped from the impact and the lid was agape. I lifted it to check inside and there, spilled from a blanket and lying on top of the spare, was a big steel cleaver with a sharpened edge. There was also a long, thin boning knife and an old rusty machete with black tape on the handle. There was a screwdriver and a small saw, a coil of rope, some duct tape. There was a small burlap sack, and even before I opened it I knew what I would see: a flat black automatic pistol.

"What's wrong?" Dani yelled. "Everything good?"

"Great," I said. I pushed everything back into the blanket and slammed the lid. It popped back up and showed me its open mouth. I slammed it again and it stuck. I went back around and got in beside her. I put on my safety belt. I smiled.

"Let's go," I said.

I reported the attack over my cell phone, and Townes met us in front of my building, along with his agents and a contingent of cops. He bought a Softee ice cream from the truck on the corner and then listened impassively while the city cops took our statements. The shopkeeper with the smashed window had called in the shots and the cops had found the slugs, but it seemed the only car anyone saw fleeing the scene was "a piece-of-shit Datsun."

"Let's recap," Townes said finally, finishing his cone and tossing the napkin into Dani's back seat. "You evaded the FBI, then illegally gained entry to crime scenes—crimes, by the way, in which you yourself are a suspect—and you are now claiming to have been shot at, presumably by the real killer, who's after you because you're getting too close."

"Yes," I said. "Exactly."

"Which conveniently proves your own innocence, or rather it would, if anyone else saw it."

"Are you saying I shot at myself?"

"Let's see," he said. "Do you own a gun?"

"No."

"Do you have access to one or know anyone else who does?"

I couldn't help glancing at Dani, who sat on the hood of her shitty Datsun, but she didn't notice. She was too busy glaring at Townes.

"No," I said. "I don't think I do."

61

"Hello? Claire? Are you home?" I shouted, as I stepped through the door. "You'll never believe what happened." I bolted the lock and got the chain on.

"In here," she called from the bathroom. "Come in. I can't get up."

"What's wrong?" In a panic, I pushed open the door. She was taking a bath, tucked chin-deep in the bubbles.

"Sorry," I said.

"No, I want to hear." She brushed a puff of suds from her nose. "Sit."

So I sat on the toilet lid. She listened wide-eyed to my whole story and almost sat up, splashing over the rim, when the shoot-out occurred. Then I told her about Dani's trunk.

"Maybe they were just in there from a long time ago," she suggested.

"OK, fine, but why?"

"Well, she's a stripper. In your book *The Stone Cold Deadly Fox,* that stripper packs a rod, remember? She has a holster built right into her G-spot."

"G-string. Don't quote my own books to me. That's just some bullshit I thought up."

"So what do you think she's up to?" She faced me through her steam and froth. Her toes appeared over the tub's rim like a little row of pebbles. I shrugged.

"I don't know what to think anymore," I said, shutting my eyes to try and clear my head. I yawned and sniffed the air. It was warm, moist and oily. Some familiar feeling was drifting back to me and I yawned again. I was infinitely tired.

"What's that smell? Where did you get the bubble bath stuff?"

"It's bath salts," she said, holding up a frosted bottle. "I found it under the sink."

It was an ancient bottle of Jean Naté.

"You smell like my mom," I said. "It's sweet and creepy at the same time."

"Look who's talking. At least I'm sweet."

Smiling for the first time that day, I went into the kitchen, poured Coke over ice, and then went to my office. I got out a fresh yellow legal pad and a new Uni-ball Vision fine point and sat down to think. Nothing happened, which is generally the case. I tried writing up notes of the day's events, making columns down the page for an easy chart to refer to, but got discouraged when, three pages later, there was still nothing but a question mark in the column entitled, "Clues." I finished the Coke and got a refill. I told Claire to hurry up because I had to use the bathroom. Then I remembered the Fontaine letters.

Honestly, I had been putting it off: the erotic correspondence of a dim-bulb psychokiller and his newly slaughtered would-be paramour wasn't something I looked forward to digging into. I just wasn't in the mood that night. I was sufficiently depressed and freaked out already, with enough ugly ideas in my head to last a lifetime. Anyway, I opened the box. The letters were all neatly folded in two stacks. I picked one at random and took it from its envelope. It was, like my own mash letter from Clay, handwritten in blue ballpoint on cheap lined paper, the kind with the thick lines and chips of wood, like for kids.

When Claire finally got out of the bath, an hour later, and came in wrapped in a towel, I was still reading.

"You can pee now, sorry. I had to wash my hair."

"What?" I didn't look up. I slammed a page facedown and read the next. "Motherfucker," I grunted.

"What's wrong?"

I looked up and my expression made her frown. "This goddamn motherfucker."

"What? Who?"

"Clay," I said, waving the letter.

"What about him?"

"The goddamn fucking sick bastard is a better writer than me."

62

In the morning, I left to go see Clay again. I'd slept only in snatches, waking up from dreams that I was glad not to remember, and my nerves were strung between fear and anger. My unknown stalker was now trying to kill me; my protector, Dani, was a potential nutcase; and still I was no closer to the truth. My one clue was the letters, which made Clay himself my only hope of solving the murders. That thought didn't mix so well with my breakfast of coffee and vitamins. It sat like a stone on the bottom of my stomach.

So when I left for the subway, with a small travel bag over one shoulder and my briefcase-computer-bag thing over the other, and I began to get the creepy feeling that I was being followed, I wrote it off as nerves and ignored that little something that made me wriggle, like a tongue on the back of my neck.

It was the wind, I decided. The changeable weather of that spring, which kept trying and failing to break the grip of winter, had backslid again, and after a warm morning, suddenly it was cold. This is always when I get sick. I soldier through winter's assault, then collapse at the first caress of spring. I stopped to get out a sweater. A man walking behind me—tall, in a navy sweatshirt with the hood up—stopped in his tracks for a second, then kept walking around me. He went into Macy's. I pulled on my sweater and popped into Flushing Noodle for some pork buns to take on the trip (four for a dollar, the best deal in town), then went down to the subway.

Approaching Manhattan from Queens on the elevated track is, in my opinion, the most beautiful way into the city, especially at dusk or on a day of variable skies. The train emerges from the depths of the subway to float above the roofs, then sinks once more under the river. The outer edge of the raised railway platform has no guardrail or boundary; you sail along among the water towers and antennae and peer down into the streets. You can see a long way out, over brick apartment blocks full of living windows and warehouses swarming in graffiti, past the train yards like a nest of track, all the way to the wide green belt of Flushing Meadows Park, with the steel globe big as a building. You pause at Shea Stadium (Oops, sorry dear editor: Citifield now, alas), asleep amid vast parking lots and auto graveyards all day, but on game nights suddenly alive and close, a giant bowl of light. And beyond that, drawing nearer, as we fly in out of the east, is the city, showing its older, braver, gray and silver front: the Empire State, the Chrysler Building, the bridges and docks and the massive orange projects of East Harlem.

We slid then into that darkness, beneath the earth and the river, and when we emerged, with everyone on the train half dazed, Times Square felt feverish, the sudden blast of sound and people and bad light. I changed for the 1 to Penn Station and was still shaking off the fog as I crossed the open concourse to catch my train upstate.

That was when I saw him again, the guy in the sweatshirt. I was mixed up like I always am at Penn, walking back and forth to find my train on the big board overhead, and I turned to check the track and there he was. This time I showed no reaction but simply walked as fast as I could, choking the urge to run. I cut through a magazine shop, rode up and down an escalator and then, in a surprise burst, hurried to my train and climbed aboard. Only then did I let myself look back. He was gone. Or at least I couldn't see him. If I really had seen him at all. I was now rethinking it. To be honest, I could barely describe the guy, just a white face, stooped shoulders, jeans. And after yesterday I was certain to be jumpy, seeing unreal things, like a hooded figure ghosting me, the ghost.

I slid low in my seat and pretended to read the paper until the train left, and even then I didn't really start to breathe normally until we cleared the city, slipping through a series of tunnels and tracks that ran behind the backs of blocks, as if the train itself were trying to slip away unseen. But there were no more sightings. I got out at Ossining, took a cab to the gates, went through the by now familiar procedure of clearing security, and then, in the visitors' waiting room, ran into my pals, Theresa Trio and Carol Flosky.

"What the hell are you doing here?" was Flosky's greeting.

"What do you think?" I said. "I'm here for a haircut."

Flosky grinned, showing some gold. "I assumed you would have figured it out for yourself, but work on the book is suspended until the legal issue is resolved."

"Which legal issue? Catching the killer? Or is that irrelevant now?"

"That's the cops' job. I thought we were clear on that. My job is freeing my client, who didn't kill anyone."

"Well, someone did. And yesterday they tried to kill me too."

Her smile faded. For a moment she really looked like she gave a shit, but she recovered. "That's very unfortunate. I told you my fears. You should inform the police."

The guard appeared in the door, and Flosky went in to see Clay. Theresa smiled apologetically, but I could tell she was in a happy mood.

"What's with her?" I asked. "What legal issue?"

"Didn't you see the news last night? We were in court all day."

"Sorry. I was distracted by getting shot at."

"Really?" That paused her. "Well, the judge granted a temporary stay while her petition for reopening the case is considered. It looks like Darian has a chance at a new trial."

"I see," I said, and sat down.

63

Ten long minutes later, Flosky came out. She shrugged, took out a cigarette, acknowledged the guard's warning, shrugged again and sat down. Darian had decided to see me after all.

"I advised him not to, but whatever, he wants to talk," she told me. "But no tape recorder, no notebook, no nothing. And remember, this is all off the record."

I agreed. The guard let me store my stuff in a locker and then led me through. Clay looked cheerful in his orange jumpsuit, his slippers and cuffs, a toothpick in his mouth and a fat legal-size folder on the table. From where he sat, things were looking up.

"Hey, look who's here," he said. "My Boswell."

I laughed flatly, without smiling. I sat down. I spoke in a low, even voice. "You used me, motherfucker."

"What?" he looked genuinely surprised, and maybe even a little stung.

"The book," I said. "It was just a scheme. Part of this plan, whatever it is, to get you out or off death row."

"What're you accusing me of, exactly? I can't kill anyone in here. Not even you." He rattled his cuffs. "I used you? How? Are you saying that I, as an innocent man facing death, used you, a writer, as a way to get my story heard? Sure. Of course."

"But your story isn't being told, is it? Not now."

He shrugged. "Events intervened. That's not my fault."

"Why didn't you just write it yourself?" I asked.

"I don't understand."

"I read some of your letters. To Marie Fontaine. You can write. You're a well-read man. Boswell, indeed. The thick-skulled porn hound I met in here before wouldn't know Boswell from Hugh Hefner."

He smiled. "Well, I appreciate your opinion of my writing. As a professional to an amateur."

"Is this act just for me? What about Flosky? Does she see the dumbass or the smartass? Is it part of the innocent act? Too dumb to kill?"

He chewed his toothpick. I shrugged.

"I don't expect you to answer that," I said. "But tell me this. Why the porn stories? OK, you needed a patsy, someone to ghost your book, a desperate deadbeat writer to help with the scheme. But why the sex stories, when you were clearly capable of writing up your own little fantasies? Why did you need me?"

"Why?" He took the toothpick out. "Because I wasn't there. I never even met these fucking girls, remember? I'm Mr. Innocent. I needed you because I couldn't be there, with them, in their homes. I needed you to make it real for me." He leaned toward me now, and his eyes glittered, maliciously. "But you, you were there and still you noticed nothing, learned nothing. What did these girls sound like when they laughed, screamed, came? What did they smell like, their hair, their armpits, their pussies? Did their odor change after sex, grow stronger, sweeter? Did they sweat much? How wet did they get? What were their cunts like? The lips, the clits, the hair. Describe their assholes. What was it like in their rooms? How did the light enter during the day and the darkness by night? What sounds were in the air? Cars, birds, voices from other rooms? Did they have to hear a TV laugh track or an old lady snoring as they died? What were they wearing? Did their breath smell? Of what? What do these women eat, anyway? Are they vegetarian, and if so does this effect their odor and the color of their urine? Were they on some ridiculous, pathetic diet hoping to slim down for me? What was in their bellies when you split them open? Brown rice and organic tofu? Chocolate and wine? Piss and sperm? How did the blood look in the bed? Did they beg for their lives? Did they cry? What was in their eyes as they died?"

He flipped the folder open and shoved it across. A pile of letters spilled toward me. I saw an upside-down photo of a naked blonde. "Want to try again?" he asked. "Because they keep coming. They never stop writing to me. No wonder you're just a hack. For fuck's sake, learn to describe a little bit what life is like already. You want to be a real writer? I am reality. Describe me. You want to write literature? I am literature. You should be grateful to me."

64

When I left, Theresa and Flosky were gone. I called a taxi and spent the night brooding at the motel. The TV bolted to the tabletop, the hangers trapped on the rod, the pile of thin towels, worn nearly transparent, all made me desperate to flee but at the same time unable to move, lying immobile on the tightly wrapped bedspread till long after dark. Who knew what kind of horribly sad or sadly horrible acts had occurred on this very blanket, in this bed? This was the room I pictured Clay and his mother living in, out in Queens. A room where someone might check in to drink himself to death or eat a gun. A room where you could murder someone while the TV blared and not worry about the neighbors, snoring or fucking beyond the wall, then chop the body up in the bathtub, pack it into a garment bag like a wrinkled suit and hit the road.

Outside, the truckers were pulling in, on their way up to or down from Canada, giant semis snorting and swaying as they herded into the lot for the night. I went over to the coffee shop and ate a dry cheeseburger deluxe at a counter with several hunched truckers and one woman who I guessed was visiting a prisoner: she was dressed up nice, with a frilly synthetic blouse, a wool coat, a skirt and heels. A few of the truckers tried to talk her up but she ignored them and they let her be when they realized she'd been crying. The mix of cheaply sexy clothes and tears made her seem tragic, and I couldn't help picturing her with a steak knife between her freckled breasts. At a back table, a family of very large people, one with a little dog in a carrier, was making a lot of noise, laughing and yelling, giving the old waitress a hard time. I imagined each of them with their own severed head on their plate before them. This is what happens when you enter the world of killing, even as a detective: everyone becomes a potential victim, a body that hasn't lain down yet, walking meat.

I went back up to my room and watched TV for hours and hours until I finally fell asleep. The sound of trucks woke me early. I went out to get the free coffee and Cremora from the office, and on the way back I noticed a few women climbing from the parked trucks, lowering themselves carefully in high heels. One was bleached blond and stringy, bone white in her dirty white miniskirt but with ruddy chapped knees. A fuzzy, busty brunette was choked into dark jeans that forced her flesh to spill out in other odd places. The third was a crack-thin black woman with red hair, tiny shorts and high red boots. They were lot lizards, prostitutes who had spent the night in the truckers' cabs, but in this early air, with the blue of night still shining, it was impossible not to look beautiful. Now they tottered together toward a waiting Buick with a mismatched door. They laughed. The black girl stumbled on the uneven ground and the other women held her arms. The first rose of dawn was spread. The mountains smelled like melted snow, wet trees and diesel fuel. The asphalt shone.

I took a shower, used every towel (to me this is the real luxury of even the worst hotels) and caught the train. I was waiting for it to pull out, staring at nothing, drinking weak coffee and eating a bagel that tasted like a bad doughnut, when I saw him, my ghost in the jeans and sweatshirt. He was coming down the aisle, with a small bag over his shoulder. I was so shocked that for a second I forgot to be scared. He started too, when he saw me, and our eyes met. Then, I don't know why, but I smiled. I gave a little wave. He seemed annoyed and immediately looked away, ignoring me as he hurried down the aisle and out of the car.

On an impulse, I stood and followed him. The train lurched into motion and I grabbed the handle of the connecting door as it slid back and forth. I swung into the next car and there he was, sitting in the front row and staring up at me in surprise.

"Hi," I said.

He turned his head to the window, pretending I wasn't there.

"Hey," I said, "what's going on? Why are you following me?"

"I don't know what you're talking about," he said, without looking at me.

"All right." I shrugged. "See you in Penn Station. And then in Flushing."

He sighed, looked around, checking, I suppose, to make sure no one was spying on him, and then reached into his coat for his wallet. He showed me ID with a picture of himself in a suit. Terence Bateson, it read, FBI.

In the end, we sat together. It was easier for him than following me from a distance, I argued, and less unsettling for me. I felt safer knowing I had my own bodyguard. Terence was reluctant at first, but I assured him that I wouldn't tell anyone I'd spotted him, and once I'd promised to let him follow me back to my apartment undercover, he readily agreed. He'd been stuck on this mission solo, with no one to relieve him, and he was exhausted. We chatted for much of the ride or read in companionable silence. I told him what I could about Clay, whom he'd studied at the academy. He told me about Townes. The man was a legend, Terence felt lucky to be working for him, but, he admitted when pressed, everyone agreed he was kind of a prick.

Finally I asked him, "You don't really think I murdered those girls, do you?"

"Probably not." He ate a Tic Tac and offered me the box. I rattled two out. No doubt my breath was stale. "But Townes knew you were involved somehow, most likely as a dupe," he added amiably. "We thought that if we put the pressure on you, it would shake something loose."

"Yeah," I said. "My brains. My teeth. My kidneys."

Now he frowned. "I shouldn't have told you that. He also said maybe you're an extremely clever sociopath."

"Nah," I shrugged. "Don't try to cheer me up. I think I'm more the dupe type."

Terence smiled at this and we went back to reading magazines. Then he fell asleep—no doubt he'd been up all night watching me—and I stared out the window. His head slumped against my arm. Poor Terence. I foresaw an unrewarding career. He would be a lovable loser like me, the Harry Bloch of law enforcement, dependent on the kindness of his suspects, trusting me not to slip away or take his badge and gun. As he cuddled in closer, I thought again about what Clay had said. Homicidal maniac or not, as a literary critic he had a point. Everything I'd done in my career had been more or less a failure. At my best, I brushed the underbelly of mediocrity. If by writing as and for so many others, I had managed to wring out a subsistence-level existence, this fact only threw my true failure into deeper relief, as I admitted there was nothing worth publishing under my own name anyway. And now, handed what everyone agreed was the story of a lifetime, my own and others, I had managed to miss it. I had met the victims, seen the crime scenes, brushed up against the unknown killer; I'd met the central figure, been allowed to see, even compose, his thoughts, ideas, dreams: I had all the clues but had discovered nothing. In my hands all it amounted to was bad porn and some unfinished notes for a cheesy true-crime as-told-to.

65

When I got home, Claire was in my office, behind my desk, talking on my phone. She was in her school uniform with the white tights and working on a Twizzler. She signaled for me to sit. I dropped my bags and slumped on the couch. She hung up, crossing her legs as she swiveled toward me. She didn't eat the Twizzler, just kind of chewed it like an old man trying to cut back on cigars.

"We need to talk. I spoke to the publisher and got you an extension on the new Zorg, but they weren't happy. I know you've been distracted, but it's time to get back to work."

"Distracted? Someone tried to kill me. Twice."

"Well, now that first one was just an assault, am I right? They knocked you out and left you. But I understand. You're upset. Just let's be clear: there's really no book here anymore."

"Fuck the book. This is real life. Nonfiction. Do I look like the type who's gunning for posthumous recognition?"

"OK, but nothing's coming in. There's barely enough in your account for rent."

"I know, I know. Pride's a luxury I can't afford." I stood and started pacing. "But I was used by that bastard Clay and by that bastard Townes. I feel like a worm on a hook and . . . Wait. You looked at my bank statement?"

"I checked it online."

"I didn't know you could do that."

"I set it up for you. The code is my birthday."

"When is your birthday again?"

She stood and smoothed her skirt. "Look, I'm going to school."

"I've been wondering about that."

"But I'll be back tonight, if that's OK. Dad's in Hilton Head."

"Sure. Why not?"

"Oh, and Robertson's office sent that over." She pointed her gnawed Twizzler at a big manila envelope. She saw my blank face. "He's the lawyer? It's your stuff, back from the FBI."

She left and I made coffee, then sat behind the desk and tried to think of an ending for *Whither Thou Goest, O Slutship Commander*. I was stuck with Commander Dogstar and Polyphony, fleeing inter-galactic war and seeking a refuge for their own forbidden love, crash-landing on Earth just as the engine in their timespacecraft is about to die. But then what? Much like Commander Dogstar himself, I stared helplessly into my blank screen, feeling time crawl past me, watching the photons die. Despite what Claire said about my poverty, I was too overwhelmed by reality to focus on my made-up world, a world I deeply regretted ever leaving.

At least the books I wrote were honest lies. The characters might be familiar, reusable types, but I wasn't pretending to plumb the psy-chology of my vampires and cyborgs, any more than I pretended to understand Dani or Theresa Trio or any of the women who chased Clay. I just recounted the old themes: betrayal, vengeance, fear, escape. Love, which might as well be an arrow through the heart for all the sense it made.

In its tropes and types, genre fiction is close to myth, or to what the myths and classics once were. Just as, a century or two ago, one could refer to Ulysses or Jason and hit a deep vein of common understanding in your reader, now we touch that place when we think of a lone figure riding in the desert, or a stranger in a long coat and hat coming down a corridor with a gun, or a bat wheeling above the city at night. Reduced to their essence, boiled down, the turns and returns of genre unfold like dreams, like the dreams that we all share and trade with one another and that, clumsy and unrealistic as they are, point us toward the truth.

In the roundtable discussion I had with Dani and Claire about our favorite detectives, I had, I now realized, forgotten the best of them all, that solver and creator of mysteries, Dr. Freud. Contemporary with Sherlock Holmes, writing up cases like his own Watson, his practice and methods were oddly similar to Holmes's. They both even did coke. Always the case began with a client arriving in his dusty, cluttered study, full of books and relics, to tell the great man of what was missing or lost. Always he set out by listening, in a wreath of smoke, by noticing the clues, and by diligently, patiently, fearlessly following where they led, which was always into the past, kingdom of lost things, and where, at the end of the story, which is always the discovery of its beginning, there is always a crime.

I ripped the manila envelope open. It contained the tapes and incomplete transcripts of my interviews with Clay and the murdered women, my notebooks and files. I popped in a tape and began randomly flipping through papers while listening to Clay ramble on, in that backward tone, a voice I now knew had been put on for my benefit.

I opened the file Clay had given me: his love letters, the stack of pink and purple Polaroids and prose that he'd collected from his admirers. I flipped through, grimly entranced. Yet another kind of porn, I suppose. So many women, stretching back through time, so many faces, names, bodies. What had become of them? Any one could have ended up like the three I met. Then near the bottom of the stack, I found a handwritten note, on nice white stationery, dated three years before.

Dear Mr. Clay,

My name is Daniella Giancarlo. My sister is Dora. I know that you have always said you were innocent of her murder. I also know that she modeled for you, so you must have liked her and thought she was worthy to be in your work. She is my identical twin. That's why I felt I could be presumptuous and write to you. I was at your trial, and I think you looked at me and smiled. I kind of feel like I almost know you, since we went to the same high school, though not at the same time. I am younger, of course, and I was only there till junior year, when my family moved to the Island. I even remember your house, the foster house around the block from school. For all these reasons, I want to ask you a favor. Please, despite what they say in the papers, I am hoping you will show me you are a kind man. If you can help me find my sister's remains or learn anything about her death, please tell me. I know you have the power to help.

Respectfully yours . . .

A small head shot, like a passport photo, was included, showing Daniella or her sister (who knows?) with brown hair. The overly deferential tone, the flirtatiousness—it all suggested a freshman psych major with a book on managing psychopaths, but it still made my stomach churn. Why hadn't she told me? Why hadn't Clay? Had he written her back? He had alluded to her with me. Was he teasing me, perhaps, with a clue? Why hadn't Dani mentioned the high school and the foster home? True, she'd left that neighborhood years before the killings and there was no way she could have known Clay back then. But still.

I tore through the transcripts of my interviews with Clay and found the spot where he mentioned his foster mother. Gretchen. That was the name. Mrs. Gretchen. That bitch ought to be in prison, he said. Instead of sitting on her ass in that old house. Why would he stay informed about this woman he hated after all this time? How could he even know she was alive and still in the house? Were they in contact? Had Dani told him?

Here we come to the part I always dread writing, when the plot needs to snap together and resolve itself. The climax or whatever. The third act. It's a thankless task. Story plotting is like plumbing: no one wants to think about it until it stops working. Then everybody's a critic. But consider for a minute how unrealistic, how contrived your own real-life dramas would look on paper, how obvious the secrets and hidden motives would appear, set down in black and white for the eyes of the objective reader. For example, and be honest now, was anyone surprised by the way things went between Jane and me—except for me? So even in a true-crime story like this one, making the story part feel true is hard labor, heavy digging and burying, and creating suspense is largely a matter of covering one's footsteps. Still, looking back, I see that I let the answers slip more than once as I scattered my trail of clues across these pages.

66

Outside my building, I saw Agent Terence and another guy parked in his usual spot across the street. I was tempted to ask for a ride, but I didn't want to embarrass him in front of his pal, so I left him there reading the *Post*. It took two trains and a bus to get there, and when I emerged from the subway, I saw that Dani had called my cell, but I didn't check the message.

I had to wander for a while before I found the house. This neighborhood had gone through several lives since Clay and I were kids. It had been dying then, a faded district of run-down apartment buildings and private homes that the owners were too old or poor to keep up, clinging to the lower rungs of the middle class while the city itself slid into bankruptcy. Now it was in revival, everything bright and clean, and a house like Clay's foster mother's, with its crooked steps and sinking foundation, its overgrown shrubs and drawn curtains, was like a bad rash, the bane of the block. As I paused and checked the address outside, a young mom eyed me suspiciously from across the street. She was bundling a baby into the back of a Volvo, and her driveway and house were bordered with flowerbeds. Her irises were in full bloom. On my side the walk was cracked and weedy, and there was a dead old Buick rotting in the drive. I smiled at her and she looked away abruptly. She climbed into her car and I heard the electric door locks hiss. I didn't blame her. The place gave me the creeps too, and I looked over my shoulder for the reassuring sight of Agent Terence. He wasn't around.

I pushed the gate back and immediately I heard an enraged dog begin barking. I waited long enough to be sure it was coming from inside the house and then proceeded across the yard, past a sagging, overgrown apple tree, a bald, patchy lawn, and another dead car, this one a rusted-out VW bug pulled onto the dirt. I opened the torn screen door and stepped onto the porch. By now the dog was worked into such a frenzy that the whole zip code knew I was there, but I rang the bell anyway, for the hell of it. No answer. I knocked and the dog flung itself against the door in a murderous fit. I heard nails scratching, but that was it.

I gave up and walked around to the back of the house, where I found a heap of a garage that looked like I could push it right over, the withered remains of an ancient vegetable garden and a half-toppled fence. Two trees whose branches had grown together covered the whole rear of the yard in permanent shade, with years of dead leaves layered beneath them.

I looked over the fence. I saw a small woods, a patch of no-man's-land running behind the houses, with a highway overpass on one side. On the other side, I glimpsed a bright green field through the trees. I checked my map. That was the high school where Clay had gone and where he had learned to take photos.

I slid sideways through the falling fence and made my way into the woods. The tangle of trees above me was so thick, the sun barely broke through, starving the weaker plants on the sparsely covered ground. Instead the earth was blanketed abundantly in trash—a huge quantity of paper, bottles, mattresses, tires, unidentifiable heaps of rotten or charred matter. The thaws and rains of spring had turned big sec-tions into mud, and I had to hop and skip my way along. The woods ended in a kind of small meadow, an overgrown slope between the trees and the edge of the school property, where the grass was closely trimmed.

The scene was vaguely uncanny. It reminded me of something, like a place we've read about in a book, or as if this were my old school, which I'd forgotten and stumbled across by accident. I walked around, hearing the overpass traffic buzz and whisper like insects in the trees. Now it came to me: this had to be the field where that kindly teacher Mr. Bratwurst had discovered young Darian mooning about with a camera and encouraged him, taking him in hand. Did he take anything else in hand as well? Given Clay's background, it would seem likely. Every relationship in his life was built on victimization. The only variable was who was predator or prey. As I turned and went back through the woods, my cell phone rang and I grabbed it. "Private number" it read. I answered. The signal was awful.

"Hello?"

"Harry Bloch?"

"Yes."

"This is Agent Bateson."

"Who?"

"It's me. Terence!"

"Oh, sorry. Hi." The phone showed no bars. I was surprised it could even ring.

"Listen," he went on. "I wanted to tell you. We were called off your tail for a staff meeting but I wanted you to know that a woman in a car was seen following you this morning."

"When?"

"This morning."

"Dani?" I asked. "Is it Dani?"

"This is Terence," he said, and the phone died.

I realized then how quiet the woods were. Even the dog had stopped. Only that faint hum from the overpass. Then I heard a branch snap, or something, and I froze. Whatever was snapping froze too. If it was anything at all. I took a careful step. And suddenly from the corner of my eye, there was a movement, like a figure in the trees. I wasn't sure, but I didn't care. I bolted, and ran right into the mud. My foot sank ankle deep in the muck, and when I pulled, it sucked off my shoe.

"Fuck!" I howled, forgetting for a second that I was supposed to be hiding from someone. I reached over to retrieve my lost shoe and my other foot sank with a slurp. "Shit," I whispered softly. Feeling, I admit to you, like crying, I crouched down in the fetid slop and dug my shoe out, then carefully hopped to dry ground. I started running, guided by panic, one wet sole slopping and my other foot in a sock, clutching my shoe to my chest. Every few feet I would nervously glance behind me. I saw no one but kept thinking I heard a foot, a crackling twig, a breath. When I got to the fence, the dog exploded, and though it shocked the hell out of me, I was thrilled. I broke into a wild charge across the yard. And now I saw a dim light in the window.

"Help!" I yelled, and scurried over, waving my shoe. At the window I saw the dog. It was just a small poodle of some sort, wiry and gray, barking and jumping, bouncing its paws off the windowsill. The light was a TV with its back to me, and beyond that lay a person of some sort, a figure, gray and old, spread in a recliner.

"Help!" I called again. I banged on the glass. The little dog howled and spit like it was going to lose its mind. But the person never budged. Dead maybe? More likely sleeping or drunk. Was that Clay's foster mother, or even her boyfriend? The lump was sexless. Finally I gave up and ran on, or limped really, at this point. My foot hurt and I was out of breath. When I reached the street, I thought about banging on the neighbor's door, but I remembered she was out, and anyhow, I realized how I looked, sweaty, wild, covered in mud, stumbling from the neighborhood's haunted house, brandishing a shoe. I stopped and put it on. I tied both laces. And then, a small miracle, the sweetest sight in the world: a taxi came around the block.

I flagged it down, calmly, so as not to spook the driver, and even though according to Claire I couldn't afford it, I had him take me all the way home. Darkness fell, but slowly, now that it was spring. We sped along past Flushing Meadows Park, the lines of trees streaked by, and in the dimming light they melted into a mass of black and green. Reflected on the taxi window, my own face wavered and flowed across the woods, like a photo that had been double-exposed. I remembered taking such a picture myself, as a kid, with the plastic camera my mother gave me, when I took a summer art class, one of those free workshops the city sponsored to keep urban youth off the streets. That's when I understood, and in a flash, sitting in the cab, I solved the case.

Now, you may have noticed that, in my normal, day-to-day existence, I can be a little dense, as Claire says. I tend to stumble through life as if lost in a deep forest with an out-of-date map that I can't figure out how to fold. The trees all look familiar, animals are making scary sounds in the bushes and the sandwich in my bag isn't what I ordered. No doubt I'm not alone in this. It is because life stumps us that so many adore puzzles and games and mystery stories. Sitting on the couch, cracking the spine of an Agatha Christie, or magneting a Tuesday *Times* crossword to the fridge for Claire to ignore (or strangest pleasure of all, solving the problem I set myself in my own books, as if one side of my brain finally embraced the other like a long lost twin), I see through reality's inscrutable surface and glimpse the inner cogs and wheels as they spin. I imagine a world that I can make sense of and, just for a moment, I know how it must feel to be a genius.

But of course we have only one world, this dark and knotty one, and the truth we find when we look too deep is rarely pretty. Unlike in books, where we are all fearless seekers, in life, most of us would rather not see too clearly. And so, although the sudden rush of knowledge I felt was strong, its taste in my mouth was bitter: I knew the name of the killer now. I understood.

I pulled out my cell. It was working again, but so what? I didn't have Terence's number or Townes's. I had his card at home somewhere, I thought. Or was that Claire's lawyer? Could you call the operator and ask for the FBI? We got to my place. It was dark now, a clear, bright night. I paid and hurried in. No one followed. I took the elevator up. I opened my door and headed through the dark apartment toward my office. Halfway there I remembered that the card, if I had it, was probably still in my bathrobe pocket. So I walked into the bedroom and turned on the light.

Claire was spread naked on my bed. Her thin arms and legs were stretched to the breaking point and bound to the bed frame with my ties. Her mouth was sealed with duct tape and a line of blood trickled from a thin cut in the crook that ran across her throat. Her eyes stared at me in a horror so pure it seemed animal, a creature in a trap. Her eyes rolled.

"Claire." I stepped toward her and her head jerked wildly. She made a very soft gurgling sound that I knew was a muted scream, eyes rolling again to my right. I turned, just in time to see a huge knife coming at me. I saw a woman's red-nailed fist around the handle. And then I was face to face with Carol Flosky.

Our eyes met as the blade slashed my left arm. Pain flashed through my nerves, lit me up like lightning, and I saw a deep flap of flesh fall open and fill with blood. I howled, a wild high sound that didn't seem to be coming from me at all. It sounded far off, like a wolf. I wanted to curl up and clutch myself, but the knife went up again. That's all I saw—the blade, the arm. I put up my left hand and grabbed her arm below the wrist and we went down together to the floor, my right arm trapped beneath our weight. Now the blade was over my throat, and she was bearing down with all her strength while I held her up with my bloody arm, wrestling to free my other from where it was pinned behind my back. Shock was setting in, and there was no more pain from the cut, but my hand was numbing, and I didn't know how much strength it still contained. Our faces were only a few inches apart. She stared right into my eyes. I saw nothing in hers but total concentration on my death. A force willing me to die. Her lips twitched slightly into a near smile and I saw it, the resemblance. I never would have noticed, but now it was obvious. They were alike.

I grunted and pushed up with all my strength, trying to find some leverage to slip out or get my right arm up. She leaned her whole body against me, pushing everything down. Our eyes moved together toward the blade, its point pressing my skin, and then met again. Then there was a shot, so loud my ears seemed to go out for a second, and Flosky's eyes went big. She twitched.

"Look out, Harry," I heard Dani say. I felt warm blood seeping from Flosky to me, between our legs. She grimaced in pain. Her eyes flicked away from mine for a second and I felt my chance. Instead of pushing back, I forced my numb arm sideways an inch or so and let it fall. The blade sunk into the carpet beside my left ear, and I jerked up sharply as Flosky's face collided with mine. Our skulls knocked painfully and I rolled to the right, throwing the woman off. I heard another shot, and this time it was Flosky who howled. I looked up to see her down on the floor, scrambling back into the corner, bleeding from her leg and her arm. Dani was holding the gun in her right hand with the left supporting her wrist. She kept it on Flosky as she moved closer, eyes never leaving her target.

"Who is she?" she called out to me, loudly, as if I were down the block.

"The lawyer. She's been killing the girls. She's Darian Clay's mother." I clutched my wound now as pain throbbed back. My whole arm was stained red. Claire whimpered from the bed above me.

"Should I kill her?" Dani asked. Flosky, twitching, cringing, looked at me.

"Yes," I yelled. "Kill her. Shoot."

Dani stepped over me. She leveled the gun at Flosky's head. She looked right at her. She asked, "Where is my sister's head?"

That's when Agent Terence entered the room.

67

Ambulances came and took us all to the hospital. I wasn't hurt that badly after all—the cut had missed the important bits—but I was weak and dumb from the loss of blood and spent the night getting pumped full of various fluids while cops, nurses and FBI guys wandered in and out, never once knocking.

Carol Flosky underwent surgery. The first bullet had shattered her femur and lodged in the meat of her thigh. The second had gone clear through her shoulder, slicing muscle and nerves on the way. The cops dug it out of my floor.

Dani was briefly treated for shock and then taken in to give her statement. She had asked about my welfare but had not requested to see me.

Neither had Claire. She was unhurt except for small bruises and the cut on her neck, really a very minor, accidental scratch made when I startled Flosky by opening the apartment door. However, since the tape was removed from her mouth, Claire hadn't spoken at all. She seemed OK, responding with nods and shakes to questions, sipping juice from a straw held up by a nurse. But when I was wheeled past her in the emergency room, on my way to be sewn up, and called out her name, she just shut her eyes and turned away. Her father, who was golfing in North Carolina, had chartered a plane and was flying up that night. Her mother would arrive from Hong Kong the next day.

Townes came to see me with a whole team of agents, including Terence. They made me go over everything, the whole story, again and again. When I mentioned the Marie Fontaine letters, still back at my house, a couple of them ran from the room. They all seemed uncertain as to whether I was actually guilty of anything criminal or not, and I wondered about Claire's high-priced lawyer. I assumed he was off my case. Anyhow, I was too dizzy and weak to worry about it much. I was mostly preoccupied with Claire, and when I was told that her father had arrived and taken her away, I finally fell asleep.

In the morning they drove me home in a police car, and the neighbors all watched, opening their doors and staring in frank amazement as I was escorted down the hall and into my apartment. The place was wrecked, the police and feds having done far more damage than Flosky. Then Townes arrived, looking exhausted, worse than me. The others left, and when I offered coffee, he accepted and sat at the kitchen table with a sigh.

"Well, there's good news and bad news," he said.

"Shit," I said. Trying to make coffee one-handed, I had poured it all over the counter. Townes got up and helped, brushing the spilled grounds into the filter. I noticed some old breadcrumbs mixing in but didn't mention it.

"Good news first," I said.

"She confessed to the killings. Officially signed her statement last night."

"And what's the bad news?"

"She confessed to the killings," he said again, sitting down to watch the coffee drip into the pot. "All of them. Including the ones we're about to execute Clay for."

"Oh, I see." I sat down too. "What does she say?"

"She says that she never lost touch with her son or not for long anyway. That she tracked him down at the foster home, kept seeing him secretly. After he grew up, they were together again, mother and son, reunited. The only problem was when he started photographing women. She didn't approve. She says she knew what women were like, she'd been a whore herself, and she saw right through these girls. They were tempting him, trying to steal him away. So when he worked with these models, she would spy on them, and afterwards, she killed them. When Darian got arrested, she went and got a law degree just to help him. It checks out. He had a public defender through the trial and she took over as his attorney five years ago. Turned herself into a death penalty expert just to defend her son. She's a formidable woman, in her own fucked-up way."

"You believe her? About the earlier killings?"

"Of course not. It's her last shot at saving her boy. Do you?"

"No."

"But the problem is she doesn't need us to believe her. All she needs is for a judge to think she raises enough doubt or new evidence to warrant a new trial for her son. And then, if at that trial she testifies that she did the killings, well, the prosecutors have quite a job on their hands, proving him guilty and her innocent. He could end up with a hung jury or who knows what? A walk. Anyway, I think that's her plan."

He pulled a bottle of aspirin and bottle of Zantac from his coat pockets and shook some out. He sucked them slowly, like mints.

"Water?" I asked.

He shook his head and swallowed. "Why do you think she tried to kill you?" he asked.

"She knew I was on to her. Or about to be. There's a woods in back of Clay's old foster home where he used to take pictures for some art class. I recognized it from a photo in Flosky's office. When I saw it, everything fit. I knew she was his mom. She had to be mixed up in the killings."

Townes perked up at this. "I'll have somebody go fetch that picture."

"She must have followed me out there. Terence tried to warn me, but I thought it was . . ." I hesitated. "I thought it was someone else. Anyway, Flosky saw that I had all the pieces and it was just a matter of time. I think at that point she decided to take me out. She went back to my place to wait for me and found Claire."

"Yes," Townes agreed. "Claire was unlucky. She was there when Flosky broke in. So she had to kill her and make it look like the others. But you got back early."

"I took a cab," I said. "I never take cabs." Then I scowled at myself. Saving Claire's life with such a shoddy miracle—Cheapskate Slips in Mud, Scares Self, Takes Taxi—felt like a further insult. Poor Claire.

Townes nodded at the counter. "I think the coffee's done."

"Oh right." I stood. "Milk? Sugar?"

"Both."

I poured two mugs and put out milk and sugar. Townes loaded his up and took a grateful gulp. This was the first time he'd asked my opinion of anything. I realized that he was speaking to me, if not as an equal, at least as someone he didn't despise. But I despised myself more than ever. Townes stood.

"Get some rest. Come to my office tomorrow and sign your statement."

"I can come now."

"Tomorrow's fine. Go to bed. And thanks for the coffee."

"OK," I said, and sat without moving until I heard him leave. Then I locked the door and took his advice. I rested. But I didn't go to bed. Just the thought of stepping into that room made me see Claire again, strapped down, gagged and spread before me, a line of blood running down her throat. So I lay on the couch with the TV on, which is how I slept that night, and the next, and the next, and the next. It took a long time.

I tried reaching Claire, both on her cell and her house phone, but there was no answer on either, and my messages weren't returned.

Nor were my texts and emails. I also left a message for Dani, who called me right back.

"Hi," she said, when I picked up the phone. "How are you?"

"OK, I guess. Thanks to you."

"No. Don't be silly. It's just chance."

"Chance? You're a badass. How did you learn to shoot like that?"

She laughed. "It was after my sister died. I had this fantasy of tracking the killer down and started going to the firing range. I had a whole collection of weapons I was going to use, just like he did to her. Then when they caught Clay, I just kept it up. I guess it made me feel safer or something. Crazy, I know. Paranoid."

"Well, I'm no psych student," I said, "but I don't think it counts as paranoid and crazy when you're completely right." I told her about the letter I found, how it led me to the foster house.

"Yeah, I wrote him," she said. "I drove by the house. Repeatedly. He's the whole reason I even took psych, to be honest. I guess I didn't want you to realize how crazy I was about getting revenge. Even though he was caught, somehow in my mind I was still hunting him. What can I say? I've got a lot of baggage. I guess I can't let it go while he's alive."

I thought about the new legal problem that Dani's own capture of Flosky had paradoxically created, but I didn't mention it. Nor did I mention my own dark, crazy thoughts about her. Instead I said, "Let me buy you dinner tonight. A thank-you for saving me. Twice. So you get dessert included too. A cheap reward, I know, but then my life isn't worth that much. Even if you double it."

She laughed. "I don't know."

"Come packing heat if you want, but remember, I'm one-armed. You'll be able to take advantage of me."

She laughed again, lightly, like a small smile I could hear on the phone, but said, "That's just, it. I'm not sure we should."

"Oh, I see." I realized that she meant it. "Why not?"

"It's just, I don't know, I can't really see us ever being just a normal couple splitting a flourless chocolate cake. It's not your fault at all. You're a good guy. Like I said, I've got a ton of baggage."

"So does everybody. At least ours matches," I said, and she laughed, for real this time. "Who knows? Maybe I can lighten your load."

"No," she said, quietly. "That's not how it is. Everyone carries their own."

I said I understood and she apologized and I said not to, and after a bit more warmhearted but hopelessly awkward stumbling we said good-bye. I knew she was right about everything. We had gone too far and we couldn't cross back over that line. My own issues or whatever you want to call them—emotional problems, distrust, suspicion—had hobbled us more than she knew. And despite what I'd just said on the phone, she was most certainly crazy. Still, I couldn't help feeling that I had blown something big, maybe the biggest thing of all.

Then, since I couldn't sleep anyway, I sat down and finished writing the Zorg book. I needed the money.

68

From *Whither Thou Goest, O Slutship Commander*, chapter 24:

"There it is," Polyphony shouted, pointing to the white stone tower that appeared on the mountain's far green side. Using our last ounce of thrust, I took the ship down, trying to aim her toward a clearing.

"Hang on, Poly," I yelled, and we hit, crashing into a forest. The poor old *Phallus* plowed through the trees and came to rest its battered head against a boulder. The windshield shattered and the dials on my console froze as the pilot lights went out. Polyphony was knocked semiconscious. I forced the hatch, set my cell on mutilate, and then, uniform in tatters, Polyphony in my arms, I staggered from the smoking wreck of the *Phallus*.

I was in a glen. Sunbeams filtered down through the pine trees. The only sound was the wind. An old bearded man in a white lab coat sat on a rock, watching us curiously. He smiled and puffed his pipe.

"Welcome, friends," he said. "Welcome to the Gore Institute. I am Dr. Beamish."

After he patched our wounds and fed us, we told Dr. Beamish our story, how we'd come to Earth hoping to find a temperate planet where the love of a Master for his android sex slave would be accepted and had randomly chosen the year 2058 (5819 on your lunar-Jewish calendar) as the closest entry point on our navigational charts. Our timing could not have been worse. Earth was undergoing vast cataclysms as a result of global warming: floods, droughts, famines and pestilence, leading of course to war. We'd escaped the submerged ruins of New York, fought off the bands of psychic killer dolphins who now ruled it, then made it past the Jesus-freak tribes of the Middle States to safe haven in the Native American Free Zone, searching the whole way for the Gore Institute, in the former state of Colorado, where we'd heard scientists were working feverishly on an answer.

"I'm afraid you heard wrong, friends," Dr. Beamish said, smiling sadly. The Institute was abandoned and he himself was the last surviving scientist. We were sitting in what had once been the World Climate Command Center, high atop the rather redundantly named Rocky Mountains, but on the center's screens we saw nothing but horrors, doomed humans fighting over the dwindling resources that would let them survive a little longer until, degree by degree, human life was erased from this planet. Meanwhile, as the world's infrastructure ran down, Dr. Beamish watched his screens die slowly, one by one.

"It's funny you came here from outer space, looking for a future," he said. "The stars have been my one consolation. You see, the night sky has been growing brighter and more beautiful, as the earth goes dark."

"Dr. Beamish, is there really no hope at all?" Polyphony asked.

Dr. Beamish puffed his pipe and stroked his long beard. "My dear, as a sworn meteorologist, I quote a wise human, Kafka, and say, of course there's hope, infinite hope." He shrugged. "But it might not be for us."

"Nor for us, Doctor," I said. "Our ship's too damaged to escape Earth's gravity. We are stuck here with you."

"I'm sorry," Dr. Beamish said, "that our human foolishness should doom you to death as well. Earth was once a very pretty planet. Pity you picked the wrong year."

The dutiful Dr. Beamish went to check his readings. Poly and I stood on the observation deck, watching the beautiful, fatal sun go down. It was sixty-five degrees that evening, but it felt like sixty-three. She was crying.

"I'm so sorry, Master," she said. "It's all my fault. I selfishly wanted to live with you in realtime, and now we will both die."

"No, Poly, you were right," I said. "I have no regrets. One night with you is worth everything. You're the best slut I ever had."

She clutched me tightly, and I leaned in to kiss her, when, suddenly, her tears became laughter.

"I do have one regret," she said. "That we didn't randomly pick another year. Say 2009."

"Poly," I cried, grabbing her close again. "You wonderful droid, that's it!"

We found Dr. Beamish and brought him to the wreck of the *Phallus*. I explained my plan. He puffed his pipe excitedly and raised his fuzzy brows.

"Time travel as a way to save Earth? By God, it just might work."

"Unfortunately, the ipod only holds us two, and the engine is weak," I said, while Poly checked the systems.

"But we can manage a short hop," she said. "Maybe fifty years. Back to your 2009."

"Ah, old zero-nine," Beamish said. "If only we knew then what we know now."

"But you will," I said. "We'll find you in that place you mentioned studying at, the Universe of Harvard? We'll tell the young you what's happened. You'll have another chance to get it right. We all will."

"But what about you two?" he asked.

"We will be stranded in 2009, without the power to leave," I said.

"But then you might be doomed," Beamish cautioned. "Doomed to live and die in the present."

"Just like you," I said. "And everyone else." I secretly squeezed Poly's hand.

"The present will be time enough," she said, looking out at the night. She gazed at the beautiful, empty spaces we'd crossed and the dead stars from whence we came. "It has to be. It's all there is."

PART FOUR
May 18—21, 2009

69

If this were a classic detective story, a procedural, it would end right here, as soon as the killer was caught, the crimes explained, the final victims counted. But I'm no classic detective and my own story has one more twist still to come.

To be honest, I prefer the old-fashioned mysteries myself, with a dead murderer on the last page and no mushy stuff about the hero's private life. I always see it as a sign of decline in a series, and desperation in the writer, when a detective suddenly grows a tumor or terrorists kidnap his wife. It's unprofessional. I say, Don't bug us with your personal problems. Just do your job. In his first novels, Dashiell Hammett, the headmaster of the old school himself, didn't even bother naming his detective. The narrator was just a short, fat guy with a gun and a hat who smoked too many Fatimas. He came to town in a crumpled suit, solved his case, and caught the next train out.

But unlike the characters in the stories I read or write, it seems I'm destined to live one in which, every time I'm ready to fold down the page and toddle off to sleep, fate slips me one more surprise. Perhaps you're way ahead of me and already have it figured out. After all, the clues are right there, if you can see them. But I never do.

So, the next morning, I went downtown to the FBI offices to sign my official statement. I had not been to the Federal Building in, well, I couldn't remember how long, and the feeling was, I guess, very post-post-9/11: there were concrete barriers and extra cops, and at the same time a feeling of everydayness, as if this new fear had simply been integrated into the other old fears and become the new normal, suppressed and forgotten, as it must be, if daily life is to go on. For example, I walk by Ground Zero all the time now, without registering it as anything but one more construction site. On the other hand, I remember, not long ago, walking through Little Italy, or I guess it's now Nolita, while the trash of the San Gennaro street fair was being swept up. Suddenly, and for no reason I knew, I felt such a wave of mysterious sadness that tears welled up in my throat. As a city kid, walking on holidays down the middle of the litter-strewn street had always been a special pleasure. Not anymore. Ever since that beautifully clear September morning, empty streets full of blowing paper fill me with secret grief.

I went through the metal detector and got a visitor's pass from the desk, then waited till Agent Terence appeared to escort me up in the elevator. We shook hands warmly and I thanked him again. He blushed. We were genuinely glad to see each other, which was lucky, because as soon as we stepped off the elevator, I was pretty much attacked by John Toner.

"You," he said, getting up from the couch where he was sitting, across from the receptionist and the wood-paneled wall with the big FBI seal. A thin blond woman with large boobs put a calming hand on his arm, but he brushed her off. The second Mrs. Toner.

"What the fuck have you done?" he yelled. "Didn't I tell you?" Receptionists stopped talking into their headphones and agents walking by with files turned to look.

"Mr. Toner," I said, quietly.

"Didn't I fucking tell you?" He took a swing at me, and I jumped back, but the blow was halfhearted and Terence neatly interceded, grabbing his arm and gently pushing him back.

"Please, sir, please," he said, with real pleading in his young voice. Mrs. Toner hurried over and began pulling her husband away.

"Don't you care?" he asked me over his shoulder. "Don't you even care how you affect people? You're a bloodsucker. You live off pain." Tears ran down his cheeks. He sniffed, touching his face, as if suddenly noticing that it was wet. Then he fell silent and let his wife guide him back to his seat. Terence quickly steered me to the glass door that led to the offices.

"Vampires," he said, as he walked me down the hall. "That's what James Gandolfini said too, you know. I read it in an interview."

"Who?"

"Tony Soprano. The actor who played him?"

"Right."

"He said writers are vampires who suck the life out of people. He said it about the guy who wrote the show."

"Oh yeah?" I said. "That's really fascinating."

"This is it," Terence said, and rapped his knuckles on a door before opening it.

"Harry, good," Townes said. He was standing behind his desk, sorting through big piles of paper. "Sit down. How's the arm?"

"Fine," I said, "thanks," and sat.

"Good," he said without looking up, and waved vaguely at the desk. "There's a copy of the statement you gave at the hospital. Read and sign."

I did, while Townes flipped through files and Terence stood and watched.

"Toner's still out there," Terence told him. "He took a swing at Mr. Bloch."

Townes glanced up at me.

"It was nothing," I said. "I've had worse."

Townes didn't smile. He looked back down at his work and started turning pages. "Poor guy," he said. "He has his lawyer filing all kinds of shit. At this point he's probably just bogging things down, but you can't blame him. If Flosky helps Clay get a new trial, it will be like having his wife dug up all over again."

I signed the statement and handed it to Townes, who gave it to Terence, who left, shutting the door softly behind him. Finally Townes sat. He took off his glasses and leaned back, rubbing his nose.

"Did you sleep?" he asked me. We had to position our heads between stacks of files to see each other.

I shrugged. "A little."

"Nightmares?"

"I don't remember," I lied.

"Keep the lights on?"

"TV."

"You keep seeing it, don't you?" he asked, craning forward over the desk.

"Yes."

He blinked at me several times. He nodded. "Well, it doesn't go away. I wish it did. You get used to it." He opened a desk drawer and pulled out a big manila envelope. He laid it on the desk. It was old and worn, with coffee circles and tape along the seams.

"I don't know if you want to see this or not. But I wanted you to know that I know what it's like."

I opened the flap, and as soon as I saw the white edge of the photo paper, I understood that these were the original pictures, the ones Clay took and sent to the cops.

Townes spoke. "More than twelve years ago, I saw those girls, for real I mean, those bodies. And then the photos that fucker sent. And I probably still see them, at least for a second, every day, or maybe now it's every other day. Or maybe I won't think about it for a while, a few weeks even, and then I'll see something—a billboard, a woman on the street—and it will all come back. Or I'll be on the subway or passing by a flower shop, and I'll smell that smell. You know what I mean."

I did. "Death."

"Death and rotting flesh. That sick, sweet, bitter smell. It's in my

nose now, and my head. I suppose that's why I hang on to those pictures. I keep them here so my family doesn't see. And even here I hide
them, because they wouldn't understand why, every now and then,
I have to look. But you do, I think. Understand." He stopped talking
and stared at me and the look in his eyes was plaintive, almost beseeching. He was, I realized, begging.

"I do," I said. "I understand." I looked. The stack was thick. On
top were the normal photos, the conventionally arty shots that he'd
taken in his studio and that had been seized during the investigation.
Mostly they were proofs, sheets of small squares featuring pretty girls
in typical poses, the only pathos added by hindsight, the fact that I
knew what they could not: I was looking at the dead, and seeing them
through the eye of their killer. Then at the bottom were the other
shots, the ones sent in to the police.

They were beautiful, at first glance, pale forms like giant flowers.
Then you realized, these sculptures were made out of girls. A girl re-
shaped to look like a blossom, hands and feet and hair radiating out,
her face in the center. A girl turned into a chair. A girl with her head
emerging between her legs, so that she appeared to be giving birth to
herself. A girl sawed in half and laid arm in arm, like she was hugging
herself, kissing her own twin.

70

I left the Federal Building in a fog. I spun through the revolving door and crossed the plaza and was trying to remember where the subway was when a cab stopped before me at the curb. Theresa Trio emerged with a cardboard box and a stack of files in her arms. When she saw me, she jumped and dropped her stuff.

"My God, it's you."

"Hey," I said, trying to sound lighthearted, and bent to help. "Sorry I scared you."

"No." She laughed awkwardly. "You just startled me."

She was in her lawyer look, a fitted knee-length black skirt and a cropped jacket, but her nail polish was chipped and bitten and there were rings under her eyes. She picked a folder up backward and the papers spilled out.

"Shit." She sighed. I grabbed them up for her.

"Why are you here anyway?" I asked.

"To answer more questions. They just finally let me into the office for my things. Being there gives me the creeps. I guess that's why I'm jumpy." Her laugh was hollow.

"Let's sit a minute." I pointed out a bench under a bus shelter. We sat side by side with her belongings piled between us, watching the traffic flow past. At first I thought she would cry, from the way her breathing fluttered. Instead she took out a cigarette. The flame on her lighter was much too high and she jumped back as it flared.

"Hey, watch it."

"Sorry. Sorry." She sucked at her blackened Marlboro Light.

"You shouldn't smoke. It's dangerous."

"I know. It's gross. I don't really, but . . ." She shrugged and puffed, mightily. The huge ash fell on her skirt, and for a second she reminded me of Flosky. "I keep thinking about how much time I spent alone with her. In the office late at night. We even shared a room upstate at the hotel a couple times. God." She shook her shoulders. "She killed girls my age. What am I saying? She tried to kill you."

Reflexively, I touched the bandage under my jacket. "You know, I've been remembering our conversation on the train. About capital punishment and what was civilized?"

She nodded.

"I guess you might think badly of me," I said. "But I have to admit, if I'd had the gun in my hand, I think I would have killed her without a second thought." I glanced over at her. "I'm sorry."

She watched the smoke rising through her hand. Her voice shrank far back to a whisper. "I wish you had killed her too." She puffed on her cigarette, choked, and threw it in the street. "I guess that makes me a total hypocrite."

"It makes you normal. To be scared or angry is human. With Flosky, it wasn't even personal. I was just this thing that went from being useful to being a problem. And she wasn't herself either. I mean she wasn't the person I'd met, wasn't even there in the room." I realized Theresa was peering at me closely. "Never mind. I was rambling."

I sat back and watched a bus snort by.

"That's just like what I keep thinking," she said. "How you never know who someone really is. To be honest, it even crossed my mind that the killer could be you." She smiled at this and covered her face. "I can't believe I just said that." She peeked up at me, blushing, as if over a veil. I laughed, loudly, a sudden, inappropriate guffaw. She recoiled.

"Sorry." I caught my breath. "But I just thought of something. I don't know if I should tell you. You could ruin me." For a moment I thought how angry Claire would be, then I remembered she was gone. "Never mind. It's frivolous. Forget it."

"No, come on. Frivolous is good. I could use frivolous, believe me."

"OK," I said, trying to keep a straight face. "I am Sibylline Lorindo-Gold."

"What?" She smiled faintly. "I don't get it."

"It's me. I'm her. Sort of. She's my mom. But I wrote the books."

She sat back and narrowed her eyes, as if putting me in perspective. "What the fuck are you talking about?"

So I explained, while she watched me suspiciously. She dug into her carton and pulled out my new book. She checked the photo closely, then lifted her glasses and stared at my face. I tried to smile coyly. I batted my eyelids.

"Jesus," she said. "I feel nauseous. This is freaking me out."

"I thought you'd laugh."

"Laugh? Do you know how many times I looked at this picture without knowing what I was seeing?" She put her head between her hands. "I can't look at you. I keep seeing her. This is definitely not what I needed."

"Try to breathe," I said.

"Shut up. Just shut up."

"Do you want me to leave?"

"Yes."

"Are you sure? Will you be all right?"

She didn't answer. I hesitated, perching as far from her as I could on the bench. Another bus sailed by, its wave of exhaust glittering in the sun. Now my own mind had begun to turn around something she had said. How many times she had looked at the photo. Without knowing what she'd seen.

"And this means you wrote these books I've been reading all this time." She spoke without looking up.

"Yes," I said, but I was only half listening. Something had clicked in my head, like the feeling just before I understand where a book is going. I was answering her by reflex. My brain was writing the next chapter.

"The crazy thing is, I love your books," she went on. "Or hers. Whoever." Then she smiled up at me, makeup smeared, and said the one thing I had waited my whole life to hear. "You are my favorite writer."

I stood. "Thanks, but I have to go. I'm so sorry."

"What? You're going? Now?" She looked at me in shock, as if maybe I really was a killer after all.

"I'm sorry," I said. "Really. Do you need help getting inside? Are you OK?"

"I don't know. Just go. Jesus."

"Sorry." I took off running.

71

"You're back," Townes said, when I rushed into his office, again with Terence as my guide. "You forget something?"

"Let me see those pictures again."

Townes looked at me oddly. I was out of breath and waving my arms around. He probably thought I had snapped.

"I just thought of something. Please," I said. "Let me see."

He signaled for Terence to leave us, then took out the envelope again.

"Don't make me regret showing you these in the first place," he said, as I clawed open the envelope and spilled the ghastly pictures out. I pushed them aside and got the proofs, the sheets of regular glamour shots taken in Clay's home. I examined them closely while Townes examined me.

"What are you looking at?" he asked.

"Do you have a loupe?"

He opened another drawer and rooted around while I held the sheets under the desk lamp. This sheet was Dani's sister, posed in a ballet outfit, and it disturbed me too much, so I flipped to the next one, Janet Hicks. I peered as close as I could, with the sheet right up under the bulb, but it was too small. "Loupe, please," I said again.

"OK, I'm looking," Townes said. He was on his knees, looking in the bottom of the drawer. "Got it." He hit his head on the open top drawer. "Fuck." He stood and handed it to me. "Here's your fucking loupe."

"Thanks." I held the magnifier to my eye and peered intently at Janet Hicks's pretty face, the pout of a yearning actress. Then I went to the next shot of her, and the next, all along the rows. Then I checked the next girl. The next. I was recalling something Clay had told me about working with his models, about getting them to hold still. Like a hunter, he'd said.

"What the hell are you doing?" Townes asked.

"I got him," I said, and handed him back the sheets. "I think."

Townes looked down at the photos that he'd seen a million times, then shrugged and took his seat. "I'm waiting."

"As part of my illustrious writing career, the one you perhaps justly mocked me for, I spent a number of years writing and editing porn magazines."

"I know. It's in your file."

"I have a file?" I was both frightened and flattered.

"You were saying?"

"OK, well, as part of that job I spent countless hours staring at proof sheets like these, at girls like these, and I knew before there was something wrong with them, but I didn't know what till now. It's the eyes."

"Eyes?" He peered at the sheet.

"Every girl. The eyes are the same in every shot. No movement. The camera's fast but not that fast. You always get a shot with the eyes shut or droopy. Not here. Not a blink, not a squint. Not a glance to the side. The same fixed stare, always. Plus these are studio shots, brightly lit with big, strong lights. None of their pupils are contracted. Have your guys blow these up and measure or check however they can, but

I'm telling you. The girls in those pictures look dead. And that means they were murdered before he photographed them, not after, like Flosky says. Clay is guilty as hell."

In silence, Townes pushed the loupe to his face and hunched over the photos. He stared for a long time, moving from image to image, sheet to sheet, while I waited. Then he looked up, and for the first time since I'd met him, he smiled, revealing a discolored front bottom tooth. It didn't last long. As soon as I smiled back, he frowned, hit the intercom, and started yelling.

72

Townes insisted on taking me and Terence out to celebrate, but the place they took me to, a randomly selected Hooters-type gentlemen's club, reminded me of that other night at the bar where Dani danced, and I got depressed thinking of her. After one drink I begged off, complaining about my arm. Outside, I called Morris and went over to his place, where his boyfriend Gary cooked me an excellent Vietnamese dinner of pho: kind of like my mother's brisket, but with glass noodles, basil, and chili. Then I went home and lay awake on my couch, staring at the TV.

But I couldn't sleep. After cycling through every channel twice, I got up and went to my office. I checked my email for news from Claire. There was nothing but a couple of vampire-related items forwarded from the publisher's site that I had been too busy to read. One, a fan letter from a Dallas teen, got a standard cut-and-paste, thanks-for-writing response. The other was local, an invitation to a vampire-themed night at a Brooklyn goth club held every Monday. This was Monday, or just had been; it was a little after twelve.

Of course the invitation was to Sibylline, not me, and of course they wanted her to read or answer questions or who knows what, arrive on bat wings and bite someone, but I was restless and, I admit, scared to lie there alone. Also, I further confess, I had the dim thought Theresa might show. So I got dressed and pulled on what I thought was an acceptably nefarious black overcoat. I turned the collar up.

I found the club without much trouble, at the end of a street near the river in Dumbo. The sky was purple, the water was black, the bridges and buildings were blinking white and yellow. The building looked like some kind of old factory, shut tight and dark, with only one bulb burning over a small sign that read TO CRYPT. An arrow pointed toward a sloping ramp that led into the mouth of the basement, where another faint light glowed, behind shadows and garbage, as if in the back of a throat. I started down, leaning back against the slope, and once the street sounds faded, I heard nothing but my own heels clicking on the concrete. The ramp curved, and as I approached the blind turn, a little fist of panic squeezed my chest. I almost turned and ran. I put my hand out to steady myself, but flinched when my fingers touched the cold, clammy wall. I breathed deeply, trying to ward off what felt like an anxiety attack and remembering, ludicrously, that I was supposed to put my head between my legs. Hardly the way I wanted my dead body to be found. Bullshit Writer Discovered with Head Up Own Ass. I forced myself forward and peeked around the bend.

I saw an empty parking garage, with spaces marked in white paint and, at the far end, a metal door where a big black bouncer sat on a stool. He waved a flashlight at me and flicked it off. Adopting a jaunty air, I walked over, while he stared unmoving from behind mirrored shades. He checked my license, handed me a flyer and pulled open the heavy steel door.

I entered a long, low-ceilinged room, with a bar along one wall, tables in the middle and a dance floor in the back, all lit dimly in reds and blues. Some kind of heavy dance music was beeping and booming. The acoustics were lousy and I could hear the bass buzzing in the ceiling and feel it beneath me in the floor. The place was about half full, with the whole crowd pushed into the back. Of course, as soon as I was inside, my eyes began hunting for Theresa, but it was hard at first to distinguish people in the dark. Not to mention that they were all wearing black, with the occasional splash of red, and here and there a girl in a long white dress, fluttering among the dark bodies, the cotton lace dyed pink in the lights. I thought of Marie Fontaine's house, the white siding and dirty snow stained pink from spinning sirens, while upstairs her room was red.

Shaking the image off, I snaked a path through the crowd, hands in my pockets, scanning the faces, until I reached the back wall. Theresa wasn't there. It was just as well, and I was starting to wonder why I'd even come, when I realized that there was something odd about two women dancing near me. They were dressed the same, for one thing, in black dresses with high lace collars close around their throats, one in gloves and the other with a hat and veil. Both were brunettes, heavily made up, one pale with powdered skin and bright red lips, the other dark with dark brows and a mouth that looked purple in this light. The pale girl was shockingly thin and taller than me. Her knees poked sharply through her fishnets. Her companion was heavy, with thick fleshy arms emerging from her sleeveless dress and a wide bottom half. But there was something else about them, something that held me. Then another woman wandered by, older and blond, and she too was wearing a high-necked black lace dress, a wide hat and a veil. They were dressed like Sibylline. Like my mother. Like me.

Wearing clothes similar to the clothes I'd lifted from my mother's closet, and with made-up faces reminiscent of Claire's attempts to hide my stubble, these women were bizarre caricatures of my own imposture of my mom. It gave me the creeps, frankly, and I turned quickly away, feeling paradoxically exposed, as if afraid they would somehow recognize me. As I tried to make my way across the dance floor, the whole room snapped into focus and I saw: The girls in the white dresses were Sasha, my half-vampire heroine. The men in the black suits carrying canes were impersonating Aram, the master vampire, while those in white wigs were acting as his rival, Faubourg St. Germaine. The sultry-looking women clad in tattered black were Ivy, high queen of the vampire world. And of course, the men in the black overcoats, with the collars turned up (like me!) were playing Jack Silver, the vampire hunter, who couldn't help giving his heart to young Sasha. I squinted at the card the security guy had handed me when I came in: "Vampyre Monday," it declared. "This week a salute to Sibylline Lorindo-Gold."

Now the panic attack came back for real, and while I tried to breathe deeply, inhaling perfume, sweat, and beer, I found myself fixated on their passing faces. Sheened in sweat from the lights, yelling over the noise, these girls and boys—with streaks and smears in their makeup, with ill-fitting suits and thrift store costumes, with pimples and bad haircuts, with stained armpits in their ball gowns and dandruff sparkling in the blue light—they all gathered here, a dark coven, drawn together by their shared regard for a badly selling trash horror series, and met, in a nondescript, boring bar on a dismal night, seeking not blood, or eternal unlife, or an evil Sabbath, but that most mysteriously mortal of our dark desires: simple connection with another human being.

When I got home that night I checked my email, nothing, then opened my buddy box. VampT3, the only buddy I had, was AWAY. On her vampire blog it said she was going out of town to visit friends for a while and would be off-line.

73

Townes called early the next morning. The results had finally come back: inconclusive. The lab guys all agreed with me, but there was no way to prove with certainty that a person in a still photo like this was dead. Fortunately, certain proof wasn't what we needed. It was Clay who was trying to use his mother's confession to reopen his own case. The expert testimony of the FBI photo lab was enough to tip the scales and convince the judge that Clay's new evidence wasn't sufficiently compelling. That evening we learned that his request had been denied and that the stay on his execution had been lifted. He would die after all.

It was a victory, but somehow the call just left me empty, and even Townes, who'd been laughing and toasting the night before, was subdued. I left Dani a message with the news. I checked the mail, puttered around, showered and shaved. Then in a sudden rush, as if answering an urgent request, I packed an overnight bag and hurried out to catch the subway into Penn Station, and then the train upstate.

I wasn't really sure why I was going to visit Clay again. He had never intended to write any book, and he had no reason to see me, now that his use for me was over and I had actually helped ensure his end. Nevertheless, I had a hunch he would talk to me, and I was right. His ego, his sense of himself as both the subject and the ultimate author of his own adventure demanded it. If no longer his writer, I was still his ghost, and now his only reader. But the story was incomplete and I wanted to know the end, even if it would remain unwritten.

So once again, I spent the night in a crappy hotel I could hardly afford, ate a damp club sandwich, slept badly with the sound of trucks rumbling outside. I loitered in the visitors' lounge, where I'd seen Flosky and where, who knows, her own lawyer might soon be visiting while she sat on death row. I bought a stale Snickers from the machine. And then they brought me in.

Clay looked older, thinner, grayer, but he didn't look scared or even unhappy.

"Hey!" he called out when he saw me, smiling broadly and raising his cuffed hands in greeting. Then he lounged back in his chair with his legs crossed, as if he were waiting for his after-dinner coffee, or perhaps chatting with Jay Leno, and it was only by whimsical choice that he had donned an orange jumpsuit for the occasion. He didn't seem particularly worried about dying, despite his decadelong struggle to live and the lengths he and his mother had gone to, nor did he seem upset that she was now quite possibly headed for death herself because of him. He didn't even seem upset with me. He seemed eager to chat.

He did make it clear: whatever he said would be of no use to me whatsoever. The contract was null and void, if it was ever really legal in the first place. He still denied everything publicly and had specifically announced, through his new public defender, that he was innocent and all stories to the contrary were lies. I had no tape recorder, no notes. Anything I wrote might as well be considered fiction.

I told him that I understood. So he talked and I listened. He talked until the guard came and said I had to leave.

74

The first thing I ever killed was a gerbil. Or a guinea pig. I forget the difference. One of the other foster kids had it. This girl Betsy. Mrs. Gretchen favored her. She preferred the girls in general because she said they were neater. Anyway Betsy got to have this gerbil or whatever. Hamster? That's it, this hamster in a glass tank with a wheel and cedar chips, with his little turds mixed in and one of those water bottles that it drank from with the little metal drip spout. Betsy was a brat. A bit older. I was seven or eight maybe. I'd been in foster care a couple of years. They all had their favorites. But it was never me. Well, some of the men liked me well enough. Still, Betsy could have let me play with it, let me pet it, but she never did.

Then one day she stayed after school, for a play rehearsal. They were doing *Annie*, I think. Mrs. Gretchen was drinking in the yard. Her boyfriend was at work. I snuck in and got the gerbil and started petting it, holding it in my lap. I still remember how soft it was, like putting your hand in a mink-lined glove and those black eyes like buttons. It's amazing to think they're seeing, isn't it? That a little mind of some sort, a little consciousness, is watching through those pinheads, thinking its little hamster thoughts? A little life, the same as yours, as everyone and everything. Isn't it difficult to conceive, really? I'll tell you how I picture it. Like a beach after the wave crashes and recedes back out. Whether it's the ocean itself, or a wave in the ocean, or a pool left behind in the sand, or just the drop inside a tiny shell, it's all the same thing, the same water. And I remember petting the hamster, Donny, I think she called it, and feeling that little heart beating so fast, and just squeezing tighter, and thinking about how much I hated Betsy, and then feeling those little bones crunch under my fingers, and then just squeezing till it stopped. Then I put it back in the cage, in its wheel. Then I went out and played. When she found it, everyone thought it'd had a heart attack running on its wheel. We buried it in the woods behind the house.

As you may know, or guess, by now, my mother and I never lost touch, at least not for long. She tracked me down and we began meeting in secret. An illicit romance. She'd take me for ice cream after school or I'd say I was seeing a movie with a friend and go with her. She even gave me the money for that first camera I bought. Of course she was still hustling, picking up men, taking them back to her room. Sometimes I'd wait outside, or once she got a small apartment and I'd wait in the kitchen. Sometimes I watched through a crack in the door. Things went on like that for a while until I was sixteen, I think. Or seventeen maybe, a senior in high school. My mother had this trick over and he was smacking her around. There was nothing new in that, frankly. She was very casual about nudity, needless to say, and she often had bruises that I noticed when she was dressing or getting out of the shower.

I think she liked it. I'd seen her getting hit by men, and how it turned her on. But this time it got out of hand. I heard her screaming and cursing and fighting back and something crashed. I opened the door and her nose was bleeding. This guy, a big guy, at least six feet and a couple hundred pounds, was punching her in the face, full strength. She flew across the room. She spit out blood. At first I was stunned. I didn't know what to do. I was still just a kid. Then he got his hands around her throat and started choking her, hard, shaking her like a doll, and I knew he would kill her. I saw her eyes and she looked at me and just gurgled. So I ran into the kitchen and got a knife, the big serrated bread knife, and without stopping to think, there was no time to think, I ran over and jumped on his back. It was like mounting a horse, and he reached behind to swat me, he must have been surprised that anyone was even there, but I just grabbed his hair and pulled his head back and ran the blade over his throat. He bled out like an ox. Flopping and shivering while I rode his back and my mother struggling under him. That was it. It was easy. The hard part was rolling that big moose off of her and then getting rid of the corpse. She had to shower his blood off while I mopped the floor. Then we chopped him up in the bathtub and took him out in bags. We put cinder blocks and bricks in the bags and sunk him in the river. We sold his watch and rings and credit cards.

After that it just grew. I spent more time with her and went to stay for good after I finished high school and got sprung from foster care. We were traveling around by then. All over. We'd both go out and pick people up—a bar, a park, a men's room—like two fishermen, whoever bagged one first, the other would trail along. Most times that was all that happened. She'd blow the guy or let him fuck her. Or I'd let some old fruit suck me off. Get paid and call it a night. Other times I just beat him up and took his cash, his jewelry, his cards. Or

I'd sneak in and knock her trick over the head. They never called the cops. How could they? Then sometimes it went further. I got good at it too. I remember cutting my first heart out and feeling it beat in my hand. I pulled a man's intestines out while he watched. He didn't look pained. He looked, well, kind of fascinated. Why, you want to know. Why one and not the other? That's what you want to ask me, I know, but all I can say is, wrong question. They were all the same to me. Just bodies. Bodies with eyes moving in them, and a beating heart, and a little brain teeming with thoughts. A few drops of blood, floating in an ocean of gore, an ocean of blood that has been coming and going in waves for an eternity. So what if I spill it back in or I don't and that body keeps moving for another few years? Just another drop, like rain over the ocean. Like the gerbil. Like me or you.

I lost my virginity when I was twenty. Late bloomer, I know. I was handsome but I was very shy and afraid to smile around girls because of my teeth. I stuttered a little and I'd always been awkward and poor. But then one night I was in a bar and this woman picked me up, she got me drunk, and we went to her place. She was older, like thirty-five or forty maybe, and she showed me what to do. She put it in for me. Told me to go faster, slower, harder. Told me it was OK to squeeze her breasts, squeeze them hard, to pull her hair, to smack her ass like the men did to my mother. She screamed like my mom screamed and I came. I told my mother and she said, Well you better go back and take care of her. She said maybe she'd get pregnant or track me down. She said bitches were even worse than men. She said never trust a woman. Aside from her. So I went back the next night and I knocked on her door and she smiled and let me in and we did it again, but this time when I put my hands around her neck I kept squeezing. I strangled her. I choked the life out of her while I was fucking her and I could feel it, I could feel her pussy contracting as she struggled and I banged her head against the wall and then she died. My mother was waiting in the car, or so I thought. But afterward I looked up and saw she was watching. She'd snuck in to make sure I didn't need help going through with it. We wrapped her in a blanket and she helped me get her into the car and we drove out to the country and buried her in the woods with lye, so that no one could find my DNA inside her.

I've fucked a lot of girls since then. Hundreds. I don't know how many. I got good at it. After that first time I wasn't shy anymore. I knew I could have them, so I just went right up and talked to them. Hookers a lot of times, sure, I didn't care. I'm the son of a whore. They got to eat too. But also college girls, married women, waitresses, girls in shops, moms watching their kids play in the park. Some turned me down, of course, but a lot say yes, believe me. They need it and they know I can give it to them. Most I didn't hurt. I left them happy. Every so often when one would rebuff me harshly or get on her high horse, I'd laugh and think, You don't know how close you just came. I'd laugh and walk away. I'd let her go. Or not. Who cares? I wasn't angry. That's not what this is about. I don't hate women. Why should I? Because of my mother? Nigger, please! That's what the black guys say in here to each other. I think it's from some show. Anyway, I've heard enough from shrinks about my mother. Yeah, she was fucked up. So what? The only thing I ever owned is my life, and she gave me that. I've never struck a person in anger except maybe that first guy, with the bread knife, but really even then I don't recall feeling angry, just numb, like I was in shock, which most likely means I was terrified. But after that, I didn't feel fear or anger. I simply felt alive. The way an artist feels when he's working. Perhaps the way you feel writing about your goblins. I became fascinated with the endless variety of nature, the infinite beauty and complexity of bodies.

Often, I've lingered over a perfect asshole, that hidden cleft tucked within the crease of the round ass, sometimes a pale pink, sometimes a deep rose, like a tight bud ready to open, sometimes almost purple, like a plum tucked inside a peach. So delicate, so carefully brushed on, like blush. I've heard all the sounds bodies make, in pleasure, in pain. Sometimes you can't tell one from the other. I've seen their eyes roll up into their heads. I've smelled their perfume and their hair. Other times though, I would be equally amazed carving up some fat man, spilling his guts like a sack of offal, wading into him almost, with my tools, unloading his organs like a battered old pig-hide suitcase. I saw what he had for dinner, peas and carrots. Then in the cold, my breath fogging under a three-quarters moon, I went and dug a hole until the back of my neck ran with sweat. I buried his mess and by dawn was eating breakfast in a truck stop. Steak and eggs. That was West Virginia, I think. The Smokies at dawn with the mist burning off the mountaintops and then creeping away down the valleys like those invasive Japanese vines. That day I drove to Kentucky. Very pretty. Very green. A really deep shade we don't get here. Ohio to me was brick houses, old trees and the river. I worked for a bit in a convenience store, the night shift. I didn't care and that's a job you can always get. My mother picked up men in the bar, fucked them in hotels while I worked. One night I met a girl with eyes like jade, really, that milky green. At least it looked that way to me when she came in for a pack of Newports and some kind of chips. Doritos, maybe. Or Cheeze Doodles. I remember that orange dust on her fingers and her lips. Funyuns. Her hair was copper blond. She sucked an iced cherry slush through a straw. She had a smattering of freckles across a button nose and a tattoo of a chain around her ankle that she showed me by, with admirable flexibility, thumping her sneakered foot atop my counter. She had great cheekbones and a fetching gap between her teeth that embarrassed her; she laughed at my witticisms behind her hand. After my shift I went to her trailer. Fucked her mouth and cunt willingly, her ass against her will, and against her wall as well, with my hands around her throat. I hung her from the shower and cut those pretty eyes out. Then I went home and found my mother under some grunting lug in tube socks, her nails dug knuckle-deep into that white flab. I slipped in quietly and checked his wallet. He was loaded. A truck driver who'd just delivered and been paid. So I sunk the claw end of a hammer into his skull. It was, as they say, quite a night. In Mexico I sliced up two hookers that I picked up in a bar outside of Tijuana. Both had high round asses and low round breasts. Indian faces, like a Mayan stone. One had green eyes though, darker and brighter than the white Ohio girl's. The other had gold front teeth. I tied one up and made her watch while I used the other, cut her eyelids off so that she couldn't look away. It was hot, and by the time I was done I'd stripped down, naked and covered in blood. Drinking tequila while flies licked my back. I waded out in the ocean with their dismembered corpses in some bags, let them go with the tide, and then splashed around in the surf under the moon. I felt great and I recall that next morning, the butter-flies, the monarchs arrived. Have you ever seen that? A vast nation of moving orange flowers, flying down from northern California to die on their ancient land. Creatures too small to have brains, too short-lived to have memories, and yet they remember this, a homecoming to a place they've never been. They'd cover a whole tree, fluttering like leaves, like a bush of blinking eyes. Extraordinary. The coast of Michoacan in fall. In Los Angeles that year, I met a pregnant woman with a belly like a melon in her skirt. Can you believe she wanted me still? A rich man's wife. I let her live. Why not? I sent her home to hubby. She climbed into her Mercedes and drove off, blowing me a kiss. She left me laughing. In Albuquerque they overcooked my steak. I followed the waiter home and knocked him unconscious. He woke up as I was nailing him to the floor. I can't abide an overcooked piece of meat. I killed an old man in Denver. He was a bum, sleeping, drunk on the side of a road, under an overpass, stinking of wine and piss. I stopped and I cut his throat and I went. In Minneapolis a hooker named Cookie, with a C-section scar across her gut. In Memphis a couple of married swingers, tanned and waxed and buff. People are much too uptight about the human body, don't you think? Whatever their age, race, or size, I wish they could learn to appreciate the beauty of their bodies, like I do. And the inner beauty too. Have you ever seen a liver? That purplish brown, the sheen. A spray of fresh blood. The pink organs nestled in their warmth. People are horrified, nauseated by entrails, and I admit the aroma is a bit rich and takes some getting used to, but if you can set aside your preconceived notions, really the inside of a human being is quite pretty.

I'm glad we're both from Queens. Did you know Queens is really an island? Part of Long Island. I like that idea, like a kingdom unto itself. But less showy about it than Manhattan. Even though I traveled all over the country, I knew I wanted to end up back there. It's home. Home to the world. I miss the food. Amazing isn't it? Argentinean, Colombian, Chinese, Korean, Malaysian, Indian, Greek, Italian, all shoulder to shoulder. Compared to the city it feels slower, warmer, like a small town, and yet now I feel like it is the real New York, all that is left of that city we both knew growing up. Real estate developers, yuppies, Eurotrash millionaires, and trust fund snotnoses: if I had to do it all again, that's who I'd kill. You know, as a one-man crime wave, I might have single-handedly kept rents low, scared the rich off, and thereby saved Western culture. There'd be a statue of me in Astor Place. Oh well. Anyway, I don't have to tell you about Queens. You still live there, in your dead mother's apartment. Yes, I know all about you. I read your vampire literature and the crime novels. The one where the black fellow, your hero, Jeremiah Johnson, is it? Mordechai Jones, yes, the one where he tracks a serial killer who's harvesting all of the top pimp's women. Quite amusing. Though I prefer the sci-fi ones, that other planet with the sex slaves and fuckbots and such. Those are fun. I even had my mother follow you for a while, before you met officially of course, before I wrote you my fan letter. She told me you have quite the eye for the ladies yourself: that little one who follows you around, Claire is it? I hope Mom didn't hurt her too badly. She has a problem with women, like I said, especially young attractive ones. And then you also bagged our mutual friend Dani. I must say I am jealous of you there. She and I corresponded for a while and I was quite impressed. That girl has potential.

Where was I? Oh yes, the photos. The endgame. My downfall and my final, fatal girlfriends. The Queens princesses. Though I suppose in a way it was art that doomed me, not women. I never got over that itch, and it crept into my work. I'm sure you've considered how individual development is like a metonym of the history of art itself: from the infant messing about with feces, to savages finger painting with berry juice and charcoal on a cave wall, to Michelangelo floating on his back coloring the roof of heaven. Well, on a far humbler level of course, that was I. All that fooling with blood and guts, at first just butchery, I admit, it was the killing that thrilled me. Then I started wanting to create instead of just destroy, I guess, or to create through destroying. I wanted to make beauty too, you see. I worked with eyes, hair, hands, fingers and feet. I came to understand skin and what it can do. The largest and strangest of our organs. To appreciate and love the stomach, the lungs, the intestines. To know them, if you'll pardon the pun, inside out, like any craftsman understands stone or wood or clay.

Back home in Queens I decided to make some more permanent work, on film. I didn't plan to kill these models at all. I was going to simply shoot a portfolio, make normal pictures. Well, relatively. So I posted ads for models in the schools, at work, in the local papers, even shot a few. Basic stuff. Then that one girl answered. Nancy something, yes. That sounds right. I remember in the papers she was described as the quiet type, a good girl who lived at home. Well, sorry, folks, not quite. Remember I was still young and pretty then and I'd sharpened my charm, like all of us vampires must. At first she was nervous and we shot some fairly bland stuff. But a bottle of wine later, we did some nudes. Two bottles, and I was going down on her till she moaned and shook. After that she'd do anything I asked, stand on her head with flowers in her ass. Then Mom came home. Well, like I said, she doesn't trust women. And you know how it is when they get going. My God. I bet your mother was like that. Relentless with the nagging. How could I bring a stranger in our home? And a stupid slutty bitch as well. She was a danger, a liability, blah, blah. Finally I slit her throat just to shut her up. The girl's throat I mean, not Mom's. Though who knows, maybe I made the wrong choice. Know what I mean? Anyway, the rest is art history. I'd found my project. My work. I had to keep going till they caught me, like all artists. And I had to make sure that somehow my work lived on, even if only in a file in a police station basement. It will find its way, like all art does, like undiscovered paintings, unpublished novels, unsold poems. As long as it gets made, then it will live. Don't you agree?

Have I ever known love? Why not? Who says I didn't love that jade-eyed tattoo girl in Ohio? Or one of those Mexican whores? The one on the left. Maybe I loved them all in my way. After all, who else thinks of them now but me? Or perhaps in the end I love only my work. But that's the choice we make, right? The artist's choice. What are other people to us?

Material. The stuff of our work. Whom do we love more, the girl or the portrait, the thing we've made of her? We artists, we're not quite human, are we? We love no one. Nor do we hate. Does the hurricane hate the tree it snaps? Do tigers love or hate the creatures they rip to pieces? And when the tiger slows, and his teeth dull and he dies, who weeps? We artists live and die alone.

What gives me the right to do as I do? Nature itself, who creates and destroys, who creates by destroying, and who endows me with these desires. I am nature, that is all. Nature values the maggots that eat the flesh as much as the rotting saint. The only limits are those we humans impose, and why? If they are demanded by the majority, that is to say the weak, it is to protect themselves from the strong, a herd of sheep banded together against the wolf. The only law that a free, intelligent and reasonable person obeys is his own desire, and the only limit he accepts is that of his power to live that desire out. Do I regret my crimes now? Of course not. I am completely content. To be tried and punished, these are no hardships for me. In the old days criminals dressed for the gallows as though they were going to their own weddings, and the crowd threw flowers and cheered. To be publicly executed for our crimes is the highest honor that our society can bestow. Aren't we humans killers first of all? Each day we are wiping out whole species, destroying the very planet, using up our own sources of life, until through our own deeds, we erase ourselves from the world. And so what? Life will go on. The planet will not miss us.

And now we come to our little partnership, for there is one regret that I must admit: I wish I had done even more. This is the only boundary that nature herself imposes on us, the limitations on what we can accomplish, in space and time, with one body and one life. Perhaps even you know this feeling. You are with your girlfriend, your lover, that Jane perhaps or our mutual friend Dani, and you have fucked her once or twice, and you are lying there, exhausted, spent, musing like Socrates after he's buggered a few boys, and you see her bend over perhaps to get a cigarette from her purse or else go to sit sweetly on the toilet in the moonlight, and when she returns your desire for her returns too, and you want to possess her again, but you cannot. You are empty, finished, done. This is the only frustration, the only torment, that a man like me can know, for my imagination drives my desire beyond the capacities of my body, while the pleasure of my senses inflames my imagination in turn, so that from one to the next, desire to thought, philosophy to pornography, there is an endless cycle. But luckily, even here, there is a way out. If the Lover becomes an Artist, then there is no limit to how far his desire can range and whom he can reach. He can inflame the minds of others to enact the deeds he could never in a dozen lives accomplish, and by infecting generations he can multiply his desires forever through time. Think of all the words you wrote. Think of all the minds you touched, the dreams you implanted, the desires you lit. Who knows what loves and what crimes you inspired? What else is writing for? Literature is nothing more or less than an attempt to fuck the whole world up the ass. Here's a poem: I wish this page were a razor and you all had one throat.

75

After the interview, I hurried back to my hotel and, without benefit of a tape recorder, wrote down, as close as I could, a verbatim record of what he had said. I filled page after page of a yellow legal pad with my scrawl until my hand ached, and by the time I finished, it was dark. Then I checked out, paid for my room, and took the last train back to the city.

As for the veracity of what he told me, who knows? Is it possible that he really killed so many more people than anyone even accused him of, dozens at least, on a cross-country death trip that went on for over a decade? I suppose it is. After all, when someone is convicted of, say, stealing a car, we assume it is only one of many the person stole, and if his record shows five, we guess it was really fifty or a hundred. It is an unspoken element in our morality of punishment, this idea that the career criminal, by the time he gets caught, has already done more damage than we can know. This might be even more true of a serial killer. After all, a professional car thief, a bank robber, a drug addict, a man who beats his wife: all these have clear patterns, motives and methods that make it almost certain they will eventually be caught. But a psychopath who kills for no reason, or no reason we can fathom, who chooses his victims randomly, or lets fate decide, and wanders the country aimlessly, burying and sinking bodies wherever he goes—the hard truth is that it is only by luck that such a person is ever caught, and unless he confesses, it is hard to be sure which crimes to even hang from his name.

It's chilling, in this light, to consider all the people who go missing, thousands each year in this county alone. The husbands and wives who can't stand any more and take off, storming away after a fight or just popping out for a pack of smokes and never coming back. The parents who abandon their families, delinquent dads, moms who dump their babies at a hospital or on the steps of a church. The choked workers who commute back and forth to their jobs for years and then one day just skip the exit and drive until they run out of gas. The debtors escaping their bad names. The heartbroken lovers hoping to forget and be forgotten, to float off and drown in the crowd. The addicts, the drunks, the gamblers and the perverts, hiding out from themselves. All those runaway kids, armies of them, heading like pilgrims from whatever toward whatever, vanishing into our cities, our nights. We assume that they all chose to disappear, driven on by their own demons. But what if it was another kind of demon who disappeared them? What if they were not lost but found?

On the other hand, maybe he was full of shit. I have tried, where I could, to check the particulars of his statements where he mentions a place or event, and in some cases they do match up with accounts I found in newspapers or other public records: A couple found dead after a home invasion in Memphis. A missing girl, never found, who had freckles and green eyes. Then again, Clay could have checked these same sources as easily as I did and simply woven them into his story. He had plenty of free time. Perhaps he was taking credit for other people's crimes, to boost his own profile, to assure his place in history, to have a last joke on us and leave a confession that was really only another cryptic false lead, a red herring. Or maybe just to fuck with me.

The same goes for his philosophizing, if that's what you want to call it, his theorizing and self-analysis. His grand views of Art and Life and Death. Again, he had all the time in the world to construct his arguments and work out those suspiciously solipsistic and self-serving ideas. Who knows if that is really what he thought and felt while killing, or if it was all an attempt, undertaken long after the fact, to add a veneer, a coat of intellectual and aesthetic polish, to the senseless rampage of a madman? Remember, despite his claims to deep learning and artsy sensibilities, it was only in prison that he read, thought, studied. At the time he began his crime spree, he was a semiliterate ward of the state who had barely completed high school. With the education in brutality he received, he was well prepared, even groomed, for sex crime and murder and not much else. He was like a rare species bred in a hothouse: the American maniac.

And it is from this angle that I want to consider his other assertion, his supposed commonality with other writers and artists, and with art and literature, including my own minor efforts. Despite everything he said, one small but essential difference remains: he is a total nut job. And that is his blind spot.

He admits to being evil and immediately mobilizes his extremely powerful mind to demolish the moral system that makes him evil, but he never for a moment questions his own sanity. What he can't see is that madness can be rational, organized, systematic, even brilliant. Insanity can make perfect sense, as for example in paranoia, a closed system that admits no outside reality or objective truth: anyone who doubts me is part of the conspiracy, hence I can never be talked out of my beliefs. Similarly, Clay might be hyperintelligent, and I don't doubt that his IQ is higher than mine, but nevertheless there is this crack, this fundamental derangement, that prevents him from doing what I, for example, manage however humbly to do: actually write something. As a writer, Clay produced only those few letters and nothing else. As an artist, he created a handful of horrifying photographs and a bunch of other very ordinary ones.

Not that writers and artists can't be nuts. We all know that. Perhaps most of them are, to some extent. Art is an inherently cockeyed enterprise. But the part that writes is, I believe, the sane part, the part that strives to rescue the world from oblivion, life from death, by getting it all down on paper. And what is that wish to save everything and bring everyone along with us, good and bad together? What is that but love? And those of us who write genre books, with our detectives and killers, our vampires and aliens—perhaps this is why we return to the same story again and again, like children clutching a favorite, jelly-stained book: to retell the tale over until it's finally right; to keep adding new rooms to the house we built for our thoughts to live in, returning each morning with a fresh armful of sadness from the haunted woods; creating that doll-chain of pages, that endlessly forking tree, that toy city of books inhabited by ghosts, that obsession in the shape of a story, the series.

By the time we hit the city, I'd exhausted myself with these thoughts. As the train slid through the back alleys and tunnels, I found my mind slipping, back in time, to childhood. Not mine, Clay's. Half-consciously, I turned to the page where he'd told me about his origin, his first kill. The gerbil. Hamster. Whatever. It bothered me in a way that I couldn't place. That frantic wheel kept spinning in my head, going nowhere. Those little bones snapping like pretzels between my teeth. I woke up with a headache in Penn Station, one of my sweaty hands gripping the other.

I changed for the subway, and when we broke ground and emerged across the river, it was dark out and I had a message on my phone. It was Jane. She and the husband had been talking. They'd very much like to publish an excerpt of my Clay book in the next issue of *The Torn Plaid Coat*, maybe even make it the centerpiece of a special issue on crime, organize a reading, a party, the works. And although it sounded like I had a great manager already, they'd mentioned my book to their own agents and editors and they were eager to see it too. Weren't we all?

The prospect of going home to my lonely couch and my haunted apartment filled me with dread, and when I saw Morris still sweeping up his shop, I ran to bang on the window. He let me in but declined my desperate plea to buy him a drink.

"No offense, but drinking with you and those straight people is a bad influence on me," he said. "Anyway, I have plans with Gary. And no, you can't come. But here, this might cheer you up."

He handed me a bunch of beautiful irises.

"It's my new project. Home-grown. I raised and planted them right in my backyard." He handed them over with a smile.

"Genius . . . ," I mumbled.

"Really?"

"Genius." I grabbed him and, standing on tiptoes, I kissed him on both cheeks.

"You're welcome," he shouted, as I ran out, waving my purple bouquet. Rushing down the sidewalk toward home, I got my phone out and called Townes. He was gone for the day.

"It's urgent. An emergency. I mean it."

They dithered but put me through and at last he got on the line. A TV droned in the background and I heard dinner sounds, silverware and plates and clinking glass.

"Yeah, what?"

"Townes," I yelled, as if trying to reach him without a phone. "I got it. I know where he buried the heads."

76

As soon as we got off the phone, Townes dispatched units to secure the area, and by dawn the digging had begun. Agent Terence and another man picked me up, and after a quick run to Dunkin' Donuts, we arrived to find the street blocked off by cop cars parked sideways, their red lights rotating in silence. Vans and more black government Impalas filled the street, and a backhoe was idling nearby. Big lights flooded the house and yard, throwing the woods into stark relief. The chaos had woken the neighbors, who came out to watch, lining up on their porches and driveways, as if the circus had come to town and decided to set up across the street. As the cops waved us through, I saw the young mother from my last visit, standing beside her Volvo, staring at the run-down house across the street, the one she always knew was haunted. Now she would learn by whom.

We parked and got out. There was a predawn chill in the air. Agents in black coats, uniformed cops and forensics people in white paper space suits all gathered around our car, grabbing coffees, mixing milk and sugar from the pile we laid on the hood, and rooting in the giant box of doughnuts, which was warmed by the still-cooking engine.

The door to the house opened and Townes appeared, lured perhaps by the smell of coffee. He nodded to me but spoke to his agents first, muttering in low tones, then came over as they dispersed.

"I've been talking to the foster mother, Gretchen," he said, pulling a coffee from the cardboard carrier and lifting the plastic top. Steam spilled up.

"Yeah?"

He flapped two sugar packs and poured them into his coffee, then added two creams. He took a long sip, sucking the hot coffee over the rim, and put the top back on. He sighed.

"She's barely coherent, but yes, Clay came around now and again, to visit and look in on her. Helped with the mortgage sometimes too."

"That's suspicious," I said, "considering that he hated her guts."

"Yeah, and that her ex-boyfriend got arrested for child abuse."

"Where's he?"

"Dead from lung cancer fifteen years ago."

"You think she knew what Clay was up to?"

He shrugged. "Probably not. We're taking her in for a full interrogation, but I figure it's more like she didn't want to know. Easier to just drink her gin and watch *The Price Is Right*." He glanced at me. "And keep the blinds down when Clay said he was going to work in the yard."

"What? She said that?"

"Yeah. Helping out around the yard."

"But it wouldn't be the yard, I don't think. The woods. That's where he said they buried the gerbil or whatever. That's the spot he photographed. That's his place."

"Yeah. I know. Come see."

As we made our way between the vehicles, another agent rushed up and whispered to Townes, gesturing toward the steadily growing crowd behind the tape. Reluctantly, the gawkers parted as some cops escorted a small party to the front. It was the families: Mr. Hicks, the Jarrels, and John Toner, all blinking and gazing around them as if suddenly woken from a deep sleep.

"Just a sec," Townes said. He took a big gulp of coffee and went over. He held each of their hands in turn, giving the men a firm pump, Mrs. Jarrel a kindly squeeze. They huddled around him, and as they whispered together, one by one they stole a glance at me. Mr. Jarrel blinked blankly, with the same fish-eyed stare as before. Hicks nodded and I nodded back. Mrs. Jarrel stared right at me and then smiled, sweetly, and lifted her fingers in a little wave. I smiled and waved back, with an unaccountable feeling of gratitude. Toner alone avoided my gaze, as if out of embarrassment after our last encounter. He focused on Townes and kept jotting in a small notebook, until his cell rang and he turned away to answer. Townes returned, nodding to me, and as I followed him across the street, I saw Dani, on the other side of the crowd, standing alone. I raised my hand in a wave, but she didn't acknowledge me. She remained completely still, as if seeing right through my skin.

"Come on," Townes said. "This way."

We trooped through the gate, and once again I passed the overgrown bushes, the rotting Buick, the shuttered, sinking house, all of it now swarming with people in blue windbreakers and surgical gloves, poking, wiping, peering at who knows what. In the backyard, a section of the fallen fence had been removed and another strip of red tape was strung across it. A cop nodded and lifted it for us as we stepped through.

The woods were still dark. Light was entering slowly, shifting sideways through the trees or falling from above, where it was split and filtered by the leaves. It touched one shadow at a time, revealing it in turn as a branch, a stone, a shining face, a hand. The technicians who were digging still had their flashlights and helmet lamps burning. They moved and worked as if attached to the earth by these beams, which they switched off one by one, as the air grew brighter. They'd marked off the woods and the small meadow with tape in a kind of grid, with little flags waving and numbered plastic stakes. The air around us buzzed with static and constant radio chatter.

After that, nothing happened. We waited. The sun rose and it was full day. I took off my jacket. Agents kept coming up to whisper with Townes, and his radio and cell kept buzzing, causing him, each time, to stick a finger in one ear and yell into the device, but mostly he just stood there like me. He finished his coffee and looked for a place to throw the cup. Finally he gave it to an agent passing by with a plastic bag full of excavated dirt. After another hour he looked at me and shrugged.

"What do you think?"

I shrugged back. "I don't know." I hesitated, looking around, and then lowered my voice. "Listen, I have to pee."

He frowned. "Can't you hold it?"

"I'd rather not." In fact I'd had to go since I arrived, but there was no chance of ducking behind a tree without stumbling over the FBI.

Townes sighed. "I guess go in the house," he said. "We can't have any accidents."

"Ha. Ha. Is she there?"

"Who, the foster mom? No. She's downtown."

"OK. I'll be right back."

"Yeah. Take your time."

I walked back the way we'd come, carefully stepping around the marked ground, and went through the fence into the yard. If this property had once had the childish aura of a ghost house, then like most scary places it now seemed small and sad in the grown-up light of day. Still, the idea of going inside made me slightly nervous, and I hesitated on the rear steps, my hand on the rusty knob. I peeked through a dusty back window to check for the dog.

Then I heard a commotion in the woods. Nothing too loud, just a general rise in the radio buzz and the movement around the yard, but it was enough for me to know they had found something. I turned and ran back, through the fence, through the trees, to where all the cops and agents were now gathered around like the crowd of curious onlookers who needed to be held back. I elbowed my way forward and found Townes.

"Townes," I shouted. He looked over his shoulder and waved me up. The others let me by.

He was standing over a trench, a few feet deep, in which agents in coveralls and white booties were carefully digging, using brushes and pans and tiny knives, as if they were treasure hunters excavating an ancient ruin.

"You found something?" I asked. He just pointed at the ground. They'd struck gold. A tooth and an earring. Both were crusted with dirt and lying on a white cloth while photographers shot away. You could still see the white root where the tooth had been attached to the jaw. The earring was a thin, dangling fan of yellow lace.

"Can't say yet about the tooth, of course," Townes told me. "But that earring. I know the description better than my wife's engagement ring. It belonged to Janet Hicks."

They kept working, inch by inch, while we all stood watching, and half an hour later, they found the first head. It emerged slowly. At first someone noticed just a few thin hairs. Carefully, they combed them out, separating each strand from the dirt. Then came the top of a skull, a cracked white dome, like a dinosaur egg sleeping under the ground. A heavyset man, wearing thick glasses in black frames and looking comical in his white feetsy pajamas and shower cap, knelt down and brushed it off with a sable paintbrush. With a dental tool he dug around it. He leaned over and blew. Five minutes later, the skull was clear up to the eyes, the empty sockets peeking at us over the soil. Something gleamed.

"Here's that other earring," he said. He leaned back and let the cameras whirl, then went on, brushing off the cheekbones, cleaning the hole that was once her nose.

"Over here," called a woman who was crouched a few feet away.

Until then, I'd thought she was a man. She looked as shapeless as her colleague in a matching white space suit, white booties, white hair bag and goggles. But when she pulled off the goggles and looked up at Townes, I realized she was really a small freckled girl in her twenties. "Another skull," she said.

Over the next hour, they unearthed three human skulls in all. They were buried in a triangular formation, surrounding the skeleton of what the experts insisted was a guinea pig, not a gerbil or hamster, and a cat as well.

"Did Clay mention a cat?" Townes asked me. We stood side by side, staring.

"No."

"Maybe he forgot. He's got a lot of bodies to remember."

"No. He doesn't forget."

"No," he agreed. It was something to say. We were all just standing and looking at the three heads. Once these were people, with faces, and behind the faces, thoughts. Now they were empty, like broken china, cracked bowls out of which the brains and blood had flowed, with holes that had seen or smelled or breathed. Three jawbones grinned at us, about to laugh. One, with a few gold molars, belonged to Nancy Jarrel, Townes guessed. He knew the dental records by heart. One had what, despite the dirt and cracking, must have once been a dazzling set of white teeth. Dora Giancarlo. Dani's twin. Townes said she had had no cavities. Miss Perfect.

The scene was quiet now. People moved around, spoke in low tones, the cameras whirred. No one said what we were all wondering. Where was the fourth head?

"Did you go deep enough there?" Townes asked, pointing a few feet away. The heavyset guy in the bunny suit shrugged. "It's rock under there, sir. No way he could have dug that without dynamite or a jackhammer."

Townes nodded, hands in his pockets. Another hour went by, and still three heads stared at us, a meager crop that, having been planted so many years ago, was finally ready for harvest. We'd been waiting all this time, for just this revelation, but now that it was here, the empty sockets and leering mouths offered no answers, only questions. Why us? Why not you? They had no wisdom to offer except the one fact we all know already, the obvious stupid truth: everybody dies. Everyone, they said, ends up like us. Here in the skull orchard, the bone yard, the garbage hole, the vacant lot, the dump.

77

Townes went to talk to the families. They were still digging, but he'd more or less given up hope of finding another head that day and the experts were busy bagging the evidence for transport back to the lab. Ahead was the long work of identifying and investigating, reconstructing through forensics as much of the narrative as they could. Townes would need DNA from the relatives, and at least one of the families was also faced with the prospect of finding out that their loved one remained unfound. I saw Dani, still by herself, and told Townes I'd talk to her.

When I waved her over, the cop at the barricade let her right in, as if I were some kind of deputy, and neither of us could help smiling a little at this, my promotion from contemptible muckraker, to murder suspect, to junior G-man, now that it was all over anyway and didn't matter.

"You found them," she said immediately.

"They found three. One is missing. They'll need DNA to tell who. But I think . . ."

"You think what?"

"Never mind."

"What? You can tell me."

"It sounds weird, and if I'm wrong it will just make it harder. But I feel like I saw your sister."

Dani smiled. She squeezed my hand quickly and let it go. She cleared her throat and I realized, when she spoke, that she was choked up.

"So what do I do?" she asked. "To give the sample?"

"They'll drive you over to the lab. Or you can go down yourself. I can come with you." I touched her shoulder. "It doesn't have to be right now."

"I'm fine," she said. "I could use a drink of water."

"Let's go in the house."

"No. I'm fine. Don't bother."

"Don't be silly. It's no bother," I said, guiding her through the gate. "To be honest, I'm desperate to use the bathroom."

We climbed up onto the creaky porch and opened the door. I held it for her, but she shook her head.

"You first," she said. "It's creepy."

"It is creepy, right?" I said, walking in. The place was filthy and smelled like dog shit. There were newspapers stacked around a recliner patched with duct tape and a TV tray covered with pill bottles. Someone had been busy dying in here. It was like a tomb. We went into the kitchen. Empty gin bottles were lined up on the drain board, like she was into recycling. A free Chinese restaurant calendar hung from a nail above the sink, still showing April. I rinsed a glass and filled it.

"Thanks," she said, frowning, and took a skeptical sip. Just then the little dog padded in and I flinched involuntarily, but he didn't even bother to bark now.

"Hey, look," Dani said, and knelt to pet him. He licked her hand, gave me a dismissive look, and disappeared back into the house. "You know what's weird?" she asked me.

"Everything."

"Yeah, but in particular. Why wouldn't Clay bury that head with the others? It's not like him to be random. If you know what I mean."

"I do," I said. I thought about how that was the weird thing, how we'd all come to know each other so well in this short, weird time. How long had it been? Six weeks?

"Hey," I said. "When we got shot at, out in Brooklyn?"

"Yeah. It rings a bell."

"What date was that?"

"Date?"

"Yeah. Do you know?"

"The fourteenth of May."

"How can you be so sure?"

"Because I got my period the next day, and I was worried. It was late."

"Oh," I said. I raised my eyes to hers, but she glanced away. I went to the calendar on the wall. I counted under my breath, tracing my finger up and down the dates. Dani looked at me, dubiously. "It wasn't Flosky who shot at us," I told her.

"What? Why not?"

"Because she was upstate. In court. Arguing for Clay, remember?"

"Fuck," Dani said.

"Yeah. Fuck is right."

"Who do you think it was, then? Who else wants you dead?"

I thought it over. "No one really cares that much."

She rolled her eyes, like Claire would. "Seriously, it has to be someone else who didn't want that case solved. Someone else was afraid of what we might dig up."

"That's it. You got it." I grabbed her hand without thinking and she didn't pull away.

"What did I get, Harry?" She looked excited.

"You said dig up. Someone didn't want us to dig up the heads and see that there were only three. When we know who's missing, we'll know who shot at me."

She took her hand back and started pacing. "Who do you think it is?"

"I pick Toner. Husband Number One."

"You think his wife is the one missing? Why? Just because he doesn't like you? Don't be so touchy." She laughed, and I wished I could take her hand again.

"Scoff if you want," I said, "but maybe that's why he hates me. He did everything he could to stop me from the start."

"But why? What is he hiding?" Now she sat on the table, cross-legged, and I began pacing the floor.

"Think about it," I said. "Maybe the reason Clay didn't bury her head was that he didn't kill her. He never even mentions her. Just the other three. But he did say he wasn't going to kill them at first. He only did that because his mother caught him and nagged him into it. He said he shot a couple before his mom found out."

"Shot a couple of girls?"

"No, I mean with a camera," I said. "Hold on." I couldn't wait anymore. I went into the bathroom and shut the door halfway. Finally, relief. "Look," I yelled, "how come there were no postmortem photos of her? Just living ones? The cops said because she was last, but what if she was the first? He was working there, meets her, she's a wannabe actress, he has no intention of killing these models so he has no reason to worry about the connection, maybe it will even butter her up, get him in with the boss, so he shoots her. Photographs her, I mean. Then the murders start. Later, Toner sees the news, the warnings, the sketch, watch out for a photographer trying to recruit pretty girls, in Queens." I flushed and quickly washed my hands. There was no towel so I dried them on my pants. "He puts it together, he sees his chance to get rid of the wife he's sick of or who he married just for her money. So he kills her, copies the MO he read about in the paper. Chops her up. And it's done. Everything is good until I come along." I opened the door and stepped back into the kitchen. "Is that crazy? What do you think?"

"I think you're a fucking pain in the ass," Toner said. He was standing behind Dani, with one hand over her mouth and the other pressing a gun to her head. She blinked at me. The little dog stood in the doorway blinking too. He sniffed Toner's shoe and Toner nudged him away.

"Hey," I said, putting my hands out. "Come on."

"Come on what?" Toner asked. "I fucking warned you. I practically begged you. Jesus, it's your own fault."

"Look, this place is crawling with cops. You can't get away with it. It's over."

"No. It was over. You dug it up. Now when I bury you, it will be over again."

Dani stared at me, pleadingly, like Claire had. Her eyes teared up. The poodle settled down on the linoleum between Toner and me, listening intently.

"They'll know your wife's head isn't there," I said. "They'll figure it out."

"Sure. And they'll assume Clay just buried her someplace else, or fucking made an ashtray out of it. Who knows? He's a goddamn nut. Without you bugging the shit out of everyone, they'll have no reason to work the rest out. And if they do, it will take months. I've got enough socked away. I can leave the country. The only thorn left in my ass is you. And the stripper here. So open that door there, and turn on the light."

"Listen . . . ," I began, though I had nothing to say.

"Do it." He pressed the gun hard against her skull. Her tears ran into his hand. I did what he said. I opened the door and found a switch. There was a staircase to the basement and a dim hanging bulb. The dog immediately dashed down and began exploring the steps.

"Now go down," Toner said. "Very carefully."

Hands up, I made my way downstairs, trying not to trip over the dog. It was a small square room of crumbling concrete with a dirt floor. It was musty, and despite the warm day, it was chilled. There was a boiler and pipes and some stacks of junk that if you knew to look you realized had once belonged in a darkroom. There was a heavy black curtain over the stairs that Toner drew as he came down, pushing Dani before him. She had one arm bent behind her and her face was red. For the first time since I'd met her, she looked scared.

"See," Toner said. "Nice and private. No one will hear a thing."

There was a flicker, like a silver fish in a pond, and before I had time to register what she was doing, Dani's arm came out from behind her back. Her switchblade was in her hand. The blade flashed out and she cut Toner across the arm that was holding her mouth. Toner grunted and pulled his arm away, and Dani screamed for help.

I charged toward them, trying for the gun hand, and then there was another, much brighter flash, and the booming sound of a shot echoed in the small room. The dog yipped loudly and ran up and down the steps. Dani gasped and slumped between us, as if Toner and I were both helping to hold her up. I didn't know where she was hit or where the gun was. Toner tried to push free. Dani's head rolled on my shoulder and I felt her press the knife in my hand.

The gun fired again. This time I heard the bullet ring as it hit the boiler. Now Dani moaned softly as if she were crying in her sleep. I gripped the knife and with my other hand I dug my way through the grappling limbs, pushing past Dani's limp body toward Toner. It all happened very slowly, like trying to budge on a packed subway. I felt the dog brush my feet. I found Toner's chest. Then with all my strength, I pushed the blade in, past his open sport coat, through his blue dress shirt, into his skin and the flesh and bone underneath. He grunted sharply, like a bark, and struggled, bucking against us. I leaned in harder. Blood squirted out, hitting my face, and he squirmed away. Dani slipped free and crumpled to the floor. Blood streamed from her neck and the dog jumped up on her chest and began to lap it up, in short quick licks, like from a fountain.

I forced my way forward, over Dani, and now Toner and I were face to face. He looked right at me, an inch or two away, and his gaze just seemed curious, surprised, whether by me or by death I can't say. Blood rolled down my forearms and seeped between our clothes. My fingers were slippery and I had to grip the knife hard. I looked back into his eyes and saw the last light leave them as they went still. Then I drove the knife all the way in, right up to the handle. I stabbed him straight through the heart.

PART FIVE

Epilogue: July 9, 2009

78

We sat in a kind of theater, on bleacher seats, staring at a window in a cinder block wall painted green. Beyond the glass hung drapes of the thick fabric type I associate with chain hotels. Back there, Darian Clay was being prepared for death.

Lethal injection is a four-step process. Strapped down, with sensors attached to his chest, he would have two needles inserted into his veins, one as a backup, and connected to long tubes. At first a saline solution would be fed through, to keep the lines open. Then, when the warden gave the signal, the drapes would be pulled. Next, Clay would be injected with sodium thiopental, an anesthetic, which would put him to sleep. Then flows pancuronium bromide, which paralyzes the entire muscle system and stops his breathing. Finally, the flow of potassium chloride stops the heart. Death is from anesthetic overdose and respiratory and cardiac arrest, suffered while the condemned person is unconscious. We think.

The Jarrels and Mr. Hicks were there, sitting in the front row. This time they all shook my hand and expressed shock about Toner. They asked about Dani, whom they had previously dismissed as a drug-addled hussy. I told them that she'd been lucky. After Toner fell dead, I had dragged her up the stairs and into the kitchen, where I saw the blood draining from her neck. Screaming for help, I pressed down as hard as I could, feeling her life slide helplessly though my clenched fingers. Fortunately there were a dozen cops and medical techs within a few yards. They stabilized her quickly and a small motorcade raced to the hospital.

She would be OK, eventually. Toner's bullet had passed through her throat, missing the jugular by millimeters, just nicking the carotid artery, and doing some small damage to the spine on exiting. But the surgery was long and the rehabilitation would be painful. In a moment of delirium, standing over her bed, I had asked her to move in with me. Why not? I thought. Maybe this was what I needed, a sexually depraved girl who never went anywhere unarmed. But she passed on my offer. Her father and stepmom had flown in for a bed-side reconciliation and she had already agreed to move in with them and finish her rehab in a special facility out in Arizona before eventually returning to school, although she no longer wanted to be a shrink. She'd had enough of crazy people.

Townes was at the execution as well, sitting with the families, shaking hands with the reporters and local law enforcement big shots who made up the rest of the audience. He had turned in his resignation and was developing a possible TV series based on his adventures. We joked a bit about my working for him someday, but then a reporter grabbed him and he went to pose for a photo. We had decided to like each other at last, but now that the case was done, we had nothing left to say. Unless someone else I knew got murdered, it was unlikely we'd meet again.

It was a nice day at least. If it had been, say, a stormy night, I would have been tempted to lie, just to avoid the cliché. Instead it was bright summer, and everything was alive. The air itself was thick and soft, and I felt it against my skin, as if it were pressing back for a moment before yielding. On the train ride up, the trees along the tracks had been waving, and the flowers by the station were open so wide they seemed dizzy, like cartoon drunks with their tongues hanging out. Even along the road to the prison, all blacktop and concrete and fence, I saw a stand of glorious sunflowers, defiant, blazing, tall. Like our own honor squad, ready to fire away. All of this, one wanted to say, is what Clay will be missing out on, forever. That is his punishment. Each of these lost moments. But he didn't seem reluctant to kiss this world good-bye. For his last meal he'd ordered rare steak and lobster and chocolate cake, which he shared with the guards. Then he read a magazine for a while and fell asleep, apparently with no trouble. I don't know what the magazine was. I like to imagine it was an old *Raunchy*.

When we arrived at the prison gate, we encountered a small group of about twenty or thirty protesters, some with signs. It was an odd mix: aged hippies, a nun, two Buddhist monks, both white with shaved heads, a few young people, earnest and hairy, and among them, standing quietly, without a sign, was Theresa Trio, whom I hadn't seen or heard from since that day on the bench. I waved, but she didn't seem to see me, and then the gate rolled shut.

I had however heard from Claire, at last. I'd gotten an email a few nights before, after I'd pretty much given up hope:

> Hey Sibylline,
> What's up? Remember me? Sorry I didn't call or write to you. Of course I wasn't mad. You saved me. I think I was scared. Not of you. Never. You were my best friend!! I think the world just suddenly got scary and I had to go home, go back to being just a kid, which is what I guess I am. I'm out in Lawn Guyland for the summer at my dad's place at the beach. I hate it but it's OK. Then I'm going to boarding school in Switzerland. Which is weird I know but I'm kind of psyched. Is that totally lame of me? Maybe I'll hate it who knows. Then maybe I will sneak out and come stay with you. Will you still let me? Thanks for letting me hang

around so much. Thanks for everything you did. Thanks for everything you didn't do too. Thanks for taking such good care of me. Sorry I can't take care of you anymore. But you don't need me. Not really. Thanks for pretending. XOXO C.

At five the warden gave the signal and the curtain rolled back. Darian Clay was strapped to a black table with arm extensions, in a kind of crucifixion pose, or as if in some S&M massage chair. The IVs ran from his arms into a hole in the wall, behind which unseen technicians were controlling the drips. Though I knew this hideout was the modern equivalent of the axman's hood, it still struck me as inane. Were they frightened of having the dead man know who killed him? Did they think he would come back for revenge from beyond the grave to haunt them or wait for them in hell? If so, would ducking behind a wall really fool a ghost?

Clay looked around, smiled at us, and lifted his fingers in a little wave. Everyone stirred nervously and I looked at the row in front of me. Mrs. Jarrel's hair was thinning. Mr. Jarrel had dandruff on the shoulders of his suit. For some reason, these two details made me unbearably sad. This isn't going to help, I thought. Nothing would ever make these people feel better, except perhaps the slow dulling of time and the sweetener of some new small joys. And as the memory faded, that fading would in itself be a further sadness. And although the crime was solved and justice done, the mystery, the real mystery, would never be explained. Perhaps this was already dawning on them, even now, as they sat watching, holding hands. The warden asked Clay if he had any last words. He nodded and muttered something. The warden frowned.

"The prisoner's final statement is, 'No hard feelings.'" He cleared his throat. " 'I forgive you all.'" Then he quickly spoke into the intercom and gave the command. The anesthetic flowed into Clay's bloodstream. He responded almost immediately, lifting his head like he'd been startled, and then slowly lowering it. His body seemed to relax. Then, as if fighting the urge to sleep, he craned his head again and looked at us. He looked at the Jarrels and at Hicks. They looked away. He looked at Townes, who stared straight back. Clay nodded at him. Then he looked at me, and I looked back, trying as best I could to see something, some message from his side, whatever there was to see. He smiled, I think at me. But who knows? He was pretty high by then. Then he shut his eyes and his head fell back onto the table.

The warden gave the signal and the next drug washed in, paralyzing his muscles, and we could see his fingers twitch and stop. We could see his chest rise and fall and then not rise again. Then they released the final drug and stopped the one thing still moving, the heart. We stared. A few minutes later a doctor entered the room and, at 5:12, declared him dead. I got up and left. I didn't wait to say good-bye to anyone. I didn't want to see their faces when they turned around, or show my own.

79

I cleared security and walked outside. Clay's death had just been announced. A small group of protesters were praying in small clutches, holding hands or lighting candles. Others were already loading their signs into their cars. I'm sure it was difficult for them. No one was really sorry he was dead. Theresa was standing apart from the group. She smiled when she saw me and gave a short wave.

"Hey," she said. "I was wondering if you'd be here."

"Clay invited me. Weird as it sounds."

"I guess I felt like I had to see it through too," she said. We began walking together toward the parking lot.

"What about Flosky?" I asked. "If she ends up here, will you come and protest?"

"Yes." Her eyes met mine briefly and then turned back to her feet. "If I don't stand by my convictions, who am I?"

Me, I thought, but I just said, "Good for you."

"What about you?" she asked. "What will you do?"

"I have no convictions that I'm aware of. Only trials."

"No," she smiled. "The book."

"There is no book. The only hook was the confession, that it was a memoir in his own words. No one cares now. And in case you didn't notice, he's not exactly big news anymore."

"Oh well," she said.

"Oh well," I repeated. "Now a Flosky book might have a little traction, but I think I've had it with real life for a while. It's a major pain in the ass." She laughed, and I continued, "I'd better write something quick, though. At this rate I'll wind up teaching junior high."

We walked through another gate and were in the parking lot, where the prison employees parked their cars. Some of these people would end up serving more years here than the convicts.

"Hey, I have an idea," she said, brightening and touching my arm. Was that the first time? "Why don't you turn it into a vampire book? Like a vampire serial killer. Or wait, even better, a vampire cop who ends up having to hunt down a serial killer."

"Yeah," I said. "That might work."

"I think it would be great," she said. "I mean, it's a great start and that's probably the hardest part, right? The beginning?"

"Not really."

"Or the end."

"Neither," I said. "It's like real life. The hard part is the middle."

She grinned, and I grinned back, and for a second I almost thought I could get away with kissing her, if the setting weren't so utterly inappropriate. I heard a loud honk and jumped back as a Subaru wagon pulled up, full of cheerful young do-gooders.

"Come on, T!" a scruffy boy with a beard and nose ring yelled.

"Got to go," she told me.

"OK," I said. "See you in the city maybe?"

"Sure, call me up sometime." She grinned. "Or look for me online."

I laughed. "So that was you, vampT3?"

She shrugged. "Maybe, maybe not." She climbed into the back of the car. The door slammed, and I turned to find my own way out, but I heard her call my name.

"Hey, Harry!"

I turned. She was hanging out the window as the car started to roll.

"Yeah?"

"Keep writing. We need you." She waved and they drove away.

80

I don't know about you, but I hate coming to the end of a mystery. It's been a problem since childhood, when alone in the library one day, I discovered Poe, the first grown-up writer I really loved. Besides his great horror and fantasy tales, he was the inventor of the detective story, and ever since then, no matter what else I read that was supposedly more realistic, or experimental, or psychological, I kept drifting back to mysteries, long before I was forced to write them for a living. Nevertheless, there is always a certain dilemma: I prefer the beginning to the end. I love the mystery and am vaguely let down by the solution.

The tough part of writing mysteries is that they are actually not mysterious enough. Life defeats the form literature gives it, whether the climax of a thriller or the three-act cake of most literary plots. The real risk and danger of life comes from never knowing what will happen next, from living in an absolutely contingent present, where each moment is unique and unrepeatable, and about which we know only one thing, that it will end. Hence my disappointment with most detective stories and the fictional answers that never seem equal to the vast questions they uncover.

The conventional view of mysteries, as explained by Auden, for example, is as an essentially conservative genre. A crime disturbs the status quo; we readers get to enjoy the transgressive thrill, then observe approvingly as the detective, agent of social order, sets things right at the end. We finish our cocoa and tuck ourselves in, safe and sound. True enough. But what this theory fails to take into account is the next book, the next murder, and the next. When you line up all the Poirots, all the Maigrets, all the Lew Archers and Matt Scudders, what you get is something both far stranger and more familiar: a world where mysterious destructive forces are constantly erupting and where all solutions are temporary, slight pauses during which we take a breath before the next case.

And yes, I would have a next case, despite all my failures. Not for any noble reasons, or anything Jane or even Theresa would say, but just because I couldn't stop myself. It was too late. For both Clay and me, the course was set in childhood, in little rooms in Queens with our moms. About his, enough said. About mine . . . well, isn't it obvious? I was the lonely little boy who hid his head in books. Decades later, I'm still at it. But I'm no psycho who thinks his private, inner world is real. Instead, I admit my world is nothing, next to nothing, mere fiction, but go on anyway—poor, lonely, despairing, depraved, bitter and neurotic—and I persist in holding my books up to the face of reality, like a mirror that reflects only dreams. Every work of literature is a great victory over oneself and a small act of resistance against the world.

I thought about these things on the train home, while I tried, with Clay's story over, to outline some new chapter for my own. I would go back to my mother's apartment, to my empty bed, and in the morning, most likely I would begin another book. And since a cheap hack like me can't afford to waste a good story, I would salvage what I could from this one, retelling the story as fiction, changing the names and other details. But one name would be real this time: my own.

Clay had said that we were all just little vessels, holding a drop of life, and that breaking us was nothing, like letting that little drop flow back into the ocean that it came from. That was how I thought of him now, lying there, asleep too deeply to even know he was dead, that this last current flowing through his blood was the one that would take him with it.

His story was like anyone's: a swift dark river that runs, through rapids and falls and forests, to spill into a vast and mysterious sea. Only then, when speed becomes stillness and we float free at last, do we realize that we have been carried all this way, and are now far out, and infinitely beyond our depth. But then it's too late. We have read into the night, and have reached the end of our story. We have come to the empty page.

Maybe you've figured out which of the real-life characters I altered or combined, or who never existed at all and what facts and dates changed. Maybe you feel you know me, like the trusty narrator in a novel, or maybe, like the novelist behind the book, I'm only a ghost. But for now, let's just say that I was on a train one evening last summer, that the train was approaching the city, that from the window, I could glimpse the black river running between forested banks, and that all of it was slowly disappearing into a darkening sky. Now close the book and put out the light.

Acknowledgments

I would like to thank the following people for their invaluable assistance, without which this book would never have seen the light of day: my agent, Doug Stewart, for his wisdom and perseverance; the intrepid and irrepressible Seth Fishman; my editor, Karen Thompson, for her insight and belief; my teachers and classmates, from P.S. 69 to Columbia and everywhere in between, who showed me what was possible; my friends, too abundant to mention here, who read everything first, and second and third, and whose understanding and indulgence always amaze me; my Jens, of course, for their kindness and grace; and most of all my family, whose love, support, patience, and generosity are infinite, and who I promise are nothing like the characters in my work.

About the Author

David Gordon was born in Queens and currently lives in New York City. He attended Sarah Lawrence College, holds an MA in English and Comparative Literature and an MFA in Writing, both from Columbia University, and has worked in film, fashion, publishing, and pornography. This is his first book.